RISING SNIPER

A World War II Thriller

DAVID HEALEY

INTRACOASTAL

RISING SNIPER

By David Healey

Intracoastal Media digital edition published 2022.

Print edition ISBN 978-0-9674162-6-7

Cover art by Streetlight Graphics.

BISAC Subject Headings:

FIC014000 FICTION/Historical

FIC032000 FICTION/War & Military

This one is for Dad. We miss you.

"Our sights are set."
—James Forrestal, US Secretary of the Navy, 1944

CHAPTER ONE

Pearl Harbor, December 7, 1941

JASPER COLE always did have keen eyes, which meant he was the first one to see the planes coming in.

The young man from Tennessee was among several crew members who had the bad luck to be on duty this Sunday morning, while others got to sleep in a little later in their cramped bunks in the depths of the battleship USS *Arizona*.

Low in the sky, the early morning sun glinted off the waters of Pearl Harbor, forcing Jasper to raise his hand and shade his eyes. Truth be told, the light felt like glittering shards hitting his eyes, and his head ached with a dull throb. That was to be expected, considering that the night before had been spent ashore, visiting the bars that sailors frequented for cheap beer and a chance at female company.

There was plenty of one and not much of the other. Of course, female company could be bought for a price, but so far Jasper had resisted the urge, having heard horror stories from his fellow sailors about being given three minutes to get the job done. Then there were the required visits to the sick bay for an embarrassing exam to prevent venereal disease.

He'd stuck with spending his money on beer, with no regrets.

One thing about Pearl Harbor—the locals had made an art of getting every last dime out of the sailors stationed there.

Despite the revelry of the night before, he had been on duty bright and early. That was just fine with him, considering that none of the senior officers would be around on a Sunday morning. There were only a few hungover petty officers and junior officers, none of them inclined to shout at the sailors because of their own aching heads.

"We almost needed a winch to get Ostrowski out of the bar last night," said one of the sailors working alongside Jasper. "You should have seen him. Of course, he had to pick the biggest marine in the joint to pick a fight with."

"Sounds like Ostrowski. He ain't got no sense," Jasper said, grinning in amusement at the story. He looked around and didn't see Ostrowski on deck. "Where's he at now?"

"In sick bay with a broken nose and a hell of a hangover."

"Is that right? Some guys will do anything to miss out on a little work."

On deck, the sailors traded a few more stories that would never appear in letters home, bragging about exploits that were typical of young men far from home and looking to blow off steam.

Listening, Jasper chuckled and bent to his task, which involved arranging large lines on the deck into neat coils. Other crews were oiling the *Arizona*'s vast teak deck, a space so expansive that the entire crew of more than a thousand could be assembled there. Beneath the wood lay several inches of steel decking, but the wood provided a better grip and was a throwback to the days of wooden sailing ships.

He had developed a fondness for the ship and found its sheer size, as well as the sight of the massive guns, to be more than reassuring. There wasn't anything on the sea as mighty as a battleship.

It wasn't hard work that he was doing, but he was already starting to sweat in the semitropical heat.

He didn't mind. Despite the heat and the early hour, Jasper considered himself to be a lucky man. He felt grateful to be in the navy these past two years, having escaped the Depression-era hills and mountains back home, where there were no jobs and sometimes not even anything to eat. Nobody ever went hungry in the navy, even if the pay wasn't all that great.

Two years ago, what he knew about ships and the sea wouldn't have filled a teaspoon, but the navy had taken him on anyway. He was just grateful to have a purpose and a job, however inconsequential that job might be in the overall mechanism of the United States Navy.

Finally, he was just grateful to be alive on this December morning, watching the sunlight at play over the warm waters. As he worked, his headache faded.

Back home, the creeks would be starting to freeze over, and there might even be snow on the mountains. In the mountains, winter was a time to survive. Getting through the season was a daunting challenge that went back to the first settlers and their log cabins. Before that, the Indians who had once occupied those hills found winter to be a season that must be endured.

Here in Hawaii, things were different. The tropical warmth didn't pose challenges to anyone except on the rare occasions when the heat and humidity got to be a bit much. Then again, Jasper supposed that he didn't have much to complain about when he looked around at the palm trees, green lawns, and blue waters.

"Quit lollygagging and pay attention to what you're doing," the petty officer grumbled, probably in a bad mood because he, too, had been out on the town and was paying the price this morning. "The last thing I want to be doing right now is nursing you worms."

Jasper redoubled his efforts, hiding a smile at the thought that the petty officer was likely suffering from a wooden head. Nearby, he could also see a grin on the face of one of his buddies, Jim Butler, who, like Jasper, had the bad luck to be on deck this morning. Neither said a word as they focused on their task. Never mind that these ropes were already neatly coiled. They had been neatly coiled yesterday, and they would be neatly coiled again tomorrow. There was never anything sloppy about the navy, that was for sure.

That was when he saw the planes.

Something caught his eye, or maybe it was a sound carrying on the morning air. He straightened his back and shaded his eyes to watch the squadron approach.

"See them planes? I reckon we ain't the only ones out and about this morning," Jasper said.

"Huh, looks like the flyboys are doing some kind of exercise. I'll bet they were none too happy about it being Sunday morning."

"That's for sure."

Something about the planes didn't look right. He couldn't say what, exactly. It was more like a feeling.

Maybe it was the way that the squadron appeared to be heading right at them. Just behind the first group of planes, he could see another squadron, and another behind that. This in itself was unusual.

What was going on? That's a lot of planes for a Sunday morning.

Jasper raised his hand again and squinted intently into the azure bowl of the sky. He had sharp eyes like everyone in his family. In fact, he couldn't even think of a Cole who had ever worn eyeglasses, not even Granny Cole, who was eighty years old.

He began to realize that the color of the planes was all wrong.

They were angled to come in low, awfully low. They weren't supposed to be this close to the ships.

"Here they come. Mighty low. I guess those flyboys are showing off again," Butler said. "There's gonna be hell to pay for that."

"Something ain't right," Jasper said.

The planes kept on coming, close enough now that they could hear the menacing whine of the engines, sweeping lower and closer.

And then a curious thing happened. He saw tiny objects begin to fall away from the aircraft and splash into the harbor.

"What in the world is going on?" Butler asked. "Are those supposed to be fuel tanks or maybe dummy torpedoes?"

They had all seen planes on training exercises drop dummy bombs, but never in the harbor itself.

Somebody laughed. "Geez, those flyboys must be really hungover. Don't those guys know they're not supposed to bomb our own vessels in the harbor!"

Jasper stared, a feeling of horror going through him.

"Those aren't dummy bombs," he said, pointing to the white trail of wakes that the torpedoes were leaving in the water.

Nearby, the petty officer hadn't shown much interest in the planes at first. But now he, too, had spotted the torpedoes in the harbor.

"Holy hell," he said, his voice stricken.

The torpedoes were headed right toward the hull of the *Arizona* and other ships in the harbor. There wasn't time for anyone to do a damn thing about it.

Moments later, a huge explosion rocked the ship. The sailors were all thrown from their feet, scattered like bowling pins across the deck. The massive deck itself heaved into the air and rippled like a sheet snapped over a bed. The beautifully oiled teak shattered and splintered.

Dazed, Jasper looked up as a plane passed overhead. He could clearly see the red circles on the wings—the rising sun symbol of the Japanese empire.

"Those are Japs!" he shouted, as if anyone could still hear, or if anyone hadn't figured that out by now.

He couldn't believe it. They were being attacked by the Japanese. It seemed such a strange thing, considering that they weren't even at war with Japan. Sure, people had talked about it, but now it was actually happening. He stared in disbelief at the carnage all around him. The petty officer lay nearby, impaled through the belly by a teak board. Jasper thought that maybe he would wake up, and all of this would be a bad dream.

But like they used to say back home in the mountains, wishing don't make it any less so.

More planes came in, dropping bombs and torpedoes. A few sailors had managed to get on the antiaircraft guns and were firing back.

"Get to your stations!" someone yelled, although to Jasper, it seemed too late for that.

He ran to join a gun crew. Like most sailors, he had been cross-trained to serve in many positions.

The gun was firing up at the sky, unleashing a frenzied line of tracers that barely showed against the bright sky. However, the nimble Japanese Zero planes were almost impossible to hit, so small and fast as they zipped overhead after decimating the fleet. Their single Mitsubishi engines propelled them at more than three hundred miles per hour—three times the speed of a fastball pitch. By the time anybody got a Zero in his sights, it was almost instantly out of range.

Another explosion ripped through the ship, and Jasper found himself hurled away from the gun, clawing for a grip as the deck tilted at a precarious angle.

Where was Butler?

Gone.

Everything seemed to be on fire. Nearby, he saw a badly burned man who looked like meat that had been left on the grill too long. Jasper wrinkled his nose at the smell of burned flesh.

He fought down the urge to vomit. He had more important things to do, like get off this burning ship, but it was easier said than done. The smooth teak-covered deck was gone. In its place was a wreckage of splinters and gaping holes through which flames leaped. Jasper wouldn't have thought it was possible for anything to penetrate the armored steel. His eyes were seeing it, but his mind still couldn't register that this was real.

The whole ship was on fire. The sight was terrifying. At this point there was no more thought of fighting the Japanese, only of surviving. His sole hope was to get off the ship and into the water as quickly as he could.

Crawling and sliding on the tilted deck, he made his way down to the gunwales and stared at the water below, weighing his chances.

Other survivors were doing the same, then leaping into the water.

He looked below and his heart sank.

The still, blue waters of the harbor were gone. Instead, a sea of flaming oil surrounded the ship. He heard screams as the men who had jumped into the harbor were consumed alive by the flames.

Did he really need to jump? The deck tilted yet more, and it was clear that the mortally wounded ship was threatening to "turn turtle" and capsize. If he didn't get clear, he would be sucked down as the ship sank.

His only option would be to dive down through that mess of burning oil and try to swim beneath it to safety.

He looked in the direction of where the burning oil ended and there was clear water again. It seemed an awfully long way to swim underwater, but he didn't know what else to do.

He had to at least try.

Taking a massive deep breath, Jasper slid off the deck feet first, pinning his arms to his side, and spiked into the fiery water below. He felt the heat of the burning oil. He let the momentum of his dive carry him as deep as possible. Even so, some of the flaming oil was not extinguished right away and followed him down in a trail of fire.

Jasper did not panic. That was not how he had been raised or trained by the navy. As unreal as this all seemed, he forced himself to stay in the moment. Rather than clawing for the surface, he fought against every instinct and swam deeper into the darker waters of the harbor. Only when he was far enough down did he begin to swim laterally, trying to get out from underneath the flaming waters above him, but there was nothing easy about it.

Swim, boy, swim.

His lungs began to ache for air. His legs hurt too. He realized that he had been torn open and wounded on the deck above. In fact, one of his legs wasn't working right at all, which slowed him down. When he tried to kick, it hurt him painfully.

He had no choice but to keep going, because to rise to the surface would mean certain death in the flames. He kept swimming, but it was too far, too much distance to cover underwater. He became disoriented and had no idea where the flames above ended. He couldn't even remember which way to swim. He realized that he had been swimming in circles under the flames rather than escaping the burning oil above.

He was still in disbelief that just twenty minutes ago he had been enjoying a beautiful Hawaiian Sunday morning.

And now he was staring into the depths of hell, burning sea above him and darkness below.

The Japanese, he thought, a sudden burst of hate and anger running through him. They did this to me. They killed me.

They didn't just want to kill him. They wanted him to burn alive. They wanted him to suffer.

Jasper was having none of it.

He was almost out of air. His lungs ached to inhale, and in the end he knew from his navy training that no matter how hard he tried, he would eventually open his mouth to let in the sea, and that would be that.

Instead of swimming up into the flames, desperate for air, he pivoted and swam deeper into the harbor, down into the depths of the black water. It was his way of denying the enemy their victory. He would die on his own terms. After all, there never had been a Cole who wasn't stubborn by nature.

The depths of the harbor were cold and dark, but oddly peaceful, far removed from the carnage of war above.

His last thoughts were of home. He remembered a spring morning in the mountains, the soft, fresh air. It smelled of a new rain, the morning sunlight warm on the new leaves.

Jasper let himself sigh, and then his world went eternally black.

CHAPTER TWO

LIEUTENANT COMMANDER TOM O'CONNELL looked out at the Pacific, enjoying the fresh sea breeze that cleared the morning fog from his head. Far out at sea, the USS *Northampton* was on maneuvers, part of the USS *Enterprise* carrier task force commanded by Admiral William "Bull" Halsey Jr.

O'Connell watched the sharp bow of the cruiser cutting through the blue waters. The bow wave rolled out across the otherwise calm surface of the sea. The ship and its crew were far enough away from the rest of the task force that they felt all alone out here, which was a feeling that the young officer enjoyed, but that was also a little daunting. The United States mainland was at least two thousand miles away. Tokyo? Another four thousand miles.

The cruiser should have been back at Pearl with the rest of the fleet, but they had put to sea for yet another training cruise. So here they were, many miles from base, the sharp bow cutting a wake through the blue Pacific.

Although the cruise had its own rewards, such as this moment staring out at the Pacific with a hot mug of coffee in hand, it meant that the crew and officers had missed out on a weekend of shore leave.

He doubted that there was any place on earth as lively as Oahu when all the ships were in port.

But things weren't all bad. In fact, he had gotten into a good poker game last night. Considering that he had won twenty dollars, he supposed that he had come out farther ahead than he would have during a night on the town.

Being a good card player not only helped pass the time, but it had been something of a necessity for supplementing his meager salary over the years. He had graduated from the United States Naval Academy at Annapolis in 1933, barely hanging on as the peacetime navy cut officers during the Depression era, then getting married and starting a family on paltry pay.

He was fortunate that his parents, both Irish immigrants, had become fairly well off back in Cambridge and weren't about to let their grandchildren starve. But the poker money helped.

"Don't look so smug, you damn card shark," said Lieutenant Smith, approaching with his own mug of coffee in hand. The hot coffee managed to steam in the morning air. The very fact that they had a few moments to themselves to enjoy the view and their coffee indicated that this was a very relaxed cruise. "Just because you won twenty bucks off me, you don't have to stand there grinning like the Cheshire cat."

O'Connell laughed. "You can win it back from me next time. At least you can try."

"You must be one lucky Irishman is all I can say."

Even coming from Smith, who didn't mean any harm by it, the Irish remark was a little galling. The United States Navy officer corps was very much a WASP club that was hard for an Irish Catholic with an ethnic name to break into, even as an Annapolis graduate. O'Connell was sensitive to that. Then again, he knew that Smith was just giving him a good-natured ribbing.

Despite the headwinds he sometimes faced in his naval career, O'Connell didn't regret the choice that he'd made. After graduating from Cambridge High and Latin at the top of his class, it had come down to deciding between Harvard, which had been almost literally in his backyard, or Annapolis. Although his parents had some money and could be proud of what they had accomplished after coming to

America without a dime to their names, they were far from being wealthy.

The young son of immigrants had been under no illusions about his chances of fitting in with the Boston Brahmins who populated Harvard. He had decided on a free education at the United States Naval Academy.

No matter where you went to college, it still made you a member of the elite, educated class—scarcely 1 percent of all Americans held a college degree in 1941. O'Connell had heard that fact somewhere, and it still awed him.

"If it makes you feel better, I'll buy you a beer when we get back to shore," O'Connell said with a grin.

They stood in companionable silence, drinking their coffee and gazing out to sea. The calm seas made drinking coffee on deck relatively easy, which wasn't always the case when the Pacific was really rolling. They nodded at the chaplain, who came by, preparing for the Sunday-morning service.

Gazing across the Pacific, they noticed smoke rising in the distance, in the direction of Oahu. The island itself was too far away to be visible.

"Is that coming from Pearl?" O'Connell asked, puzzled. He couldn't think of anything on Oahu, other than the navy complex, that could be on fire and produce that much smoke.

"Maybe they're burning off the sugarcane."

"I don't think so," O'Connell said. On occasion, there had been big fires when the old sugarcane was burned off by the plantation managers, but this looked different. "Look at that smoke. It wasn't even there a minute ago."

Indeed, the smoke was thick, black, and heavy, rising in massive columns from multiple sources. Oil smoke, not burning cane. Even this far out to sea, it was an incredible amount of smoke.

"You know what? I think that *is* Pearl," Smith agreed. "What the heck is going on?"

"Your guess is as good as mine," O'Connell said, just as puzzled.

Just then, the call sounded for general quarters. What had been a calm, even relaxing, Sunday morning aboard ship dissolved in a flurry of action as sailors poured out of the hatches and ran to operate the cruiser's guns. Except for the thick pillar of smoke on the horizon, it all still felt like a drill, considering that the sea and sky surrounding them looked as empty as ever.

O'Connell stopped another officer rushing past, hurrying to tug on his flotation vest and helmet. More sailors streamed toward the big guns and to the antiaircraft batteries, taking their stations.

"Hey, Jimmy, what's happening? Is this another drill?"

"Hell no, this isn't a drill," said the officer whom O'Connell had stopped. The man looked almost frantic. "Don't you see the smoke?"

"Sure I do, but that's way the hell over there. Besides, doesn't anybody know it's Sunday morning?"

"Tell that to the Japs. They just attacked Pearl Harbor."

At O'Connell's elbow, he heard Smith choke on his last swig of coffee. He took one last swig of his own coffee, then hurled the mug into the sea and ran to his post.

The ship that had been so sleepy only minutes before had now come fully alive. The drills that they had run through so many times meant that the call to action went smoothly, but this time there was a new urgency. This time it wasn't a drill. This time it was for real.

Next to a battleship, a US Navy cruiser was one of the most powerful vessels on the sea in terms of sheer firepower. Designated as a heavy cruiser, *Northampton* was just a hair over six hundred feet in length and was armed with nine 8-inch guns, four 5-inch guns, torpedo tubes, and several antiaircraft batteries. If she gave you her full attention, you'd notice.

The United States Navy was relatively small, and most of the Pacific Fleet had been at Pearl, *Northampton* being a notable exception. Considering that WWI had been mostly fought in the trenches by the time the United States got involved, the navy hadn't seen any real action since the days of Commodore Dewey and the Spanish-American War. That had been four decades ago.

As for the attack on Pearl, nobody knew any details. Rumors flew around the ship. They heard everything from the attack being an air raid, to a naval bombardment, to a full-on invasion of the Hawaiian island. What was actually happening was anybody's guess. The sailors and officers scanned the skies and the horizon, expecting at any moment to see enemy planes or the silhouette of the Imperial Japanese Navy fleet.

More troubling was the thought of a Japanese submarine prowling these waters, waiting to launch a torpedo at the cruiser. *Northampton* and her crew weren't afraid to go toe-to-toe with anything on the sea, but it was hard to fight an unseen enemy like a Jap sub.

The base at Pearl Harbor had been attacked, but it was frustrating that there was nobody to strike back against, which was any red-blooded sailor's natural inclination. It was like a punch had been thrown out of the dark, and there was nobody to punch back against.

"Here we are on a goddamn cruiser and there's nobody to fight," O'Connell grumbled.

Instead, there was only the clear blue Pacific stretching all the way to Japan. He thought about that for a moment. He knew that the distance to Japan was nearly a tenth of the circumference of the earth from this spot. Had the Japanese somehow managed to cross that vast distance without warning and attack Pearl Harbor? That was a long arm, all right. He had the uneasy thought that even the West Coast might be within striking distance now.

"I don't see any Japs," a sailor muttered.

"Keep your eyes open," O'Connell snapped. "They're out there somewhere."

But try as they might, all they saw was the distant black column of smoke, growing darker by the moment, rising ever higher into the blue sky.

O'Connell realized, the war that everyone had talked about finally seemed to be happening.

IN NEW YORK CITY, newspaper columnist Ernie Pyle stood at the hotel window and looked down at Fifth Avenue. He couldn't hear the people from up here, but he could sense their excitement in the way that they scurried about the street. He'd already heard the news on the radio, and the newsroom had already called.

"It was only a matter of time," he said. "It's war. It's what Roosevelt wanted, and now he's got it."

"Against the Japanese?" asked his wife, Jerry, taking a drag on her cigarette. Both of them smoked like fiends, and their hotel room seemed to have a permanent fog of tobacco smoke. Overflowing ashtrays littered the dining room table, bedside tables, and coffee table, right beside a few empty mugs and glasses, some holding the dregs of old coffee, others that smelled of bourbon or gin.

"Against the Japanese and the Germans, both at the same time," Pyle said, sucking deeply on his own cigarette. "It's a world war. Gee, we haven't had one of those since the last war that was supposed to end all of the others. The Great War. You'd think we'd have learned our lesson."

"What are you going to do?" she asked.

It was a natural question, but one that was fraught with tension.

Pyle had worked himself to the bone as a reporter, seemingly always traveling or always on the job, working all the time, which created tension at home. For the last several months, he had been in London, covering the Battle of Britain. He had recently returned to the United States to spend more time with Jerry, who had been unwell.

"What am I going to do?" He repeated the question, pondering the answer. "Well, maybe I'm not too old to be a sailor."

His wife snorted at the very idea of her husband in uniform. "You a sailor? Ha! I'd like to see you do a push-up."

"Very funny," he said, without taking any offense. "The navy might not have me as a sailor, but I can still go to war. Cover the war, I mean."

"Will they need you?"

"Believe me, generals don't go to war without an army of journalists to take their picture and write down their quotes."

"If you want to write about the war, then you'd better hurry," she said. "This war might be over by next week."

Pyle shook his head, looking down at the street. People hurried to and fro, scrambling to buy the latest edition of the newspaper, with the news of the attack on Pearl Harbor plastered across the front in headlines so big that Pyle could almost read them from their hotel room.

As a journalist, he probably knew more than most of the people down there about the coming war. America and the other democracies of the world were like a little island, surrounded by despots. In Europe there was Hitler and the Third Reich, intent on creating a new empire. A lot of Americans had wanted to stay out of the fight, figuring that it was Europe's problem, not ours. America had already paid its dues fighting in the Great War. If England and Europe had gone and broken that peace, that was their problem.

It was troubling that not all Americans even disagreed with Hitler. An organization called the Bund had even staged huge rallies in support of National Socialism, right here in New York. Of course, many Americans also had German heritage and were proud to see Germany doing so well economically. For FDR, war against Germany was a tough sell.

But the Japanese were a foreign power that Americans could easily vilify and hate. By striking Pearl Harbor, the Japanese had also shown that someplace like Seattle or Los Angeles could be next.

President Roosevelt had wanted America to get into the war. For the president, Ernie knew, the Japanese attack was like a gift.

In the street below, he could see that the news had stirred everyone up like a nest of ants poked with a stick. Already, men were eager to get into uniform—and even some women were asking about how they could sign up as nurses or join the Red Cross. He felt a lump in his throat, prouder than ever to be an American.

Pyle took another deep drag on a cigarette. "There's no hurry," he said. "Darling, this war is going to go on for years. Thousands of people are going to die. Hundreds of thousands. Maybe even millions."

She shuddered visibly. "And you want to be part of all that?" she asked, although deep down she thought that she already knew the answer.

"It's what I do," he said. "This war is going to be America's greatest chapter. Anyhow, somebody needs to tell the story, and that somebody might as well be me."

CHAPTER THREE

Thirteen Months Earlier, Autumn 1940

DEACON COLE WAS HUNTING. With his dead pa's rifle held in hands calloused from farmwork, he watched the morning light spread across the mountains. He was on the trail of a big buck he had seen once or twice from a distance while roaming these hills.

Most days in the woods, he carried a shotgun with him, an old Iver Johnson double-barrel, because it was usually small game that he scared up, rabbits or squirrels that chattered down at him, scolding, until he settled things with the shotgun. If he was lucky, he'd startle some quail or a pheasant.

Whatever game he brought home helped to feed his mother and sister, Sadie, back at the Cole family's hardscrabble farm. Like most people these days in the mountains, they were barely scraping by. Sadie was just as good of a shot, but she had stayed to help their ailing mother.

"You go on, Deke," Sadie had said.

He felt his belly rumble. When was the last time they had eaten a decent meal? Sometimes Deke thought that he should be like his cousin, Jasper, who had joined the navy. He was out in Hawaii, a place so distant and exotic in Deke's mind that it may as well be the moon, eating regular, and sending money home. But there was more than one boy in that branch of the Cole family to work the farm. Without Deke, what would his ma and Sadie have done?

He smirked at the thought that Sadie would inform him that she could take care of herself just fine. Deke had to admit that she'd be right about that. While it was a toss-up as to which one of them was the better shot, there was no doubt that Sadie was his equal when it came to farmwork. The trouble was, there was a lot more work than the two siblings could do.

With their pa gone and Ma so sick, he and Sadie had done the best they could to keep the farm going. Having fallen into a struggle for subsistence, there wasn't much to take care of anymore: some hogs and a few chickens, a couple of horses to pull the plow over the rugged fields. The rocky land was stingy, and their crops hadn't been good for years.

The Depression had sunk its teeth into the mountain people like a mean dog, and it hadn't let go. Pa had taken out a mortgage on the land that the Cole family had owned since at least the Civil War. That mortgage had turned out to be a disaster.

To be sure, he had distant relatives all over these hills and mountains. The Coles were Scotch Irish, having settled the area when there were still Indians in the woods and valleys. Mostly, it was poor land that nobody else wanted. It had suited the extended Cole clan just fine.

You might say that the Coles didn't live all that much differently from the original settlers. They ate whatever vegetables they could grow in the thin soil, sold firewood or made moonshine, and relied on hunting for meat. Rumor had it that the rest of the world moved faster and faster, but here in the mountains, life was very much the same as it had been for a hundred years or more.

With the farm not making any money, Pa had been desperate to pay back the bank. He had managed to get a job down at the sawmill, but that was dangerous work.

It had fallen to the county sheriff to drive out to the farm with the news that they all feared might come someday.

They knew that something was wrong as soon as the dusty county car pulled into the barnyard. The sheriff was a big man, but his shoulders seemed to droop as he took off his hat and approached the door.

"Mrs. Cole, I'm afraid that there's been an accident at the sawmill," he had said, his brown eyes sad in his broad face. "Your husband has been killed."

"He's gone?"

"I'm afraid so, ma'am." The sheriff seemed relieved that Mrs. Cole didn't ask for the details. He looked around, apparently taking in the ramshackle house, the barn with a sheet of canvas covering a hole in the roof, the forlorn chickens scratching in the yard.

Their mother had nodded once and gone back into the house, leaving the sheriff on the front porch, hat in hand.

"Sadie, Deke," he'd said, nodding at them. "I'm real sorry about your daddy."

The sheriff's eyes had wandered down to the boy's bare feet. Deke could have explained that his pa had needed the one pair of boots they could afford to work at the mill.

The sheriff looked up and opened his mouth as if to say something, then closed it again. There were times in his job where words failed him. His whole county was dotted with farms just like this, where families were barely hanging on. A man could do only so much. He got back in his car and drove off, raising a cloud of dust as he went.

* * *

WITH PA GONE, it seemed like everything had rolled downhill faster and faster, like a boulder bound for rock bottom. There was some insurance money to pay the mortgage for a while, but when that ran out, payments to the bank had been sporadic. Ma had taken to bed, the payments to the bank got further behind, and there wasn't anything to eat unless Deke or Sadie found it in the woods.

In a sense, Deke had fled to the woods this morning. Just last week, the bank had foreclosed on the farm and scheduled for it to be auctioned on the steps of the county courthouse. Once again, it had fallen to the county sheriff to drive out and give them the news that they had one week to vacate the property. This time, he wasn't alone, accompanied by a man wearing a suit and shiny shoes.

The sheriff introduced the man. "This here is Mr. Wilcox from the bank. He's the one who called in the note on your farm. Well, I ought to say, the bank's farm now."

Mr. Wilcox didn't say a word, but he looked around with a lordly, proprietary air. He frowned, clearly not pleased by what he saw. He approached the porch, stepping carefully around some chicken droppings so as not to get any on his fancy shoes. He gave Deke and Sadie a look similar to the one he'd given the chicken shit, like they were just another annoyance.

Their mother hadn't risen from bed, so it fell to Deke and Sadie to meet the sheriff once again. "I'm sorry about this, son," he said, handing Deke a document. "That's an order of eviction. It says you need to vacate the premises within seven days."

"I'm being generous," the banker spoke up, not bothering to take off his hat in Sadie's presence. What did a banker care about a mountain girl without any shoes?

"Where will we go?" Sadie had asked.

"Not my problem, darlin'," he replied. "You just be off this property by Tuesday noon next week, or I'll have the sheriff here throw you off."

"We can get the money, mister," Deke had said.

"How? You gonna sell those chickens, maybe? No, the bank waited for its money long enough. This is a done deal." The banker narrowed his eyes as he noticed Deke's scars for the first time. "What the hell happened to you, boy? Looks like you tried to shave with a rusty razor —or maybe with a garden rake."

The banker looked away, taking in more of his new acquisition. Deke had been splitting firewood and held an ax, the edge sharp and bright. He glared at the banker. Deke's eyes were a startling shade of gray, like rainwater. Those eyes held a cunning animal glint, the feral eyes of a fox.

Deke shifted his grip on the ax and took a step toward the banker.

The sheriff looked up in alarm, realizing he was too far away to prevent what was coming next. "Son—"

But Sadie put a hand on Deke's arm, a gentle gesture that stopped him before he could take another step.

"That'll do, Deke," she said quietly.

"You can keep the chickens if you want," said the banker, barking a short laugh. He hadn't noticed the ax in Deke's hands or the look in the boy's eyes, apparently oblivious that he'd come within a heartbeat of having his head split open like a ripe watermelon.

The sheriff knew, though. He'd seen it all. The thing was, he couldn't bring himself to blame the boy.

"Come on, Mr. Wilcox," he said sternly to the banker. "We've delivered your letter. Let's go."

That had been nearly a week ago. Tomorrow, they would need to be off the land. This morning, Deke planned to hunt here one last time. It was his way of saying goodbye.

"Now, where'd you get to?" he muttered, pushing thoughts of the future from his mind and turning his attention back to the hunt. "I know this is where you like to be."

He had brought the rifle this morning because he wasn't after squirrels or quail. He was hunting the big buck that he had seen a couple of times over the summer. That much meat would have gone a long way toward feeding them right into the winter—maybe with some left to share with the neighbors.

Deke focused his sharp, searching eyes on the woods. The gray-brown coat of the buck with its splashes of white would blend perfectly with the trees, so he would need to keep a sharp eye out. If he wanted this hunt to be a success, he would need to see the buck long before it saw him. It occurred to him that his family had been hunting these deer for generations on this same ground.

He moved through the woods quietly, carefully, his footsteps silent beneath the whisper of the breeze in the barren trees. Winter was coming on fast. There had already been several hard frosts. It had been a lean harvest, and their milk cow was nearly dried out. In the morning, there was ice to crack in the water trough. A trip to the outhouse was invigorating, to say the least. Soon there would be snow, and real winter would arrive in the mountains.

For the deer, he needed the rifle. He doubted that he could have gotten close enough to the buck to take him with buckshot. The rifle was an old Winchester that had been owned by his father. Lately, Deke had realized that he was starting to forget his father's face. It was no more than a vague memory, like a half-remembered dream. But when he held the rifle, he could remember clearly. The rifle was the best connection to his father that he had, because his father had handled this same wood, and his eyes had used these same sights. It was strange, but when Deke carried the rifle, he felt as if his father walked with him. It was his father, too, who had taught him to shoot. Here in the mountains, it was one of the first and most important lessons that a father taught a son—or a daughter. Pa had also taught Sadie to shoot.

The rifle gave Deke power. It made him the equal of any man. As long as he held a rifle, and was willing to use it, to stand up for himself, there was nothing that Deke needed to fear. His father had passed along that lesson too. What did a man have if you took away his ability to defend himself?

Out of habit, he touched the deep scars on the left side of his face. They reminded him of furrows in a plowed field, still angry and red after all these years. The scars ran down his neck and across his torso. He always kept his shirt collar buttoned up tight and usually wore a bandanna knotted around his throat on the rare occasions when he went into town, but there was no hiding the scars on his face.

He followed a game trail deeper into a thicket, the brush closing in around him, the smell of musk rising from the damp earth beneath his worn boots. He emerged into a mountain meadow. He kept low, crouching, not wanting to spook the buck that he knew must be just ahead.

He scanned the meadow and caught sight of the buck. The deer stood on the far edge of the meadow, head dipped to graze on what remained of the green grass.

Deke raised the rifle to his good shoulder and put the sights on the deer. His arms were sinewy with muscle from hardscrabble farmwork, so that his aim held steady. It was a long shot, but Deke didn't fret over that. He rarely missed.

All at once, the buck seemed to be alert to something. He raised his magnificent head, the antlers held high, catching the morning light. The broad chest turned to Deke like a challenge. Up here in this remote mountain meadow, there wasn't much that this big buck in his prime had ever needed to fear.

Deke lowered the rifle. It had been an easy shot—there was no doubt that he could have taken the buck.

The buck held his eye, some primitive glimmer of acknowledgment there, then bounded away.

Normally Deke would have wanted the buck to be hanging from the big tree out back long before then, which would mean the difference between a hungry winter and a starving one. But where would they be spending the winter? Not on the farm. Not anymore.

* * *

THE DAY HAD COME and gone when they'd had to leave the farm. With nowhere else to go, the three of them had had to move into a boardinghouse in town, sharing a single room. For someone who had loved to roam the woods and fields, the cramped room might as well have been a prison cell. Deke slept on the floor, while Sadie and his ma shared the lumpy bed. The money that they'd gotten for the pigs and chickens had been enough to pay a month's rent in advance—and that was all the money that they had.

He'd thought about joining the navy, like his cousin Jasper had done, but he hated to abandon Sadie like that. With no alternative, Deke had gone to the sawmill where his pa had worked and asked for a job. The foreman had been reluctant, saying that they didn't have any work because the Depression was hanging on, but he had relented. It seemed like the least he could do, considering that the boy's father had died in an accident at the sawmill.

And so Deke had worked there for almost a year now, the noisy mill being a long way from the fields and woods of the farm. He hated that place. It was too hot in summer, and bone-cold in winter. The relentless spinning blade was always present, as threatening as an insatiable monster, a reminder of his father's death on the cruel steel.

Ma had passed that fall. The doctor couldn't even say what her ailment had been. It was as though she had just given up and faded away.

But Deke and Sadie had to go on living. The days continued for Deke, each of them passing as miserably as the next, his pay barely enough to cover the rent at the boardinghouse. In his pain, feeling sorry for himself, he sometimes bought a pint of cheap whiskey and drank himself to sleep, hating himself for that when he awoke with an aching head the next morning, as miserable as ever. Sadie didn't approve.

Then again, she had been too tired to do much about it, working herself to the bone as a maid for one of the few families with money in town. Each day she seemed to grow thinner, a shadow of herself.

Life in town wasn't easy, and he felt like an outcast. The scars on his face that made people so nervous around him didn't help.

Once, he had seen the banker who had evicted them driving by in a big car. He had glanced at Deke without any recognition, as if his gaze had gone right through him. In the banker's eyes, Deke was not worth noticing. Deke balled up his fists at the anger that went through him. If you didn't have money, it seemed like you weren't worth anything.

Deep down, he knew that he was grieving for his parents—and for the farm, a way of life that had been lost to him and Sadie. He needed to get out, to do something different, but he felt helpless as a bug caught in the current of a mountain stream.

And then came the December day when the foreman had shut down the sawmill. This in itself was unusual, and the men had gathered around as a strange quiet settled over them. Beyond the mill, people filled the street, and he could hear excited shouts. It was clear to Deke that something big had happened.

"What's going on?" one of the sawmill crew asked.

"The president just gave a speech over the radio. Congress voted, and we're going to war," the foreman said. "They're setting up a recruiting station on Main Street, and I'm sure that some of you men will be signing up. Don't expect to be paid for the time you're gone doing it."

Like everyone else, Deke had heard the news about Pearl Harbor the day before. He was worried about his cousin, who was stationed in Hawaii. He hoped that Cousin Jasper was all right, but for the first time in months, Deke felt a sense of purpose. If the United States needed soldiers, he'd be the first in line.

The big saw blade was still spinning silently when he walked out of the sawmill without saying a parting word to anyone.

He didn't know anything about war or being a soldier, but he was about to find out. He enlisted the next day. Two days after that, Sadie was on a bus bound for Washington, DC.

Later he would realize that the war had saved him, and maybe Sadie, too, and started him on the greatest adventure of his life.

CHAPTER FOUR

Guam, August 1944

AT LONG LAST, the war seemed to have receded like the tide as the fight for Guam slowly came to its bloody end. It didn't mean that the Japs were completely licked. Holdouts sheltered in the mountainous forests. From time to time, bands of Japanese troops still ambushed or harassed the soldiers.

But for the moment, the men of Patrol Easy weren't concerned about a few stray Japanese soldiers. They had been designated Patrol Easy during their reconnaissance of Guam, and the name had stuck.

Now, for once, they were truly living up to that name. The men lay sprawled on the beach, enjoying some long overdue R & R. Although the war was far from over, with a large swath of the Pacific still in Japanese control, it had taken a respite in this corner of the world, and the men were taking whatever R & R they could.

"You know how I can tell this ain't the Jersey Shore?" Philly asked. "Not a girl in sight, that's how. There was this one time, I met a girl on the boardwalk named Wanda—"

"The other three times you've told this story, her name was Betty," Deke interrupted.

Philly just shook his head, as he often did when he was buying himself some time to make something up. Deke had been around him long enough to know Philly's tricks. "Sure, there was that time with *Betty*, under the boardwalk in Atlantic City," Philly said. "Maybe three or four times, come to think of it. But I'm talking about *Wanda* now. Wanda was a whole different situation, let me tell you."

Deke just shook his head and tuned Philly out, which was easy to do. That damn city boy—*Philly* was short for "Philadelphia"—never shut his mouth. Then again, Deke couldn't help but smile at Philly's stories. There was something comforting about hearing Philly talk, like listening to a familiar radio program.

Deke looked around at the sun-washed beach, which was still a strange sight for him, about as different from the mountains where he had grown up as one could get. He missed those mountains, with their brooding, rocky faces and crisp autumn woods. On this Pacific island, the damn sand got into everything, and the air dripped with humidity.

Still, they were able to enjoy a few hours on the beach because the fighting on the island of Guam had subsided, except for pockets of resistance deep in the jungle-covered hills, where a few die-hard Japanese didn't have the sense to give up. You had to hand it to those Jap troops—they were nothing if not fanatical. They would readily make a last-ditch banzai attack or even starve to death, all in an effort to die for the Emperor, rather than give themselves up. Lieutenant Steele had explained that the Japanese saw their Emperor as a god, not to be questioned but only obeyed. He might be a living, breathing man, but Emperor Hirohito was the heart and soul of Japan.

Deke could understand the determination of the Japanese to fight to the death, even respect it. As a stubborn young man from the Southern hills, he knew what it meant to have your back against the wall and keep fighting. In a sense, he should have been dead a long time ago, and he had the scars to prove it. Deke was a natural-born fighter.

But even if he respected the enemy, he sure as hell didn't *like* the enemy. The Japs had killed too many Americans for that, starting with their sneak attack on Pearl Harbor. They had killed Americans on Guadalcanal, sent thousands of sailors to their deaths in Ironbottom Sound, and killed thousands more on Guam. One of those dead had been Ben

Hemphill, shot by a Jap sniper within minutes of landing on the beach. Deke had taken Ben's death bitterly. They had gone through training together, and Deke had promised himself that he would look out for Ben.

Deke had failed, and something in him had snapped. In a blind rage, he had bayoneted the Jap sniper until the body had more holes in it than a rusty bucket. Even that son of a bitch Sergeant Hawley had been taken aback by the sight of that.

The way Deke figured it, if the Japs were so eager to die for their Emperor, Deke was glad to help. He sure had helped that sniper down the road to kingdom come, or wherever it was that dead Japs thought they ended up.

Nobody knew for sure how many Japs were hiding out and refused to give up. Lieutenant Steele had passed along that it was anywhere from several hundred to maybe even a few thousand.

Some of these enemy troops managed to organize occasional raids on the beachhead, but those amounted to little more than suicide missions. Otherwise, the island was firmly in US control.

One of the more comical incidents involving these Japanese hold-outs had taken place a few days before, when a makeshift outdoor movie theater had been erected. In the tropical darkness near the beach, the troops sat on logs or on the ground, swatting mosquitoes and smoking cigarettes, watching a movie shown on a bedsheet. The movie had been *Stage Door Canteen*, and right in the middle of a scene with Guy Lombardo performing, someone had noticed strange laughter. Hell, the Japanese even *laughed* different. To their surprise, they found a diminutive Jap soldier who had sneaked into their midst to enjoy the movie. He had smiled and put his hands up. The shocked GIs had given him a cigarette and escorted him to the prisoner stockade. Apparently, Hollywood had won him over.

Every now and then, they heard a distant burst of fire or the whump of a mortar. But those sounds were too far off to worry about. Philly had finished up his story about Wanda, which wasn't any more believable than the one that he'd told about Betty. The only thing they knew for certain was that they were all a long, long way from New Jersey.

"Anybody got any canned peaches left?" Yoshio Shimizu wanted to know. "I've got cigarettes to trade."

"I'll take those cigarettes off your hands, kid," Philly said. "They might stunt your growth."

"You can have them for a can of peaches."

"Deal."

Yoshio tossed over a pack of smokes and caught the canned peaches that flew in his direction. Eagerly, he went to work on the can, using his combat knife, punching a hole in the top so that he could drink the sweet syrup.

He passed the can around because Yoshio was generous that way. Deke took a drink, along with "Rodeo" Rodenbeck and "Alphabet" Pawelczyk. Deke savored that hit of the sweet juice, enjoying the luxury of peaches canned on the other side of the ocean.

"Thanks, kid."

None of them were friends—or not exactly. That was the army for you, throwing men together from all sorts of places and walks of life, guys who wouldn't normally give each other the time of day. Deke was just a dumb hick. Philly was a wiseass from Philadelphia. Yoshio was a Nisei, a Japanese-American who could speak the language of the enemy and served as an interpreter—if and when there were any Japanese prisoners.

No, Deke thought. They were not friends. They were something more. They were family. You couldn't choose your family, either, but you would do anything to protect your family. That was the kind of loyalty that Deke understood.

Despite their differences, they knew each other better than brothers, at least to the extent that they could count on one another in a fight. They might not know each other's religion or what their favorite baseball team was, but they knew that Yoshio could dig a foxhole like nobody's business, that Rodeo and Alphabet kept their cool when the lead was flying, and that despite all his bluster and baloney, you wouldn't find a man braver than Philly. As for Deke, they knew he could hit anything he could see with his Springfield rifle. He could be a mean son of a bitch, ornery and sullen, and he wouldn't tell anyone how he'd gotten his scars, but he was *their* son of a bitch.

They were missing one man out of their original sniper squad. Ingram was dead, killed by the Japanese marksman they had nicknamed the "Samurai Sniper." Rumor had it that Private Egan would soon be leaving. He was a war dog handler assigned to them for their scouting mission into the jungles of Guam, before the last big push against the Japanese. His dog, Whoa Nelly, had been killed while saving his life near Yigo. It was only a matter of time before the army figured out what to do with him and he was reassigned.

Then there was Lieutenant Steele. He sat apart from the other men on the beach, smoking a cigarette. He looked tired, his thoughts a million miles away.

They had all left their weapons nearby to go for a swim, with Deke and Lieutenant Steele being the exceptions. Both men kept their weapons between their knees, muzzles up, butts in the sand. Deke held a Springfield sniper rifle with a telescopic sight, while the lieutenant had a shotgun between his knees.

Unlike the others, Deke wasn't watching the ocean. Instead, his gaze never left the line of jungle that began far up the beach. That was Deke for you, always switched on and never relaxed. So far, it was a quality that was helping to keep him alive out here.

"I'm going for a swim," Philly announced.

"Shark bait," said Pawelczyk, whose nickname was "Alphabet"—for good reason, considering that his Polish surname seemed to include most of it.

"What do you care? You can't swim, anyhow."

"It ain't swimming if you're only knee deep, which is as far out as I ever plan to go in the water. But you go on ahead and feed the sharks."

"Nah, I'm too stringy for sharks. Anyhow, I hear it's dumb Polacks like you that they really like to eat. Like caviar for sharks, you know?"

"Aw, do me a favor and duck your head under for a while. Like maybe an hour."

Philly laughed and shucked off his pants. Like a lot of soldiers, he no longer bothered with the hot, cumbersome army-issued boxers and wore nothing under the button-fly fatigues when in the field, giving rise to the term "going commando." He ran down to the ocean and threw himself into the waves. Left behind on the hot beach, Alphabet and Rodeo found the sight of Philly cavorting in the surf too much to bear, so they shucked off their own fatigues and joined him in the cool ocean waves.

Yoshio and Egan looked at each other, shrugged, and ran down to dump their clothes at the water's edge. Pretty soon, all of them were splashing and generally playing around in the waves, shouting their fool heads off. It was a reminder that, in reality, they were all barely more than kids.

Only Deke and Lieutenant Steele were left sitting on the beach, both a ways apart, looking on. It was clear that neither one of them intended to go for a swim. Steele was an officer, after all. As for Deke, he hated the damn ocean. The sight of all that water wasn't natural. Give him hills and mountains any day, but not the sea.

They had been cavorting in the waves for maybe five minutes when a rifle shot cut right through the sound of their laughter with an angry crack. A bullet struck the water, raising a white welt on the surface of the blue Pacific, quickly followed by another.

Patrol Easy had been caught out in the open, most of them as defenseless as they could be.

"Sniper!" Yoshio shouted, then dove underwater.

A bullet plucked the water where his head had been an instant before. The Jap sniper's aim was improving.

Deke was already on his belly, elbows dug into the sand, rifle to his shoulder, looking for a target. A bullet zipped overhead, so close that it left a metallic taste in Deke's mouth. He worked his hips even harder than he had ground them into that hooker during shore leave on Oahu, trying to sink a fraction of an inch deeper into the sand. The boys in the water were doing their best to stay ducked under, but every time they came up for air, a bullet struck nearby.

He didn't put his eye to the riflescope yet but scanned the line of jungle scrub that began beyond the beach. Most of the taller trees were ragged or their trunks were snapped off as if they had been caught in a typhoon, though it hadn't been a storm but the results of heavy shelling from the cruisers and destroyers assembled off the island in the warm waters of the Philippine Sea. Lower down, the scrub was thick enough to hide any number of Japanese snipers. The Jap would definitely be armed with an Arisaka, a rifle that made up for its lack of sheer firepower with its stealth—its lighter cartridge made the shooter's location tricky to pinpoint. Its lighter load didn't make it any less deadly, just quieter.

Plus Deke was already going a little deaf from all the damn shelling. After a few weeks of combat, Deke's eye was practiced enough to search for any bit of movement or the glint of the sun off the glass of a scope or the gleam of a rifle barrel. It didn't help that the heat rising off the sand made the view flicker and shimmer. The Jap sniper could have been anywhere—and nowhere.

Nearby, Lieutenant Steele was doing much the same thing, although his shotgun was next to useless at this range.

That single sniper had them pinned down good.

But that wasn't the worst of it. Like a bully kicking sand, a long burst of machine-gun fire churned up the sand near Deke's head. Another burst made the tropical water near the swimmers seem to boil. The sniper wasn't alone. The Japs also had a machine gun trained on the beach. Things had just gone from bad to worse.

"Cover me," the lieutenant shouted. An instant later, he was up and running, his boots kicking gouts of sand across the beach. He was heading for the tree line.

Deke watched the crazy bastard charging at the Japs. He fired at nothing, hoping against hope that it would make the enemy soldiers keep their heads down long enough for Steele to make it to cover.

Steele juked left, then right, moving fast. He was the oldest man on the beach by far, but he was in good shape. Either that or the fear of being stitched by the machine gun had given wings to his feet. Another burst kicked up sand all around him, but Steele kept going.

Deke fired at where he thought the machine gun was hidden, once again praying for luck. Then Steele reached the jungle's edge off to the left and disappeared from sight. One moment he had been there, and the next he was gone. *Where the hell is he going?*

Deke turned his attention back to finding the sniper. Some part of himself thought, *Hell, this is a lot better than splashing around in the ocean.* He pushed the thought from his mind and scanned the jungle's edge for any sign of the enemy marksman. The man was well hidden.

But he couldn't hide forever. Deke held still, hoping for any sign that would give the sniper away.

The machine gun was still chattering away, alternating between bursts near Deke's position and the men in the water. Another gout of seawater erupted whenever one of the men raised his head too long.

Although the men had initially been splashing in the surf, they had been forced to move into deeper water, where they could duck under and have a fighting chance of staying out of the enemy's sights. But it wasn't easy going. They swam out even farther, closer to where the big ocean swells broke against the edge of the coral reef. There was no way they could go beyond the point where the waves churned in a rush of powerful fury. Still, some of the men were in over their heads.

"Help! Help!" he heard Alphabet shouting. "I can't swim!"

"Get your feet under you!" Philly shouted back at him. It was easier said than done, with the tide tugging them out to sea and bullets coming at them from the other direction. To make things worse, the coral shelf was sharp and unforgiving, cutting their bare feet.

If the Japs didn't shoot them, it sounded as if at least some of Patrol Easy might drown. Deke stared even more intently into the shadowy jungle's edge. *Where the hell are you?*

Finally, he saw the smallest movement. It might have been dismissed as a bird flitting through the brush, or a flicker of a leaf in the breeze, but Deke caught sight of the outline of a helmet, bent over a rifle sight.

He lowered his eye to his own riflescope and put the crosshairs where he had seen the motion. Had he imagined the glimpse of the helmet? He saw only a patch of jungle now through the scope. Still, he squeezed the trigger, and the rifle bucked against his shoulder.

Through the scope, he saw something droop and realized it was the Jap sniper's body, sagging under its own deadweight. One down, one nest of machine gunners to go.

As if they had read his mind, the Japs let loose another burst that churned even closer to his head. Sand flew into his eyes, momentarily blinding him. *Son of a bitch!* How was he even supposed to shoot back?

An instant later, he heard the deep boom of Lieutenant Steele's shotgun. Then another boom. The machine gun fell silent.

One thing for sure—the Japs wouldn't be bothering them anymore.

Swiping at the sand and sweat stinging his eyes, Deke still managed to see a figure emerge from the jungle's edge. It was Lieutenant Steele, carrying his shotgun cradled in the crook of his elbow, not seeming to have a care in the world, like maybe he was returning from a pheasant hunt. Deke couldn't help but grin.

Now that the shooting had stopped, the rest of the men made their way back in from the sea. Alphabet had to be half dragged, half carried out of the ocean by Philly and Rodeo. He sputtered and coughed up water.

But that didn't stop him from managing to stammer, "Goddamn sneaky Japs! I can't wait to kill every last one of 'em!"

The others nodded. It was pretty much how they all felt.

Rodeo pointed. "Hey, look! Someone's coming."

A jeep had appeared, racing toward them across the beach, sticking close to the waterline, where the sand was more compacted. Every now and then the driver had to yank the wheel sharply to stay ahead of a wave.

"Ain't it just like the cavalry to show up too late."

"Maybe they'll give us a ride back to HQ."

"Don't get your hopes up."

As it turned out, the jeep wasn't there to help them fight the Japanese or give them a ride. An officious-looking young staff officer looked them up and down.

"Are you men swimming? What the hell! Don't you know there's a war on? There must be a thousand Japs still hidden in the jungle."

"Don't worry. Now there's a few less."

But the officer wasn't interested in the tale of their firefight. In fact, from the look on his face, it didn't even seem like he believed any of it. He had come with orders for Lieutenant Steele. "The colonel wants to see you. That is, if you're not too busy swimming and working on your tans."

"Yes, sir. Any chance of getting a ride back?"

"Sorry, no room. You'll have to walk." With that, the officer nodded to the driver and the jeep lurched through the sand in a slow semicircle, giving a clear glimpse of the empty back seat, and then began racing toward HQ in the distance.

"Friendly guy," Philly said.

"Never mind that. Let's move out." Lieutenant Steele started to walk away but then paused to stare at Philly. "Philly, put some clothes on. The army has a reputation to uphold, son. If any marines see that short limb of yours, we'll never hear the end of it."

"It's the cold water," Philly grumped, tugging on his trousers.

Yoshio and Egan looked around, but the tide had carried off their fatigues.

Still laughing, Steele tugged off his shirt and tossed it to Egan. "Wrap that around you, for God's sake. Somebody give Yoshio a shirt."

Nearby, Yoshio was starting to shiver as the sun dipped behind a cloud.

Deke sighed. "You are a sorry sight, Yoshio," he said. Since he was the only one left with dry clothing to spare, he took off his shirt and tossed it to Yoshio. With his shirt off, the angry red scars raking down his torso were clearly visible against his pale Scotch Irish skin. They were old scars, not from something that had happened to him in the Pacific. Philly stared and opened his mouth to comment, but for once he seemed to think better of it.

"Thanks, Deke," Yoshio said, wrapping the fatigues around his middle.

"What a bunch. Anyhow, let's go," Steele said, nodding in the direction of the disappearing jeep. "It sounds to me as if the war's not over yet and somebody found a job for us to do."

CHAPTER FIVE

MORE THAN A THOUSAND miles away across the blue Pacific, on the island of Leyte in the Philippines, the Japanese were preparing to meet the threat of invasion.

A key aspect of the coastal defense was being constructed at Guin-hangdan Hill. Rising more than five hundred feet above the coastal plain, the hill offered a commanding view of the beach and Leyte Gulf beyond. From the Y-shaped crest of the hill, the sleepy town of Palo and the slow-moving Bangon River were in plain view.

The ancient volcanic core created a natural fortress, and the Japanese forces had taken advantage of that by gradually adding to its defenses since occupying the Philippines in 1941.

"Harumph," grunted Major Hisako Noguchi, surveying the work that had been done. On the one hand, he was amazed that they had accomplished so much. But on the other hand, there was still so much to do.

He watched with a dispassionate gaze as an officer beat a slow-moving Filipino laborer with a stick. Such cruelty did not bother him. Noguchi concerned himself only with the results.

With his engineer's eye, Major Noguchi studied the placement of the artillery positions, some of which had been designed to accommodate "disappearing guns" that could fire and then roll back into a cave, out of sight, making them frustratingly difficult targets.

In the last few months, construction efforts had risen to a fever pitch. Every available Japanese soldier had been put to work, trading their rifles for shovels, picks, and wheelbarrows. Mechanized equipment that was so familiar to US forces was virtually nonexistent here in the Philippines.

Instead, alongside the soldiers, work details of conscripted Filipino men of all ages had toiled from dawn to dusk, under constant threat of swift punishment if they appeared to slack off for even one moment under the brutal heat and torrential tropical rains.

If the Japanese troops were underfed and treated poorly, then it was far worse for the Filipinos, who were considered to be little more than slaves. Weakened men were pushed aside, and fresh conscripts took their place, although these were often boys or very old men. No matter—the desperate Japanese occupiers treated them all harshly. A mass grave near the base of the hill, not far from the nearby town of Palo, now occupied by the Japanese, was testimony to the backbreaking work and the treatment that the Filipinos received at the hands of the occupying force.

Those almost inhuman efforts had produced incredible results. Gun pits and firing positions now honeycombed the promontory. Extensive caves, complete with electric lighting and ventilation systems, ensured that not even the heaviest enemy air or naval bombardment could reach the defenders. They were well prepared for an attack that they were sure was to come.

The man in charge of this operation, Major Noguchi, was an artillery officer, one of those men who could instantly calculate a complicated firing azimuth in his head. He also had a talent for building fortifications and a sly cunning for managing to disguise them from the enemy.

The smell of freshly dug dirt and curing cement hung over the hill. Noguchi nodded in satisfaction. *Let them come.*

He was a squat, unimposing man—even a little chubby, and he wore thick glasses. But it would be a mistake to dismiss Noguchi on appearances alone. Within him burned the spirit of a warrior.

Noguchi walked on, huffing and puffing with exertion as he made his way up the hillside, the soldiers he passed barely acknowledging him.

It was no wonder. On more than one occasion he had been reprimanded for wearing simple work clothes rather than his officer's uniform. He did not bother with carrying a sword, like many officers, but preferred a shovel, sometimes joining in alongside the soldiers who were busy digging and carting loads of soil.

It was grueling labor. After all, there was no heavy equipment to do all this work. They had built it all by hand, as if they were laborers from a thousand years ago. Their efforts were so different from those of their enemy, who brought along ships filled with bulldozers and even backhoes as they advanced across the Pacific, ever closer to Japan.

"Faster, faster!" he admonished a group of soldiers digging a sniper pit. "You will wish that you had already dug ten more of those once the Americans arrive."

The soldiers looked past Noguchi to the expanse of empty ocean beyond. There was a cloud or two on the horizon, but no sign of enemy ships. They didn't dig any faster. One or two stopped digging to wipe their brows or take a drink of water.

Another soldier approached. He was younger than Noguchi, and not any taller, but he was far more graceful, moving like a fabled Tsushima leopard cat through the construction zone. He was not an officer, but a *gunsō*, or sergeant.

"You heard him," the sergeant said. His voice was no more than a purr, but there was menace in it. "Dig faster. My men and I are the ones who will be in these pits, while you are safe underground. Make it deep, and then dig another."

Immediately, the soldiers bent to their work with fresh energy. They didn't fear Noguchi, with his shovel and his dusty clothes. But they all knew Sergeant Akio Ikeda. He carried a rifle with a telescopic sight. He commanded the *sogekihei* squad—men with special ability as sharpshooters. Rumor had it that he sometimes drank too much sake and sat up here on the hill, picking off Filipino laborers in the distance.

"Thank you, Sergeant Ikeda," Noguchi said.

"You should hit one with your shovel from time to time," replied Ikeda. "Show them you're the boss."

Noguchi shrugged. "Maybe you are right. But you must admit, the men have worked very hard overall."

Even Ikeda had to agree. He gave the officer a rare smile. "*Hai*. The Americans will break upon this hill like the sea dashing upon the rocks."

"Indeed," Noguchi said.

Together, the two men continued their inspection of the defenses. It had been an intense matter of debate and even disagreement, but General Yamashita, overall commander of Japanese forces on Leyte, one of the nine main islands that made up the Philippines, had declared that the American invasion should not be met with defenses at the shoreline.

To many military minds, this seemed like an unnatural way to defend an island. Shouldn't the defenses be at the shoreline? Wouldn't the Japanese want to meet the enemy at the beach and hurl them back into the sea, preventing them from gaining any foothold on Leyte? Many officers could be forgiven if they didn't understand why this strategy was being abandoned in favor of allowing the American forces to land with relatively little opposition.

General Yamashita had ordered that the beaches be left undefended for the most part. He had sound reasons for this strategy. Any defenses at the beach itself would be out in the open, vulnerable to the naval bombardment that would surely precede the American landing. No matter how many men and guns they put on that beach, there might be nothing left but churned ground by the time the enemy guns fell silent.

Instead, General Yamashita had moved the bulk of defenses inland. The Americans would land, but they would soon be drawn into a deadly trap. Hidden in the hills and jungles, the big guns could do little against the well-entrenched defenders.

But this did not mean the landing would be met with a welcome mat. There would be more than a few machine-gun positions close to the beach. It would be fairly easy to move the machine gunners into position after the American bombardment ended. With overlapping fields of fire, the machine guns would exact a bloody toll before they were silenced.

Guinhangdan Hill would be another thorn in the Americans' side, anchoring the Japanese coastal defense strategy. The hill itself was what remained of an ancient volcano. Much of the volcanic stone had been hollowed out for defensive fortifications. The stone was almost made to order for this purpose—hard enough to withstand enemy shelling, but porous enough that it could be dug away by men using picks and shovels.

From up here, the artillery could fire down on the beach and also at the invasion fleet itself. No matter how much firepower the Americans threw at the hill, no matter how many planes flew overhead to drop their bombs, Major Noguchi had helped ensure that the only way the hill could truly be taken would be for those troops to march inland and storm it—at great expense.

Still, even someone as steadfast in his duties as Noguchi could not ignore the fact that the island might be overrun in the end. Other islands had fallen under the American advance. Would Leyte be different? Whatever the outcome, he was sure that the Americans would be very sorry that they had come ashore. Noguchi would *make* them sorry, as would Ikeda and his snipers. He smiled with satisfaction at the thought.

Ikeda had noticed the officer's smile. "I know what you are thinking, sir."

"Do you?"

"You are thinking that you are very glad that we are not the ones who will have to attack this hill."

Major Noguchi barked a laugh. "You would be correct in that assumption, Sergeant Ikeda."

The two men continued to climb the hill, Ikeda moving easily up the slope, while Noguchi huffed and puffed. He paused from time to time to catch his breath and to inspect what was ultimately his handiwork. Groups of men labored to dig sniper holes or to add a few more sandbags to the entrance to an artillery position, passing the sandbags up the hillside in a daisy chain that reminded Noguchi of a line of ants.

It was quite a variety of ants, considering that the growing manpower shortage meant that men of all ages had been conscripted into the Imperial Japanese Army. Some of the soldiers were barely more than teenagers, while a few had hair shot through with gray. The older soldiers might easily have been the grandfathers of the youngest conscripts, considering that men from ages fifteen to sixty were now being drafted. Under the old rules, national service had been limited to ages seventeen through forty.

In truth, the army was something of a catchall for men who wouldn't hold much promise as pilots or sailors—but a man of just about any age could hold a rifle or throw a grenade. This did not mean that the soldiers lacked fervor—almost each and every one of them was ready to sacrifice his life for Japan and the Emperor—so much the better if he took a few enemy soldiers along with him.

Most of the men worked in their undershirts or had even stripped to the waist in the heat. Their pants and boots were covered in dust, making some of the men almost indistinguishable from their surroundings. Each night, they went to sleep grimy and sweaty in fetid quarters, then rose at dawn to do it all over again.

Noguchi did not trouble himself too much regarding the welfare of the men. They were simply a means to an end, which was the construction of this fortress against the impending American attack.

Yet even he had to admit that the work was taking its toll. Sadly, many of the soldiers looked too thin, their rib cages showing or their chests hollowed out. They had spent endless hours laboring on this hillside, and the truth was that they lacked decent rations. Most of them were surviving on a bowl of white rice a day, with a small serving of some meat or fish or canned crab perhaps every other day. It was barely enough food to sustain a child, let alone a Japanese soldier doing hard labor all day. These underfed soldiers would soon be expected to put down their shovels and pick up their rifles. Would they even have enough strength left to fight?

Noguchi felt a little guilty about his own sturdy frame, if not exactly corpulent, then definitely well fed. Then again, officers had access to much better food, and the major had never been one to deny himself. As for Ikeda, the major wondered if the man needed to eat at all—he seemed to have endless reserves of energy to fuel his wiry strength. The man reminded Noguchi of a coiled steel spring.

Noguchi paused for breath, taking the time to observe a group of men working nearby. One of them seemed to only be poking at the soil with his shovel rather than actually digging. In fairness to the soldier, he appeared to be nearly as thin as the shovel handle. "You, there, put your back into it," Noguchi said.

The man bent to his work, but the tip of his shovel still only scraped ineffectually across the rocky soil, resulting in the unpleasant sound of metal screeching over rock.

Quick as a flash, Ikeda stepped forward and swatted the man in the side of the head. "You heard the major. Dig! You are a lazy disgrace!" For good measure, Ikeda kicked the man so hard in the seat of the pants that it raised a cloud of dust from the soldier's dirty trousers.

"*Hai! Hai!*" the soldier shouted, redoubling his efforts. The soldiers around him also worked harder to avoid Sergeant Ikeda's boot. Dirt flew. In the Japanese military, physical punishment of soldiers was common. When Japanese officers heard that their American counterparts had to respect the individual rights of servicemen, they were astonished. How could the Americans hope to fight a war? And yet, somehow, they did. A war that they were winning.

Finally, the two men approached the summit of Guinhangdan Hill. The view was impressive, with the sweep of the beach below clearly visible. Aqua water broke in gentle waves upon the shore. It was an idyllic scene and almost impossible to imagine that it would be interrupted all too soon by the sight of an invading force.

Near the summit stood Noguchi's pride and joy, a sight even more rare than a coveted black pearl. A massive cave had been carved into the volcanic rock, yet the entrance was so cleverly disguised that it was hard to spot from the air or even from the sea. Like the hollow eye of a massive skull, the cave managed to disguise its contents. In a sense, this cave and its contents were Noguchi's masterpiece as a military engineer. From within the cave, like the head of a hydra, jutted the muzzles of three massive guns. Their sheer size made them monstrous, dwarfing any of the artillery on that hill—or anywhere else on Leyte, for that matter.

It was a mystery why the guns had been sent to Leyte, clearly part of some master plan that Noguchi was not privy to. But he had obeyed his orders by putting them into position, and he knew how to use them well enough.

These were Type 94 eighteen-inch naval guns that had been designed for the *Yamato*, the largest of Japan's naval ships. Only a very few guns of this size had been manufactured. Each gun could fire a three-thousand-pound shell up to twenty-six miles, delivering a truly devastating blow. The guns had also been designed to use special "bee-hive" antiaircraft rounds that could sweep clear entire sections of sky. If the Americans planned an aerial assault on Leyte, they would be in for a nasty surprise.

Installing the guns had been a tremendous task, considering the overall weight of the battery. It had been akin to dragging an entire section of a battleship up the hillside, all done with ropes, pulleys and chock blocks, and sweat.

But Noguchi hoped that the effort had been worth it. If Leyte's defenses had been impressive before, they were now downright formidable.

An artillery officer approached, scrambling down from the cave mouth. "Sir, we have reports of a target off the coast."

"A target?"

"An American ship, sir. It is just within range. Forty thousand meters."

Noguchi nodded. Could this be the first of the American invasion fleet? He could see Ikeda peering out to sea, as if hoping for a glimpse of the American ship, but that was impossible at this distance. He even put his rifle to his shoulder and peered through the telescopic sight.

"Stop wasting your time, Ikeda," Noguchi said.

At that distance, the ship couldn't be seen by the most powerful binoculars, because the destroyer was hidden by the curve of the earth itself. It was like holding an upside-down bowl in front of your eyes and trying to see what was on the other side.

But that did not mean the American ship was out of reach of the battery, which some had nicknamed Orochi after a multiheaded dragon from children's tales.

"Captain, I think that this would be an excellent time to exercise the guns."

"*Hai!*" The younger officer snapped off a salute, his excitement evident from his broad grin as he turned back toward the cave.

"Sir, you are actually going to shoot that thing?" Ikeda asked.

"Even better, Sergeant Ikeda. We are going to sink an enemy ship."

Quickly, preparations were made. It required a tremendous crew to operate the guns, with more than twenty men assigned to each gun. A clever mechanical system carried the heavy shells and gunpowder up from the armory deep within the hill itself. The guns were not quick to load, and each could only fire approximately one round per minute. Noguchi smiled, thinking that the slow rate of fire would be more than compensated for by the sheer firepower those guns delivered.

As the guns themselves were loaded by their crews, the artillery officers made firing calculations. Noguchi left them to it.

"Come," he said to Ikeda. "Let us get inside the cave. We do not want to be standing out here when those guns fire, believe me."

Noguchi sent another officer to order the men off the slope in front of the guns, offering a clear line of fire. Although the muzzles would be elevated, he didn't want anyone near the guns when they went off.

It was a curious thing that artillery crews on both sides were not offered any sort of hearing protection. Some men were smart enough to stuff cotton in their ears, but the accepted practice was simply to cover your ears with your hands. As a result, the most common word in any artilleryman's vocabulary was, "What?"

"Ready, sir," the artillery captain said, looking at Noguchi. The major gave a curt nod.

All around them, the men put their hands over their ears—except for the artillery captain and Noguchi, who both kept high-powered binoculars trained on the horizon. The captain also wore a headset that put him in radio contact with the spotter plane that had sighted the American warship. The report from the spotter would be the only way that they would know if they had missed. They might then have a chance to adjust their aim, but by then the ship would be zigzagging across the surface, trying to present a more difficult target for any enemy submarines or planes. The only thing visible out there was ocean and more ocean, stretching to where the sea met the horizon, another reminder of the vastness of the Pacific. The crew of the ship probably thought that it was safe. The massive guns would be quite unexpected.

In rapid succession, the three guns fired. The entire hill shook, rattling the men to their very bones. Firing these guns was nerve-racking enough due to their immense power. It was hard to even begin to imagine what it must be like to be on the receiving end.

Considering the distance involved, it took a minute and a half for the heavy shells to make their flight. Their ears ringing, the gun crew waited with tense anticipation, ready to scramble into action to reload the massive guns.

The radio headset crackled into the ringing silence. "One splash! Two hits!" the artillery captain shouted. "The enemy ship is sinking!"

A cheer rang through the cave. Noguchi grinned with satisfaction, then patted the captain on the shoulder. This had been the first firing of the battery in anger, so to speak. The success promised to be an omen of good things to come.

The captain had more details from the spotter plane. "The spotter says that the enemy ship was broken in half and has already slipped beneath the waves. He can see a few men in the water, but no lifeboats —there wasn't time."

"Are there any American ships in the area to rescue the survivors?"

"No, none very close."

"That's too bad. We might have claimed another target. Still, sinking a ship was an excellent outcome. The men did well, Captain. You did well. Orochi did well."

It might not have been acceptable military practice, but the younger officer couldn't help but smile. "Thank you, sir!"

Beyond the mouth of the cave that sheltered the battery, medical personnel could now be seen on the hillside beneath the guns. They were tending to a handful of soldiers who had been too slow clearing the area and had found themselves close to the muzzle blast. They had all suffered concussions. Curiously, the men were naked, or nearly so. The shock wave caused by the force of firing the tremendous guns had ripped their clothing from their bodies. The men wandered in a daze, their eardrums bleeding. It was yet another reminder of the powerful nature of this battery.

Noguchi turned to Ikeda, who had observed the firing of the guns with just as much amazement as anyone. His own rifle felt puny by comparison to the massive power of those artillery guns. "You are not the only one who is a sharpshooter," Noguchi observed with pleasure.

"How would I ever hit a ship with a rifle?"

"That is why these guns are so important. With one volley, we can destroy a ship. Imagine what we will do to the invasion fleet."

"That may be true, sir." Ikeda gave a rare smile. "But when the Americans eventually come ashore, you will be glad of my rifle to protect your precious guns."

"Of that I have no doubt, Sergeant Ikeda. You and me, we are a team."

Ikeda looked the short, stout officer up and down, as if contemplating that possibility. Noguchi had demonstrated the power of his impressive guns, but soon enough Ikeda knew that he would be able to demonstrate the ability of his snipers.

"Yes," he finally agreed, tightening the grip on his rifle.

CHAPTER SIX

IN TYPICAL ARMY FASHION, it was a case of hurry up and wait. Despite the jeep that had come looking for them, nobody important seemed to have time for Lieutenant Steele, who was left hanging around the command area, awaiting orders.

"Any word, Honcho?" Philly asked. They were all eager to hear what their next assignment would be. "They've sure got you cooling your heels."

Steele just shook his head and lit another cigarette. If there were two things that they never seemed to run out of, it was bullets and cigarettes. The army kept them well supplied with both.

"It sure as hell beats getting shot at by the Japanese on that beach," Steele said. "Now get out of here before someone puts you to work."

Philly didn't need to be told twice. He caught up with the rest of Patrol Easy and filled them in. "Nothing doing yet," he said. "But I'm pretty sure we aren't being sent home to do a War Bond tour."

Yoshio and Egan took the downtime to draw new fatigues, considering that their old ones had been swept out to sea. Seeing them in fresh uniforms, even new boots, was a strange sight. Just about every soldier who had been on Guam for any length of time had a uniform that dripped with sweat, was stained with mud and worse, and was ripped in several places by the tropical thorns.

Philly whistled at their appearance. "You two look like a couple of green beans!"

"Don't worry about that," Egan said. "Hot and humid as this place is, we'll look just like we used to in a couple of days."

"You got that right," Philly agreed. "It's hard to stay looking pretty in this place."

It was true that the tropical weather took its toll. It seemed to rain on a regular basis. Already, jungle rot was becoming an issue for troops in the field for any length of time. Then there were the swarms of insects. Some just liked to get into your ears and nose and mouth, while others liked to bite.

Sitting nearby, Deke shook his head. He spent the downtime cleaning his rifle. It wasn't really necessary, considering that he'd taken only a few shots with it this morning, but it gave him something to do. The sand was more of a culprit than gunpowder residue. Here on the beach, the sand seemed to get into everything. Besides, he'd gotten superstitious about it. Some guys had a lucky rabbit's foot. For Deke, the equivalent was a spotless rifle.

"Do you always have to make the rest of us look bad?" Philly complained, watching Deke run yet another swab through the barrel. "This isn't boot camp anymore, you know. Nobody is going to inspect that rifle."

"You didn't complain about my rifle when I shot those Jap snipers this morning and saved your ass from getting swept out to sea."

"Point taken," Philly agreed. "How many did you shoot this morning?"

Deke shrugged. He didn't feel that killing people was something he wanted to keep track of, even if they were the enemy. Some guys did keep count, but Deke wasn't interested.

Philly didn't press. He knew that if Deacon Cole wasn't feeling talkative, then it was best to leave him alone.

"Mail call!" a clerk shouted, and the soldiers on the beach gathered around. While it was true that everyone did their part, the combat soldiers couldn't help but view clerks, cooks, and other support staff with more than a little disdain. But the clerk's arrival with a sack of mail had made this guy a hero for the moment, as if he had swum all the way from Hawaii tugging that mail sack after him.

The clerk started calling out names. He managed to stumble through Alphabet's last name. "Pawelczyk! I sure hope someone sent you some vowels."

"Very funny," Alphabet said, stepping forward. Grinning, he accepted a small package. "I hope to hell it's socks!" he said.

Philly's turn came, and he received a letter that smelled vaguely of perfume. "Look at that," he said, waving the letter. "Here I am on the other side of the world, and the dames can't leave me alone."

"Aw, it's probably from your sister," Rodeo said.

"You mean *your* sister, don't you?" Philly said.

"Geez, I hope she'd have better taste than that."

The letters and packages were a welcome break in the monotony and a reminder that someone back home was thinking of them. Those who received mail were thrilled, and those who didn't were disappointed, but they took some satisfaction in the news from home and packages being shared by others. It went without saying that mail delivery was a huge morale booster. It was also a commentary on the American capability to drop a letter in a mailbox several thousand miles away and eventually have it delivered to a beach on the island of Guam.

Just when mail call seemed to be over, one last name was called. "Cole!"

Surprised, Deke set his rifle aside and retrieved a package from the clerk. His surprise was nothing in comparison to the astonishment of the rest of the squad. Deke wasn't one to get much mail, much less a package. The only one who had ever written to him was his sister, Sadie, and those letters had been few and far between.

"What the hell did you get?" Philly wondered, gathering around with the rest of Patrol Easy.

"Socks?" Alphabet asked. He'd gotten a tin of cookies that was quickly being devoured by soldiers who were all too tired of their combat rations, but not the dry, fresh socks that he craved.

"No, it ain't socks," Deke said. He was just as mystified as the others, and he sure as hell didn't like the attention. "I reckon it's too heavy."

That was when he noticed the return address. The package had been sent by Hollis Bailey, who had a forge in the hills back home. He knew Hollis mainly by reputation. With growing curiosity, he tore off the paper and opened the package to reveal a bowie knife. The gleaming, razor-sharp blade was nearly a foot long, with a handle made from stag horn. The bowie was a knife design straight out of American history. There was no comparison at all between this knife and the standard blades that they had been issued. To be sure, the army-issue knives were sturdy enough, but this knife was like a Cadillac compared to a Chevy.

Philly whistled. "That's no butter knife."

"I'll be damned," Deke said. He got a good grip on the handle and turned the knife this way and that, enjoying the heft of it in his hand. It wouldn't be a bad blade for hacking his way through the jungle if it came down to it.

Deke couldn't have known it, but Hollis had made a similar knife for Deke's cousin, Caje Cole, who was fighting in Europe. In fact, Hollis was making knives for any local boy who was off fighting the war.

The knife had come with a sturdy leather sheath. The bottom of the sheath included a thong so that he could secure it to his leg. Deke had to hand it to Hollis—the knifesmith had thought of everything.

Quickly, Deke strapped on the sheath. With that knife and his rifle, he was equipped for anything that the jungle—or the Japanese— could throw at him.

Deke would have thought that no one back home really gave a damn where he was or what he was doing to help win the war. It looked as if he'd have to change his thinking on that.

Along with the mail, a shipment of USO refreshments had arrived, including bottles of soda pop nestled in ice. The exposed necks of the cool bottles dripped with condensation in the tropical heat. It was such a strange sight, considering that just a few days ago, they had been fighting for their lives in the jungle. The refreshments were already drawing quite a crowd, considering that most of the men were sick and tired of drinking nothing but canteen water—usually flavored with the lingering taste of halazone tablets.

"I'll be damned," Philly said. "Let's get a bottle of soda before it's all gone."

He and Deke headed for where the sodas had been set out. Another clerk had attempted to form the men into a line, but the thirsty combat veterans were having none of that. Instead, they had descended in a scrum around the soda pop tubs, where they plucked a bottle or two from the ice and hurried off to gulp it down. One thing for sure was that the supply wouldn't last long. There were far more soldiers than there were bottles of pop.

"Hey, one to a customer!" the clerk shouted, but he was generally ignored.

"I think we're actually going to get one of those," Philly said as they surged closer. There was some pushing and shoving as men jostled to move ahead, but so far no actual fights had broken out. The truth was that after several days of combat, most of the men simply didn't have the energy to fight. "I never thought I'd want a soda so bad. I can almost taste it. The only thing better would be a cold beer."

"Philly, if that was beer, I reckon there would be some shooting going on."

But Deke knew what Philly meant. It wasn't just soda. It was a taste of home.

There were two marines directly in front of them, recognizable from the camouflage coverings on their helmets, which they hadn't taken off despite the heat. Considering that this was an army sector on the beach, the sight of two marines was a little unusual. What were they doing here?

From their grimy uniforms, it was clear that these marines had seen some action. Both carried M1 rifles slung over their shoulders. Deke couldn't help but notice that one of the marines was quite tall, well over six feet, while the other couldn't have been more than five eight. What the shorter marine lacked in height, he made up for in width. The guy had shoulders like a bull. Seeing them together, Deke was reminded of a baseball bat and ball—or, better yet, a bowling ball.

"Almost there," Philly said, fending off an attempt by another soldier to slip in front of them.

Just ahead, the two marines had reached the tub of cracked ice that glittered in the sun. The tall marine reached in and plucked out the last two bottles of soda, handing a bottle to the short marine.

The tub was now empty. A sigh of disappointment went up from the crowd. Some soldiers cursed. Others contented themselves with grabbing a handful of the ice and rubbing it over their hot faces and necks.

The marines had turned away from the tub, carrying their prized bottles of pop. Angrily, Philly confronted them.

"Hey, you took the last one!" he blurted.

The tall marine looked down at him. "What about it?"

Philly glared at him, not moving out of the marine's path.

Deke nudged him in the ribs. That was one big marine. "Let it go," he said quietly.

Finally, Philly stepped aside.

"Yeah, that's what I thought," the marine said, giving Philly a smug smile. His gaze fell on Deke, and his smile faded as he met Deke's eyes, which were every bit as cold and colorless as the ice in that tub. *Maybe it was the scars,* Deke thought, but some of the marine's attitude ebbed, and he turned away into the crowd, followed closely by the shorter marine.

"Damn jarheads," Philly said.

"Damn *big* jarheads," Deke pointed out. "Did you want to get punched in the nose over a bottle of pop? Here, grab some ice."

Some of the soldiers were now flinging the rapidly melting ice at one another, laughing at the novelty of the cold stinging their faces. It was the next best thing to a snowball fight on a Pacific island.

Deke popped ice into his mouth, sucking on the cold. For an instant, he was transported to a winter's morning in the mountains back home. He thought of all the chores on the farm, carrying heavy buckets through the snow to water the cattle. The trees would still have snow frosting the branches, with the sun just coming up over the mountains beyond.

He remembered Sadie coming to help him, her breath steaming so much in the cold that she resembled a locomotive following its tracks through the snow. "You don't have to do everything yourself," she said. "How long have you been out here? You look half frozen. You can ask for help, you know."

Deke had shrugged. "It don't bother me none."

Sadie had fixed him with one of her see-right-through-you stares, the kind their mother had been so good at before she had taken sick. "You don't let anyone else in that head of yours, do you?"

Deke hadn't been sure how he was supposed to answer that—if his sister even wanted an answer. He just liked to do things himself, was all. There was no point in counting on anyone else when you needed something done.

He'd picked up his buckets again and started toward the barn. With an exaggerated sigh, Sadie had headed back toward the house.

At the time, Deke had to admit that hauling water out to the barn seemed like an onerous task on that winter's morning. But now, he'd do anything to be back on that farm. Not that it would ever happen, because the property that the Coles had farmed for generations was now owned by a greedy banker. He clenched his jaw and cracked the ice between his teeth.

Slowly, the men drifted away from the tubs of ice and back toward their various bivouacs. Foxholes had been dug everywhere in the sand, with shelter halves strung up to provide protection from the beating tropic sun, which seemed to disappear just long enough for a downpour before the sun came out again, leaving the very air steaming.

By some miracle, Rodeo had scored a bottle of pop. He passed it around so that each man in the squad could take a drink. When it was his turn, Deke took a sip of the pop, letting the cold, sugary taste linger. Growing up in the Depression era, a bottle of pop had been a rare treat.

The empty bottle was placed atop the rim of the foxhole like a trophy. But the men did not have much time to appreciate it. Lieutenant Steele had reappeared, having finally received their orders.

"What's the good news, Honcho?" Philly wanted to know. To avoid being targeted by Japanese snipers, Lieutenant Steele had insisted that his men never salute him or call him sir. Instead, they called him "Honcho," even here on the relative safety of the beachhead. "Are we finally going home for that Victory Bond tour?"

Lieutenant Steele opened his mouth to speak, his face grim. He had only one good eye, the other covered by a leather patch that Deke had made for him. Clearly, Lieutenant Steele was not about to deliver good news. But he seemed to change his mind about saying anything and just shook his head.

"Get some sleep," he finally announced. "What I've got to tell you can wait until tomorrow."

"I reckon we ain't gonna like it?" Deke speculated.

"No, you ain't gonna like it."

CHAPTER SEVEN

WHILE COVERING the war as a newspaper correspondent in Europe, Ernie Pyle had met most of the big generals, including Eisenhower, Patton, Bradley, and even the British general Montgomery—or "Monty," as the Brits called him.

Of course, Pyle was something of a celebrity in his own right, in that the generals had all wanted to meet *him*. Pyle never got bigheaded about it—he was a man who was much happier observing than being the center of attention. This trait was one of the reasons that the soldiers and sailors and airmen all seemed to love him. He didn't feel that he deserved any attention, but that *they* did.

As for the generals, Pyle had found them all impressive and competent, determined to win the war. But there was also something else that each general he'd met seemed to have in common. They all seemed to realize that they strode upon the world stage, and they behaved accordingly. Generals like Patton and Montgomery had their own personas, and they certainly lived up to them, from what Pyle had seen.

There was not a lot of drama surrounding a general like Eisenhower, although his legendary efficiency was a kind of persona in itself. There were rumors that Ike had a mistress, a pretty young driver from the motor pool, but Pyle wasn't one to dabble in such idle gossip. Besides, he wanted to write about the ordinary soldiers, not the generals or troop movements or military strategy.

Now that he had come to cover the war in the Pacific, Pyle had also met General MacArthur—or rather, MacArthur had wanted to meet *him*, which was again a change in the usual direction of how things flowed. More often, it was the humble war correspondent begging for an audience with the busy general so that he could write a profile of some sort that pleased his editor back home.

But with MacArthur, he had been invited to meet the general. Pyle suspected that this had less to do with the fact that MacArthur enjoyed reading his articles and more to do with the fact that MacArthur was well aware of the importance of how he was portrayed in the newspapers back home. It was no secret that the man had political ambitions.

General MacArthur was clearly a man who worked all the angles. Despite the well-honed cynical nature of a typical reporter toward anyone official, Pyle had been impressed by MacArthur. He certainly looked the part of a general, in that he was handsome, tall, and imposing. His age gave him gravitas. He could have been an actor portraying a general in a movie. But MacArthur was no stuffed shirt. He gave succinct orders and seemed to quickly absorb all the information that his staff brought him.

MacArthur didn't seem compelled to mingle with the men, or to be loved by them. His entire focus was on strategy, and rightly or wrongly, he seemed to view his troops as a means to an end. The end in this case was the defeat of Japan, which everyone could agree upon.

Whether or not he had actually read any of Pyle's war reporting was an open question. But the general had certainly been briefed to know all about Pyle. By the time that he left his audience with MacArthur—Pyle couldn't think of a better word for it, but it was like meeting some head of state—Pyle's head was spinning, which usually didn't happen with a seasoned reporter like himself. Knowing Pyle's style, MacArthur had tried to be casual, but it hadn't quite worked. General MacArthur projected a commanding presence without even trying.

Sitting here on the beach at Guam, waiting to ship out with the enlisted troops, he felt far more at home and at ease than he did when meeting generals. He much preferred the company of GIs, noncommissioned officers, and even the field officers over the company of any general. These men were the real deal, and there was nothing phony or contrived in Pyle's reporting about them.

He loved the ordinary troops. They were his fellow Americans, after all. This morning, he was at the headquarters of a captain who was single-handedly trying to rig some kind of HQ using weathered driftwood, a sheet of tin with bullet holes in it, and a handful of rusty nails. The captain appeared confident that these unlikely materials were somehow going to combine to keep out the sun and rain, but Pyle wasn't so sure about that.

Pyle didn't know where the captain had come across the tin or the nails here on this beach. But then again, infantry captains were a resourceful bunch.

"Let me give you a hand, Captain," Pyle said, hurrying to help him by holding the tin in place while the captain attempted to drive one of the rusty nails through the metal using the butt of his combat knife. Pyle had grown up on an eighty-acre grain farm in Indiana before heading off to college and a newspaper career, so he was familiar with cobbling things together from a boyhood on the farm.

And yet even the effort of holding the sheet metal in place left Pyle almost breathless. At age forty-four he was too thin, smoked too much, and had been known at times to drink his meals.

The rusty nail wouldn't take. The knife slipped, nearly taking off the captain's finger in the process.

"Son of a bitch," he said mildly, shaking a few drops of blood off his hand, then simply moving the nail farther along the post to one of the bullet holes, where he was able to get it secured. The nail head was smaller than the hole, so the captain ended up smacking the nail until it bent over and pinned the sheet metal in place.

"There," the captain said with satisfaction, standing back to admire his work, as if he had just finished constructing the Empire State Building, or maybe the Taj Mahal.

"Not bad," Pyle admitted. He'd been skeptical, but he had to agree that the rough shelter would at least keep the midday son from beating down on what passed for company HQ. "Captain, do you mind if I talk to some of your men?"

"Go right ahead," the captain said. He stuck his cut finger in his mouth, sucked on it, spat into the sand. "I'm sure they would love to talk with you. They're all good men, a long way from home."

"What about you, Captain?" Pyle asked.

The captain gave a short laugh. "Doesn't matter who I am or where I'm from," he said. "You go talk to the men."

Pyle nodded and moved on, leaving the infantry officer to put the finishing touches on his beach shack. If he needed to, he could get the captain's name later from one of his men.

He moved off down the beach and found a group of soldiers who didn't have the benefit of a tin shelter and were consequently baking under the hot tropical sun. The soldiers had recognized him on the beach right away, because Pyle was about as famous as any war correspondent could get. Winning the Pulitzer Prize would do that.

Plus, his appearance made him instantly recognizable: middle-aged, a bald head framed by tufts of graying hair, shorter than average, and thin to the point of looking almost emaciated or haggard.

Thanks to covering the war in the field with the soldiers in Europe and now in the Pacific, he ate the same C rations, smoked the same cigarettes, and heard the same shells screaming overhead. Of course, all this made him into a hero to the troops. Even if they couldn't read the newspapers themselves because delivery wasn't very good on the beach itself, the folks at home certainly read those papers and mentioned the stories in their letters to the boys at the front. It was a roundabout system, but word got out all the same about this bedraggled Hoosier.

"Where you from?" Pyle asked, sidling up to the nearest soldier and squatting beside him in the sand.

"Hey, you're Ernie Pyle, ain't ya?" the young soldier asked.

"That's me," Pyle said quietly. "But I'd rather know about you."

"Are you going to put me in the newspaper? Make me famous?"

"That's the plan," Pyle said. "That is, if it's all right with you. Let's tell the folks back home how you're doing. I can't make any promises about the famous part, though."

The men nearby laughed. They knew just what he meant.

"Well, you can put in that article that you're talking to Billy Smith from Little Creek, Virginia."

Pyle's keen ear picked up that the young man had a tidewater drawl.

"Pleasure to meet you, Billy," Pyle said, extending a hand. The two men shook. It helped that Pyle was one of the oldest men on the beach. It gave him an almost fatherly appearance, or, at least, that was how the soldiers typically reacted to him. "How do you like island life so far, son?"

Billy just laughed. "It's all right, if you like sand, coconuts, and Japs," he said. "Other than that, there ain't much to recommend it."

The other guys laughed as well, then added their two cents.

"And don't forget the leeches!"

"Or sunburn."

"Hey now, what about trench foot!"

Pyle just shook his head and made notes as the men had fun identifying challenges that they had lived with on Guam. Soldiers liked to gripe, which they couldn't do so much with an officer. Some of their gripes would make it into the article. Some of Pyle's reporting from Europe had gotten pretty dark, to the point that he'd had to take a leave of absence and return to the United States for a while.

Pyle understood that people loved to read about the long-suffering soldiers still getting the job done. There was an honesty in his reporting about what the boys in the field faced.

"How long have you been in the army, Billy?" Pyle asked.

"I joined up as soon as I was old enough, about a year after Pearl Harbor," the young soldier said. "I figured they couldn't win the war without me."

Billy's comment made the other soldiers laugh. "Yeah, yeah," one of them said. "Did ya ever think that maybe your girlfriend was just trying to get rid of you and talked you into enlisting?" That brought more laughter.

It was hard to see it, but these men had gone through a lot, just a few days ago. They had all been fighting for their lives against the Japanese, who were a ruthless enemy. The evidence showed in their gear, which was now battered and scratched, but clean, oiled, and well maintained. The soldiers' lives depended on that, as they all well knew.

Their boots were scuffed, and their uniforms showed various tears, stains, and even blood spatters. They had washed them out as best as they could in the salt water of the sea, putting them back on stiff from the salt.

The combat that they had seen was also evident in their faces, which had deep lines and creases, far more than someone their age should have. They had grown hard in order to survive.

One or two men in the small group simply sat quietly and stared, their eyes alone telling the story of what they had seen. Pyle knew better than to ask these men any questions, and he left them alone. He had seen the same look on the faces of many young men in Europe. Now, here were these shell-shocked boys in the Pacific.

He knew the feeling, having experienced it himself after the horrors that he had seen. This was the toll that war took, wounds that couldn't be bandaged or even seen.

Another soldier spoke up, bringing Pyle's thoughts back to the present. "Listen, Ernie, you tell those folks back home that we are going to lick the Japs and will be back home in time for the Fourth of July."

"What's your name, son?" Pyle asked.

It seemed like a simple question, but he had recently battled with the US Navy to allow him to use individual sailors' names. Navy officials had relented to an extent, allowing Pyle special dispensation to use names. That permission did not extend to other war correspondents, which was a policy that the self-effacing Pyle did not agree with.

The US Army, however, was fine with him using the soldiers' names, just as he had done while reporting the war in Europe, and he jotted down what the young soldier told him.

"Well, sir, I'm Jimmy Jones from Augusta, Georgia."

Pyle nodded. "I'll put that in the article, Jimmy, although I've got to warn you—you might get a promotion for that quote."

The other soldiers laughed, and Pyle moved on down the beach. It was the same everywhere. He could have almost made the quotes up, and who would know the difference? But that wasn't how he did things. He was here to tell their stories.

Where they were going next wouldn't be any kind of cakewalk. The scuttlebutt had it that they were headed to the Philippines. Pyle was always in search of a good story, so he traveled to the next destination, just as the troops did, eating the same chow and sleeping in the same cramped, overheated bunks.

That was just fine by him. He wondered sometimes if he would make it out of this war alive. He knew it was the same thought on every man's mind on this beach. They were united in their goal of victory, but they were also united by their doubts and fears.

Finally, there was some activity on the beach. The process of moving troops off Guam to the next operation was long and slow. A makeshift quay had been constructed for loading the men onto the transport ships. Smaller boats would take them to the vessels offshore, mostly the navy's cargo attack ships and attack transport ships, known as AKAs and APAs. Pyle knew from experience that these would be jammed with men and gear before making the long voyage to their next destination.

He grabbed his duffel bag and started to move along with them, struggling under the weight. The bag was extra heavy because it contained his prized typewriter. Pyle didn't carry any weapons, unless you counted a penknife that he used to sharpen pencils. He'd always been a little embarrassed that right after the Japanese attacked Pearl Harbor, Pyle had tried to join the navy but had been rejected for being too frail and unfit.

He was surprised when the weight in his hand suddenly lightened. He looked over to see that a couple of soldiers had grabbed hold of his duffel and were carrying it for him.

"No need to do that, fellas," he said.

"We've got it, Ernie," one of the men said, a burly soldier who threw the duffel over his shoulders as if it weighed nothing. "You just tell our story. Let people know what we did here, and why some of my buddies died."

Pyle nodded. That was just what he planned to do.

CHAPTER EIGHT

DEKE WOKE early enough to watch the streaks of morning light fill the sky. He couldn't say exactly what had woken him so early. Something tugged at his mind, maybe the remnants of a dream or possibly a premonition, but he couldn't put his finger on it. His rifle lay right beside him, within easy reach.

He did know that he had woken up with his hand clenched tightly around his new knife. He gave the knife in his hand a rueful smile. The war was supposed to be over on Guam, more or less. But the jungle was still full of Jap infiltrators who would be more than happy to sneak up and cut your throat while you slept. One thing about the Japs—they loved to operate at night.

There was no going back to sleep, so he sat up and watched the morning arrive. If he'd been a smoker, this would have been a good time for a cigarette. Instead, he took a deep breath of the fresh, salty air that had just blown in across several thousand miles of ocean. He welcomed the clear air, now that the burial details had cleared most of the dead Japanese away.

You had to give the Pacific Ocean its due, he thought—it was hard to think of anyplace else on earth with such spectacular sunrises, starting with a slow dawn that filled an endless horizon with all the soft colors of mother of pearl. The softness did not last long. Soon, the rising sun burst above the sea: hot, sharp, angry, red. It was no wonder that the Empire of Japan had chosen the rising sun for its symbol. In the Pacific, the rising sun looked both beautiful and powerful.

Any soldier loved the sight of morning. It meant that the dangers of the night had passed. Fear of the dark was a survival mechanism as old as humanity itself. There might be new terrors or challenges with the arrival of daylight, but at least he could see them coming.

He noticed that Yoshio was also awake, watching the sky.

"Beautiful, ain't it?" Deke said quietly. He wouldn't have said anything about the sunrise to Philly, but Yoshio had more of what Deke would have called a poetic disposition.

"Sure is," Yoshio replied, although it went without saying. "It's hard to believe that Japan controls everything between here and that sunrise."

"Not for long," Deke pointed out.

"That's why we're here," Yoshio agreed.

Nearby, they heard Philly stir and groan. "Will you two shut it? I need my beauty sleep."

"Then you might as well get up," Deke said. "You're gonna need more than a few minutes to sleep off that much ugly."

"You are one mean hillbilly," Philly said, and rolled over.

* * *

TWO HOURS LATER, they were eating a breakfast made from powdered eggs that nobody wanted to taste too much, washing breakfast down along with some brownish, lukewarm water that was allegedly coffee. The lukewarm eggs made Deke miss those country breakfasts from his boyhood that much more, with fresh eggs, ham, or even white gravy and biscuits. Now *that* was eating. His family hadn't had much money, but on a farm, there was usually enough to eat. Except when your Pa died, and then there wasn't.

"Whoever figured out how to take a perfectly good egg and turn it into powder ought to be shot," Philly said.

"I'll give you the bullet," Rodeo said.

"You know what I'd like right now? A big danish and a decent cup of coffee," Philly added.

Deke had gone hungry enough times as a boy that he wasn't about to complain about the food, bad as it was, but that didn't stop him from saying, "You know what I'd like? A big slab of Virginia ham on a fresh biscuit. Now that's good eatin' right there."

"You know what? That does sound better than a danish," Philly agreed. He looked at the few bites of reconstituted eggs left on his plate, sighed, and shoveled them down resolutely. They had all learned that you never knew where your next meal was coming from, so you didn't leave anything on your plate if you could help it.

They were just finishing up when Lieutenant Steele called them over to where he stood under one of the camouflage nets that had been erected to create mottled shade against the tropical sun.

"All right, everybody grab a seat. You'll want to be sitting down when you hear what I'm about to say."

Once again, the lieutenant's face appeared just as grim as it had yesterday when he had returned from receiving their orders. He seemed to study them all one by one with his good eye. The right eye that he had lost on Guadalcanal was covered by the leather patch that Deke had fashioned for him out of boot leather. The wound would have been enough to send Steele home, but he had stubbornly insisted upon staying in the fight. How he had swung that was anybody's guess. He either had friends in high places—or maybe enemies.

The look he was giving them with his one good eye this morning was enough to indicate that he clearly had some bad news to deliver.

One by one, Deke studied the others: Philly, Yoshio, Rodeo, Alphabet, and Egan. Together, they made a good team. They had already been through thick and thin on Guam as Patrol Easy. They had lost one man, killed by the Japanese marksman that Deke had nicknamed the "Samurai Sniper." That sniper had managed to slip away with the small number of Japanese troops who had evacuated from the island. Most of the rest, thousands and thousands as a matter of fact, had perished at the hands of US forces.

They had also lost Egan's dog, Whoa Nelly. The military had sent specially trained dogs to Guam to sniff out Japanese pillboxes and warn against infiltrators. The dogs had been so effective that they were particularly hated by the Japanese, and even targeted by enemy snipers. Sadly, at least sixty military dogs had died in the fighting, Egan's dog among them.

Whoa Nelly had died protecting him from a Japanese soldier who had ambushed them in the ruins of a village near Yigo, in some of the last major fighting on the island. Deke wasn't entirely sure that a dog equaled a person, but like most country people, he thought that a good dog came awfully close. Egan was still waiting to be assigned a new dog. For now, he was still attached to Patrol Easy.

They took seats on discarded jerricans and ammunition boxes. Philly plunked himself down directly on the sand like a beach bum. They watched Steele expectantly, waiting for him to drop the bomb.

"What gives, Honcho?" Philly asked.

"Hold your horses. I'm not the one who is going to be filling you in."

As it turned out, the lieutenant was not going to be the bearer of bad news. They looked up as another officer approached. Although he was an army officer, he was accompanied by two marines who stopped well short of the shaded netting as the officer went on alone. To their surprise, the officer wasn't anyone that they recognized. Although nobody had a pristine uniform at this point, and the tropical heat and humidity was taking its toll on everyone, it was clear that this officer hadn't been slogging around the jungles. He must be some kind of staff officer.

They got to their feet, but the officer waved them back down.

"As you were," he said. "I'm Major Berger, from General Bruce's staff." Considering that General Bruce was the division commander, this went up the food chain a lot higher than any of them had expected. Deke found himself leaning forward out of curiosity so that he wouldn't miss a word.

The major continued, "Lieutenant Steele here will give you the details shortly, but I wanted to tell you men that you are being asked to take part in a mission of utmost importance. Before I get started with the briefing, is there anything that you want to say, Lieutenant?"

Utmost importance. They all knew what that meant, and it wasn't anything good. Philly muttered something under his breath but clammed up when Lieutenant Steele shot him a look.

The lieutenant then took the opportunity to say a few words.

"Fellas, I should tell you that this mission would normally be something that Army Rangers would be doing, but they've been a little busy, like the rest of us," Steele said. "General Bruce volunteered us, saying that his boys can do anything the Rangers can do."

They all knew that the Rangers were typically doing unimaginable things like sneaking in ahead of everyone else or scaling cliffs just to fight a battle at the top. Famously, it was Army Rangers who had helped capture the beach at Normandy.

In other words, this was stuff that you'd have to be crazy to do. *Crap.* It wasn't much of a pep talk. Lieutenant Steele turned it back over to the major.

The major continued, "Thank you, Lieutenant. You know that we are fighting our way across this big damn ocean, hopping from island to island, getting closer to Japan all the time. Mainly, it's the airfields that we need. Each airfield that's closer to Japan will make it that much easier for us to drop bombs on Hirohito's head."

"Sir, I thought that we had captured all the airfields on Guam," Philly blurted out. He might have asked more if the lieutenant hadn't glared at him again.

"Not Guam. Not just an airfield," the major replied. "An island. We don't want to give more details than you need to know at this time. Let's just say that you can't share any details with anyone."

"Top secret, sir?" Philly asked.

Before the major could answer, Lieutenant Steele interrupted. "What the major is saying is that you need to keep your damn mouth shut, Philly. Think you can do that from here on out?"

"Yes, sir."

The major continued, but not before Lieutenant Steele had gone to stand beside Philly like a teacher who had singled out a troublesome student. "You may have heard the rumors that our next operation is going to be the invasion of the Philippines. Well, you heard right. The plan is to land on Leyte, which is one of the Philippine islands. I know that's hardly a secret at this point. It's probably where you've been expecting to go. That's where we'll start the business of taking back the Philippines, which the Japs captured from us right after Pearl Harbor. General MacArthur vowed to be back, and he meant it.

"The Japanese are not going to let us just stroll onto Leyte, of course," the officer continued. "They have had months and months to build up their defenses, which are quite formidable, I have to say. You've had some experience with that here on Guam, I know. Our intelligence indicates that they have done a much better job on Leyte —which is to say, it's going to be a lot worse."

Philly opened his mouth but clamped it shut when Steele nudged him none too gently with the toe of his boot.

"The Japanese had built the usual dugouts and spider holes for snipers," the major said. "But what really concerns us is their artillery. In fact, the Japanese have installed a battery of naval guns that gives them tremendous reach and firepower. Basically, it would be a suicide mission for the invasion fleet."

Now it was the lieutenant's turn to ask a question. "Can't the flyboys knock out those guns, sir? Or the navy?"

"They've tried, all right. But we just can't reach them. The bunker where those guns are hidden is just about impregnable. Nobody can get to it from the air. I'm afraid that the only way to get to them is to send in a demolition team. We intend to sabotage those guns, basically to destroy them one way or another. If we don't, it's going to be a slaughter when our landing fleet gets within range."

Lieutenant Steele spoke up. "With all due respect, sir, my boys are marksmen, not demolition experts."

"Don't worry about that, Lieutenant. I know that you and your men bushwhacked your way through the jungle here, dodged the Japanese, and somehow came out the other side. Those are the skills we want from you and your men. We'll have someone else take care of setting the charges."

He waved over the marines. Deke couldn't help but notice that one marine was quite tall, while the other was shorter and broad as a barrel.

As they stepped closer to the dappled shade where the briefing was taking place, it became clear that these were the same marines they had run into earlier—the ones who had taken the last bottles of soda ahead of Deke and Philly.

"Just great," muttered Philly, who had also recognized the two marines.

"I know it's a little unusual," the major stated. "But these are the best demolitions experts that we could come up with on short notice. They just happen to be United States Marines. They will be under your orders, Lieutenant." Addressing the men, he added, "Now I will turn it over to Lieutenant Steele to give you the details."

That said, the major made his exit, leaving the two marines behind. For a moment, Steele simply watched the major walking away, looking as if he might want to leave with him. The silence was broken by Philly.

"What are those details, Honcho?" he asked.

Quickly, Steele filled them in. The plan was for them to go in ahead of the main landing force, knock out the guns, and then be extracted. Rumor had it that there might even be friendly Filipino guerrillas to help them out, but running into the right guys would depend on pure luck. There was no means to communicate with any of the guerrilla forces. Finally, if extraction wasn't possible, then they were to wait until the actual landing—easier said than done.

"You mean, hide out on an island full of angry Japanese?"

"That's about the size of it, Philly." Steele looked around. "You all heard the major. This isn't going to be some cakewalk. Just the opposite. In fact, there's a pretty good chance that none of us will be getting off that island alive. I want to make it clear that this is a volunteer-only mission. If anyone doesn't want to go, you don't have to go."

Quickly, Patrol Easy was on its feet. As if on cue, each one of them took a step forward—even the marines.

"You can count on us, Honcho."

"I knew that's how it would be, but I had to ask," Steele said.

The lieutenant was interrupted by the arrival of a courier. While he was off to one side reading the message, Philly took the opportunity to get acquainted with the marines.

"You two, huh? How'd you like that soda pop?"

"I've got to say it was pretty good. It's a shame that you didn't get any."

"I'll bet. You two must have seriously pissed somebody off to end up on this mission."

"Well, you know, it's just like the army to call the marines when there's a job to get done."

"Very funny. You guys have names?"

"Cal Hartley," said the tall one. "This ugly one here is Beryl Watts."

"Pleasure," Beryl said.

"Beryl?" Philly snorted. "Isn't that a lady's name?"

Beryl glared, clearly unhappy that Philly was giving him flack about his name.

"If I were you, I wouldn't be too quick to kid Beryl about his name," the tall marine warned. "The last guy who did that is still looking for his teeth. Come to think of it, I might have helped."

"You marines don't scare me. We can see what's what right here and now."

Cal was taking Philly's measure. He had a good six inches on him, and at least thirty pounds. He smiled down at him. "Nah, you're not worth it. None of you guys could scare my grandma, except maybe him." He jerked his chin in Deke's direction. "Now that one, I'll keep my eye on."

"Why him?" Philly sounded offended. "I'm bigger than he is!"

"You don't want to mess with him, that's why. With scars like that, he's got to be a mean son of a bitch."

Deke just shrugged. He was sick and tired of hearing about his scars.

"Never mind about him," Philly said. "It's me you ought to worry about, tough guy."

"Yeah?"

Philly and the tall marine stood there glaring at each other.

Steele returned before things turned any uglier.

"Knock it off, Philly," he said, then turned to the two marines. "Listen, I know you two don't want to be here any more than we want you here. But as long as you two pull your weight, we won't have any problems."

"It's not us we're worried about, sir."

"What the hell is that supposed to mean?"

"Nothing, sir."

"Good to know," Lieutenant Steele said through clenched teeth. "I can see that we're all going to get along like gin and tonic. Now we've got two days before we ship out for Leyte. I plan to spend them training. We'll start with a shakedown hike tomorrow morning."

Philly groaned. "Is it too late to unvolunteer?"

"I hate to tell you this, Philly, but the fun is just beginning," Steele said.

CHAPTER NINE

A JUNGLE TREK wasn't anyone's idea of fun, but the soldiers of Patrol Easy found themselves heading into the forest not long after the sun was up. The only one who didn't seem to mind was Lieutenant Steele, but then again, this hike had been his idea. He seemed almost cheerful this morning, as if he took a perverse pleasure in making them all miserable.

In terms of the patrol's leadership, Steele essentially functioned as a lieutenant and sergeant all rolled into one. If he had a second in command, that distinction fell to Deke. Deke had no interest in being in charge of anyone but himself, but Steele seemed convinced that Deke at least had enough sense not to get everyone killed outright in Steele's absence.

It had rained during the night, one of the brief, soaking downpours typical of the tropics, leaving the foliage dripping and the trail muddy. Within a few minutes of starting out, they were all wet through.

Deke didn't mind. He was glad to get moving again. As far as he was concerned, they had been sitting around long enough. He was eager to get back into action in some way, shape, or form.

"You don't seem too concerned about this mission," Philly said. "Sounds to me like we got the short end of the stick."

"I reckon we'd be going to Leyte one way or another," Deke said. "Now we're just going a little early. We'll know where all the best places are before anyone else gets there."

"Best places? I hate to break this to you, Deke, but we're not going to a resort island for some R & R."

Deke snorted, then grew serious. "You know what it was like hitting the beach here on Guam. If the Japs had some big guns up in the hills, there wouldn't have been nothin' left of us. We can't let that happen at the next one. We've got to give our guys a chance."

"Honestly, Deke, sometimes I can't tell if you're the world's biggest Boy Scout or just an idiot."

"In that case, quit flappin' your jaw and save your breath. You're gonna need it. Have you seen that hill we have to climb?"

Up ahead, Lieutenant Steele was leading the way up the jungle trail. He had indeed picked a large hill for them to climb, all the way to the summit.

Not so long ago, that summit had been defended by Japanese troops. After a long, bloody fight, the Japanese had finally been defeated. Still, there was at least some threat from the Japanese remaining. Estimates varied, but anywhere from hundreds to a few thousand Japanese troops remained hidden in the jungles, especially in the mountainous regions.

These Japanese troops were holdouts who had refused to surrender. A few remained fearful of the Americans and had taken to the jungle in hopes of avoiding capture—never mind the fact that the Japanese POWs were treated well and had plenty of food. Having seen how American POWs were mistreated, the US had gone to great lengths to do just the opposite for the captured Japanese. They were given food, clothing, shelter, and medical care. It wasn't all that hard to provide for the enemy prisoners, considering that there were precious few of them.

The vast majority of the holdouts hidden in Guam's mountainous jungles were diehards who would rather die than surrender to the enemy. They were now fighting what basically amounted to a guerrilla war, attacking convoys and infiltrating American camps at night to cut a few throats and wreak whatever havoc they could. When they'd had enough, whatever was left of their group would mount their own banzai charge—essentially committing suicide. It was a fanaticism that few Americans could understand.

One thing for sure, Deke thought, *the Japanese were a tough nut to crack.*

They sweated even more as the ground rose and the sun climbed. At first, the two marines had joined Steele at the front of the patrol, probably intending to teach these army boys how it was done. But they had underestimated Steele, who, despite the flecks of gray in his hair, seemed to have a body that matched his name, his legs pumping relentlessly up the hill.

In fact, Steele and Deke were in the best shape of them all. Steele never talked much about himself, but he had dropped enough information that his men had pieced his story together. Before the war, Steele had apparently toned his muscles playing tennis and shooting trap at country clubs. Athletes often turned to flab off the field. Steele seemed to be an exception to the rule. Deke had honed his muscles growing up on a farm and later in the sawmill. When you grew up splitting firewood, digging ditches, and performing other backbreaking work on a daily basis, those lean muscles stuck with you. You also weren't afraid of a little sweat or hard work.

Winded, the two marines had drifted back until they were directly in front of Deke, who brought up the rear.

That was just fine by him. He wouldn't have rested easy with anyone else back here—and Lieutenant Steele probably wouldn't have either. He kept his eyes on the jungle, just in case any of those holdout Japs were around. It was a favorite enemy tactic to wait until a patrol passed by and then attack them from the rear when they least expected it. Deke didn't plan on letting that happen.

Overhead, the sun filtered down through the fronds of the tropical trees, creating a diffused light beneath the forest canopy. Insects buzzed constantly and birds sang overhead, oblivious to the affairs of men. It almost made Deke wonder what they were doing out here, anyway.

Deke had basically grown up outdoors and had spent countless hours wandering the woods and mountains, usually with a rifle or shotgun in his hands. He loved the mountain woods in a way that would be hard to explain to someone who hadn't had that experience. These jungle forests were so different, almost an alien world. Most of the other GIs griped and complained about the jungle, but Deke found it captivating. One moment he could be moving along a trail, and the next he could step off the trail and almost completely disappear into the foliage and gloom. The jungle might be an enemy, but in some ways it could also be a friend. When it came to the jungle, there were two sides to the coin—and two edges to the knife.

Ahead of him, the two big marines were slowing down even more as the trail climbed. Deke slowed his own pace somewhat, but he was wary of falling too far behind. It wouldn't be a good idea to get too strung out on the trail, just in case there were any enemy holdouts in the area.

From time to time, the leathernecks glanced back at him, as if to make sure that he was still there. Here in the jungle, that probably wasn't a bad instinct. He didn't attempt to strike up a conversation with the marines, however.

"You don't say much, do you?" the tall one asked after a while.

"Ain't nothin' to say."

They walked on in silence, enveloped by the natural sounds of the jungle.

Deke wasn't much for small talk. He wasn't much interested in making friends—or enemies, for that matter. It remained to be seen if the soldiers and marines could truly be a team. One way or another, Deke reckoned that they had to be if the mission was going to succeed. He supposed that one of the reasons that Honcho had organized this hike was not only to whip everybody into shape, but also to do what he could in the area of team building. So far, it didn't seem to be going very well.

A few minutes later, Deke's concerns about what the jungle might be hiding proved all too justified. They had reached a place when the canopy had opened up so that tall clumps of kunai grass grew in the sunny patches. In fact, the spot might have made a decent picnic grove. But something wasn't right. Deke crouched, scanning the dense landscape, trying to determine what had set off his inner alarm bell. His nose caught a whiff—ever so faint—of what smelled like woodsmoke. It was certainly a smell that was out of place in the dampness of the rain forest. *Where there's smoke, there's fire—the Nipponese kind,* he thought.

Even now, they might be in some Jap's machine-gun sights.

"Hold up," he whispered to the tall marine.

The two marines had the good sense not to ask any questions and instantly went on alert.

Deke gave a low whistle that imitated a whip-poor-will perfectly. He wasn't sure that whip-poor-wills existed here on Guam, but the whistle blended in well enough with the other birdsongs. It was a signal that he and Honcho had agreed upon. Seconds later, he heard a whistle in reply. The column came to a halt, and the members of Patrol Easy crouched among the sharp spikes of kunai grass, weapons at the ready.

Deke slipped off the trail, every sense alert to danger. He had a pretty good idea about where the smoke was coming from. He'd always had a nose like a hound dog, and a good sense of smell was yet another way to stay alive out here—it was one more reason to avoid cigarettes, which dulled your sense of smell.

Easing his way noiselessly through the grass, he headed toward a clump of trees where he thought that, just maybe, he had seen a wisp of smoke rising. He kept his eyes riveted on the spot straight ahead, which was the best way to detect any motion. Some guys might be worried about stepping on a snake or into a booby trap, but Deke reckoned a real, live Japanese soldier was a bigger concern. He knew that the rest of the patrol on the road was covering him, so he wasn't all that worried about any Japs sneaking in around behind him.

Silently, he reached the clump of trees. Sure enough, he could see the remains of a tiny, smoldering fire. Someone had started a fire here that was just big enough to boil water or cook rice. Bordering the ashes were two flat stones that would have been useful for balancing a pot. Dirt had been kicked onto the fire, but not enough to put it out completely.

Around the fire itself, a small area of grass had been trampled where several men had sat or even spread their blankets. It reminded Deke of hunting back home and coming across the place in a remote meadow where the deer had bedded down.

Deke couldn't feel the back of his neck itching, so he felt confident that the Japanese were, in fact, long gone.

Carefully, he made his way back to the trail.

"Well?" Steele asked.

"There were Japs here, all right. No more than half a dozen."

"The question is, Where are they now?"

Deke shook his head. "That's anybody's guess, but I don't think they're gonna bother us none. We must have surprised them, and they scattered instead of fighting. If they'd had a little more time, they might have tried to ambush us."

"You went pretty far off the trail. How the hell did you even know about that camp?"

"I smelled the smoke from their campfire." In Deke's country accent, the word came out as *camp-far*.

Steele gave him a look, then just shook his head. "All right, we'll keep going. You stay at the rear. I need your eyes and ears back there— and your nose."

Deke slipped back to the end of the column. They kept going. He relaxed somewhat when they left the clearing behind and the trail climbed even more steeply toward the jungle-covered hilltop.

The heat of the day seemed to increase the higher that they climbed. The uniforms that had been soaked by the wet foliage now seemed to weigh extra. Sweat rolled into their eyes, the salt in it stinging and blurring their vision. Even their helmets began to feel too heavy and made their necks ache.

Against regulations, instead of a helmet, Deke had opted for his Australian-style bush hat, with its broad brim pinned up on the right side so that it wouldn't get in the way of his rifle and telescope. The hat had been given to him by a wounded soldier, in gratitude for Deke stopping to give him a drink of water. The broad-brimmed hat kept the sun off and helped against the insects that pestered them in the stillness of the forest canopy.

"How come Deke gets to wear whatever he wants and I have to wear a helmet?" Philly had complained at the outset of the march.

"You get to be as good of a shot as Deke and I won't care if you wear pajamas and a fedora," Steele said. "Until then, keep your damn helmet on."

As silently as possible, the short column continued up the train until they reached the summit, where the jungle had been cleared away for the Japanese batteries. The enemy's shattered artillery now lay scattered in the open space, the heavy pieces tossed about by naval and aerial bombardments as if they had been toys.

From up here, they had a good view of the beaches beyond. It was out of rifle range, but from an artilleryman's point of view, soldiers on the beach would be like sitting ducks. Looking down, Deke had to admit that it made his stomach clench to think of the easy job the Japanese must have had in picking them off from this commanding height.

"There's a reason why I brought you up here, not just for some exercise," Steele said. "I wanted some of our mission and what we are being asked to do to sink in. If the navy and the flyboys hadn't knocked out the Jap guns up here, we would've had an even worse time coming ashore, and I've got to say, it was bad enough.

"Now think about the same situation on Leyte coming up, with the Japanese having even bigger guns in place, and us not being able to knock them out."

Philly gave a low whistle. "Not good, Honcho."

"Exactly. That's where we come in."

That was all the explanation that Honcho needed to give. He left the men to their rations, to the canteens of water that they'd brought along, and to their lone thoughts.

The tall marine was the first to break the silence.

"Hey, Deke," he said. "I've got to say, way to go back there. If those Japs had still been around, we'd never have known what hit us."

"Ain't no big thing, Bat," Deke said.

The marine looked puzzled. "Bat?"

"Yeah, you're the tall one. Your buddy here is 'Ball.' Maybe not a baseball, but definitely a bowling ball."

"Or a cannonball!" Philly chimed in.

The two marines looked at each other, then shrugged. Like it or not, they now had nicknames. "I've been called worse. Anyhow, I guess we're in the army now," Bat said.

CHAPTER TEN

AS IT TURNED OUT, Lieutenant Steele's plans for another day of training were cut short when the timeline for shipping out was moved up. In fact, the whole division had received orders to ship out in a few days, sending the beach into a flurry of activity. Already, some transports were beginning the process of taking on men, where they would likely sit at anchor for several days before embarking for wherever the army decided to send them.

Patrol Easy would be leaving even sooner. Looking around at the troops who were busy with preparations for the long sea voyage, it became apparent that if Patrol Easy wasn't successful in its mission, then these other poor bastards would pay the price.

After the grueling hike, it didn't exactly break the men's hearts that they would be spared whatever other field trips the lieutenant had in mind for them. But probably even more than Steele had expected, the hike through the jungle, even the near miss with the Japanese hold-outs, had done its intended job of helping the soldiers get to know the marines, and the other way around.

They had taken each other's measure, and they were satisfied that the other guys were solid. If they weren't exactly peanut butter and jelly yet, then at least the soldiers and marines were not completely oil and water.

The logistically tedious process of moving the bulk of troops off Guam was just beginning, but as it turned out, Patrol Easy was getting a special ride. While the rest of the massive convoy was still being loaded and organized, they were soon on a destroyer bound for Leyte, more than thirteen hundred miles away.

Chosen for its relatively swift speed, the ship was the USS *Ingersoll*, a Fletcher-class destroyer. Deke had to admit that the destroyer was an impressive sight. Built in Bath, Maine, the ship approached four hundred feet in length and was outfitted with both five-inch guns and forty-millimeter antiaircraft guns, not to mention racks of depth charges to deal with any Japanese submarines. The vessel had been named in honor of the Ingersoll family, who had served in the US Navy and lost a son at the recent Battle of Midway.

The patrol gathered on the stern of USS *Ingersoll* to watch Guam sink below the horizon. Soon, all that they could see was a very big ocean all around them.

"I can't say that I'm gonna miss Guam," Philly said.

"I reckon you just might change your tune once we get to Leyte," Deke pointed out.

Philly just shook his head. "That's what I like about you, Deke. You always look on the bright side."

"What's wrong with that? At least you ain't dead yet."

"See? That's exactly what I mean."

Deke just shook his head, not exactly sure what Philly meant at all, and went off to find a spot on the deck where he could clean his rifle in peace and quiet. He feared that it might start to rust in the salty ocean air.

He soon found that there wasn't much room to spare on the deck of a destroyer. Almost every square foot of space was covered in nautical gear of one sort or another, and the spaces that weren't seemed to be filled with antiaircraft batteries or racks of depth charges.

Unfortunately, they were informed by the crew that the Japanese continued to be a very real threat, especially from submarines and planes.

"No matter how many subs we sink or planes we shoot down, the Japs always seem to have more to send," one old salt pointed out. "If that wasn't bad enough, we're heading that much closer to Japan all the time."

It was also less than reassuring to learn that in order to save time, the captain had been ordered not to follow the usual zigzag pattern that made a ship a more difficult target for submarine and aerial attacks. A ship moving in a straight line would always be easier to attack.

Though fast enough to make a quick run to Leyte, the destroyer was also much smaller than the typical troop carrier. This meant that the crew and passengers felt every wave as the destroyer plowed through the sea at speed.

"You know what, Philly? I do miss Guam already," Deke announced, then leaned over the rail and promptly threw up. Once again, he was reminded of how much he disliked the sea.

Philly clapped him on the back. "I think it's going to be a long voyage for you, Farmboy. Although I've got to say, I don't know how anybody could miss Guam."

Deke didn't have a good reply. He just wiped his mouth with the back of his hand and nodded, looking distinctly green.

He felt bad enough that he halfway considered finding his bunk, bad as it was. While the food aboard the ship was like a five-star restaurant in comparison to the C rations that the men had been eating on Guam—when they weren't too seasick to eat—the tight quarters were something that was hard to get used to.

The men were given bunks in their own corner of the crew's quarters. With only about eighteen inches of space between the beds, sleeping aboard a US Navy vessel felt very much like being sardines inside a tin can. Deke had learned the hard way not to sit up too fast—he had already whacked his head more than once on the bunk above him. Quarters more suitable for an officer had been found for Lieutenant Steele—which meant that he shared a cramped space with two other officers.

Some might say that the bunks were better than a muddy foxhole. After all, there weren't any mosquitoes or other creepy crawlies to contend with. They didn't have to worry about enemy infiltrators coming to cut their throats at night.

However, the tight quarters were almost too much even for Yoshio, who rarely complained about anything. "I never thought I'd say this, but give me a foxhole any day," he said.

One of the ship's junior officers had gotten the bright idea that he didn't want the soldiers on deck, possibly interfering with the operation of the vessel. No sooner was Guam out of sight than he informed them that they would be allowed up on deck just twice each day for exercise, for a total of two hours out of their sardine can.

Not long after they complained to Lieutenant Steele, the officer gave them free rein to wander the deck. In fact, the officer now seemed to avoid the soldiers altogether.

"Geez, Honcho, what did you do to that guy?" Philly wanted to know.

"That's Honcho, *sir*. The navy isn't exactly informal, and I don't see any Japanese in sight, do you?" Back on Guam, the lieutenant had made it clear that he was not to be addressed as an officer in any way in order to avoid becoming a target for Jap snipers.

"No, sir. No Japs here."

His point having been made, the lieutenant continued. "That officer won't be giving you any more trouble. It turns out that we're sharing quarters, and I told him that I'd smother him with a pillow if he wasn't nicer to my men."

It was hard to know whether the lieutenant was kidding.

While it was a relief not to be stuck below, it was still no pleasure cruise. On the third day, the ship hit a patch of the Pacific studded with choppy waves that reminded Deke of a newly plowed field. The constant banging against the waves seemed to threaten to pop the ship's rivets apart, but the sturdy destroyer held up. Those shipbuilders in Maine had done their job well.

Then there was the threat from Japanese planes the closer that they got to the Philippines, where the Japanese still had a substantial force—or at least that was the concern. The closer that they drew to the occupied Philippines, the more that the crew looked to the skies with growing concern.

It wasn't long before their fears were realized. The men were lounging on the deck one afternoon, staring out at yet more endless seas, when the ship was called to general quarters. Sailors raced to man the antiaircraft guns that bristled from almost every surface, finally putting them into action. The only role that the soldiers were given was to stay out of the way.

"I don't see a damn thing!" Philly exclaimed. "What about you, Deke?"

"Nothin'."

"That's because it's probably on radar," Yoshio said. "They know these planes are coming from miles away."

Sure enough, the ship's radar must have given advance warning of approaching aircraft. Fortunately, it was not a determined air attack, but a plane that seemed to be scouting for ships. The nickname for it was a snooper. From a distance well out of reach of antiaircraft fire, the plane circled them like a hawk watching a rabbit. The plane finally disappeared, but the sky was not empty for long.

Seemingly out of nowhere, a trio of Betty bombers came racing toward them, skimming just above the waves. It was a common Jap tactic to avoid radar. They could see the flashes from the planes' machine guns, but more ominously, they could see what looked like bombs slung from the underbelly of each plane. Machine-gun rounds pinged off the deck, but it was the bombs that could sink them.

In the confusion, the soldiers had been forgotten. They scrambled for whatever shelter they could find as tracers from the Jap plane came streaming at them. They could hear the high-pitched whine of the bombers approaching at high speed.

But that was soon drowned out by the response from the destroyer as every gun on deck seemed to open up, trying to blast the planes from the sky. The tracers and exploding shells would have made a fascinating show if it hadn't been so terrifying. On the bridge, the captain had ordered a series of sharp turns to make the ship a more difficult target.

One of the bombers was hit and cartwheeled into the sea, leaving a smear of flaming wreckage. Another plane billowed black smoke before disintegrating in the air. But the last Betty bomber kept right on coming.

"He's headed right for us!" Philly yelped. Despite the danger, Philly seemed captivated by the drama unfolding above, plane against ship. Maybe this was something that the destroyer's crew were used to, but you didn't see sights like this from the foxhole.

"Keep your head down, you dang fool," Deke warned him, dragging Philly behind the shelter of a steel bulkhead. As much as any spot on the ship was safe while under attack, it at least felt comforting to have a few inches of metal between them and the plane. They could feel each concussion of the bigger guns reverberate through the ship and into their very bones. Deke could hear bullets ricocheting off the deck.

Philly had been right. The plane looked as though it was coming right at them—right down their throats. Deke saw the bomb or torpedo—whatever it was—separate from the aircraft. For a moment, the payload seemed to hang in the air—and then it plunged right at them.

Deke grabbed hold of the nearest chunk of metal and shut his eyes, expecting to be blown to kingdom come.

But either the Japanese pilot's aim was off or the destroyer's maneuvering had paid off. The bomb slanted down and struck the sea, lifting a geyser of salt water that soaked everyone stationed on the bow.

Having missed its chance at a killing blow, the Japanese pilot tried to pull up and away, perhaps to circle back for a second chance. The blazing guns of the destroyer weren't having any of that. Tracers raked the Japanese plane, and it began to disintegrate as it passed the stern. What was left of the enemy plane slammed into the ocean, leaving burning wreckage on the surface.

Everyone's ears rang in the sudden silence once the guns quit firing. It was hard to say who had fired the shots that downed the plane. In a sense, every gunner on the ship had played a part. Cheers filled the air. USS *Ingersoll* had lived to fight another day.

"I'll be damned," Deke said.

They'd been quick to say that sailors had an easy life. They wouldn't be saying that again.

* * *

EVEN IF THE men on the ship weren't looking forward to what lay ahead, they knew that everything they did, no matter how small on the great stage of war, was necessary to defeat Imperial Japan.

Much of that strategy was developed in the mind of one man, General Douglas MacArthur.

MacArthur was currently working alone in his office, looking over the latest reports. He got to his feet, glad to stretch, and walked to the huge map on his wall. War in the Pacific was like a game of hopscotch, thought MacArthur. Hop, skip, jump. Each move carrying them ever closer to Japan. Hopscotch was a child's game, but there was nothing childish about the war that was being waged across the warm, blue waters of the Pacific.

Thousands of American men had perished fighting on the sands or on the seas. *Perished* was too fine a word for it, he mused. They had died fighting, plain and simple, against a savage and relentless enemy.

His critics could accuse MacArthur of many faults, from being self-serving to having an imperious nature. But the truth was more complex. MacArthur was a soldier, through and through, every bit as savage and determined in his genteel way as a GI in the trenches. Everything in his life had been seen through the lens of strategy—whether it was his career or winning the war. To accuse him of simple vanity overlooked the fact that he was far from a small-minded man.

In his thinking and in all his actions, he had far more in common with the likes of Washington and Lee, or even Napoleon or Caesar, than the "everyman" American general favored by the press. Americans didn't always relate to MacArthur, and neither did the men serving under him, but he was going to win the war in the Pacific.

A staff officer popped his head into his office, where the general paced back and forth in front of the map. "Sir, can I get you anything?"

"Not unless you have a spare division in your pocket." The general shook his head. "On second thought, I'll have a cup of tea."

Most military men were devoted coffee drinkers who also favored cigarettes and scotch. The general preferred tea and a pipe. In a sense, the tea was a concession to MacArthur's having spent scarcely any time in the continental US for years. Through and through, he was a man of the vast Pacific.

Tall and solidly built, MacArthur was imposing in his own way. Well into his sixties, he was older than most of the command staff. For all the myth that had built up around him, he was human enough. He felt self-conscious about his balding head and, as a result, insisted on wearing a hat most of the time. The pipe didn't make him seem any more youthful.

But he was no tired old general, rather an energetic man still in his prime.

Just a few months ago, during the darkest days of the war, reaching the Japanese home islands had seemed an impossible feat. Sure, there had been the Doolittle Raid that dropped bombs into the heart of Tokyo, showing the Japanese that they were not beyond the reach of the American military. But that had been a largely symbolic act, America thumbing its nose at the Emperor and all his militant minions. But now the tide had turned.

MacArthur did his best thinking when he was pacing. He paused long enough to study the map on the wall. Something big was afoot. Soon, the final campaign to crush Japan would begin.

That campaign would start with the Philippines. There was a definite sense of justice from that, considering that the Japanese had seized the islands in 1942, after they had been a US possession for nearly half a century. The loss had been a major defeat for the United States. Japan's victory also had been a personal affront to MacArthur, who had commanded US forces there.

To be sure, he had made mistakes in the defense, such as not doing more to protect American air defenses. Japanese raids had quickly wiped out the US planes before they could even get off the ground. In years to come, historians would be relentless in their second-guessing of MacArthur and his shortcomings in regard to those airfields.

Then again, salvaging the air defenses might only have prolonged the inevitable and even allowed those planes to fall into Japanese hands. Cut off from reinforcement from the sea by the Japanese Navy, without any supplies or spare parts, MacArthur simply didn't have the resources to sustain much of an air war against the forces of the Rising Sun.

The general had a deep affinity for the Philippines and its people. It seemed to be an ideal melding of the Far East and the West. Part of that stemmed from the fact that Manila had an old-world, European feel, thanks to its Spanish heritage.

MacArthur would have preferred to stay and fight like the soldier that he was. After all, he had seen the trenches in WWI, far different from Eisenhower, who had never been in combat but now commanded Allied forces in Europe.

But FDR had recalled him from the Philippines rather than have his general go down fighting. The general had resisted the order, but in the end he'd had no choice. Wisely, FDR had not wanted the general to be captured and become another pawn of war, which might also have been a huge embarrassment to the United States.

So he had left, escaping ahead of the Japanese invaders. Several thousand US troops were not given the same opportunity. They fought desperately but surrendered in the end. The result had been the dreadful Bataan Death March, a harbinger of Japanese cruelty in the Philippines and wherever else they made their presence known.

Alone in his office, MacArthur stared at the map for the millionth time, letting the geography sink in. The Philippines itself was a series of islands rather than a single large island or continent. Beyond lay the rich resources of Asia. Whoever occupied the Philippines essentially controlled the sea lanes that brought vital natural resources to the Japanese home islands: oil, rubber, lumber, even basic food supplies. Planes stationed here were that much closer to Japan. This strategic location was why Japan had taken control of the Philippines in the first place. The islands were essential to Japan. It was also why MacArthur was going to take them back.

His master plan would begin soon, with the invasion of Leyte. The island provided deep water anchorages and beaches for landing troops, tanks, and supplies.

He knew that the Japanese were not going to simply hand Leyte over to the invaders. Even now, they were reinforcing their troops there, or attempting to do so. His intelligence experts estimated that the Japanese had as many as 250,000 troops on Leyte, and they were sending more all the time.

It was going to be one hell of a fight.

CHAPTER ELEVEN

The Bear

STUCK in his bunk aboard the destroyer, Deke slept fitfully between bouts of nausea and dizziness from seasickness. He didn't think that he would ever get used to life aboard a ship. Give him dry land any day.

When sleep did come, he was usually tormented by strange dreams or, sometimes, just by things he had worked hard to forget. One of those awful memories concerned the bear that had given him the scars that ran deep down his face and flank.

The bear must have come down from deep mountains sometime during the late summer. As autumn approached, he started stalking the farm fields and pastures, keeping to the shadows at dusk and dawn, taking what he could. He was a sly old beast, only glimpsed at a distance, but the farmers—most of them were also hunters who had tracked a bear or two—agreed that they had never seen such a big bear.

His hind paw left misshapen tracks that earned him the nickname "Ol' Slewfoot." When they went about their chores at twilight or in the darkness before dawn, they did so a little uneasily, knowing that the old bear was around.

Normally, no one worried too much about a bear. Dogs would run them off, or a shot fired into the air, but this bear didn't scare so easily.

He looked old—gray and grizzled and badly scarred along one side of his face, as though maybe the fur had been burned off in a forest fire and had never grown back. The disfigurement made him that much more frightening.

"He's got something wrong with his back foot," said Deke, who had seen the tracks behind the barn, where the bear had come prowling around the night before, setting the dogs to barking.

"Maybe he got caught in a trap," Sadie said. "Why would an old bear come around here?"

"Winter is coming on. He's hungry. I reckon it's easier to steal some chickens or a pig than it is to find food in the mountains."

Sadie shook her head. "If he eats our pig, we're the ones who are gonna be hungry."

"I ain't gonna let that happen."

Sadie looked at him doubtfully. She knew that Deacon wasn't one to brag or boast. Then again, her younger brother was just a thirteen-year-old boy wearing their older cousin Jasper's hand-me-downs, which were too big on him. Since Pa had died, he had done his best to be the man of the family, but he had a long way to go. She smiled. "Just don't let that bear eat you."

There were other things to worry about, such as getting through the approaching winter, bear or no bear. The whole country was in the grip of the Depression, hard cash as scarce as hen's teeth, and it was even worse in the mountain valleys, where times never were all that good to begin with.

The mountain people scratched out the best living that they could from the thin-soiled, rocky fields, harvested a few vegetables from their gardens, raised a pig or two. Some families learned how to live for a week off a turnip or two during the lean times in early spring, when the winter stores began to run out and the garden hadn't produced anything yet. Folks would scour the woods for anything edible, like pokeweed shoots.

But even the mountain people needed money for things like kerosene for their lanterns, proper shoes, and shotgun shells.

Most of the people had lived on this land for one hundred and fifty years, and they knew how to make do. But the land they lived on was often mortgaged, and they still needed money to pay the banks. More than a few farms had been mortgaged in hopes that when times improved, there would be money to pay it all off. The Cole family farm was one of those places.

And now the bear had arrived. He was like a shadow, a plague, come out of the depths of the mountains to haunt them.

Two days before Deke had seen the tracks, Old Man McGlothlin drove up to the farm in his rust bucket of a truck. Deke was splitting wood, and he put down the ax to watch the Model A truck approach. The truck was largely held together with baler wire, and each rut in the lane sent it shaking and rattling so much that Deke thought for sure that the old truck would suddenly disintegrate into a pile of scrap metal and bolts right before his eyes.

The truck rolled to a stop, still in one piece, more or less. The motor wheezed before going quiet, and McGlothlin got out.

"Howdy, Deacon," Old Man McGlothlin said. His voice was friendly enough, but his face looked like it might crack if he smiled.

"Howdy, Mr. McGlothlin."

"How y'all gettin' on?"

"All right, I reckon."

McGlothlin nodded. He was a withered old farmer, with his sons grown, his wife dead, and nobody left to help him work the land. Not a bad sort—just past his prime and lonely. His face was so expressionless that it might have been carved from wood. "That's about the best anyone can expect," he said. "Hard times."

"Yes, sir."

"Listen, I came around to tell you I saw that bear around my place."

"The one people are calling Ol' Slewfoot?"

"One and the same. He was coming around the chickens, and I ran him off with my shotgun. I think I done winged him. Last I saw of him, he was runnin' in this direction."

"Why didn't you track him?" Deke asked.

McGlothlin took off his hat and scratched his sparse hair. "He's an awful big bear, son. Like I said, I think he's wounded. You corner a wounded bear like that—" He shook his head. "I ain't as young or as quick as I used to be."

"I could track him."

For the first time, something like a smile crossed McGlothlin's face. "I know you could, boy. But let's just say that I'm too old for a bear hunt and you're too young, and leave it at that. Anyhow, maybe that bear has gone on back up the mountain."

"What if he ain't done that?"

"Best thing to do is to steer clear of that bear, which is why I'm here to let you know I seen him. I wanted to warn you that Ol' Slew-foot might come around here next. Don't none of you go out alone for a while—and take a dog along and your gun. I know you can shoot. Your pa said you could shoot the eye out of a crow flying. But believe me, the sight of that bear can make a grown man shaky. Makes it hard to shoot straight."

Deke stood a little straighter, although it was hard to tell in the baggy clothes. He hadn't known that his pa had said that about him. "I'll put the pig in the barn."

"That bear will get that pig if he wants him, one way or another. You just make sure that bear don't get *you*, or your sister or ma."

"I ain't scared of that bear."

"I reckon you're full of piss and vinegar, just like my boys was at your age." The old farmer made a noise that might have been a chuckle. "Just keep in mind that Ol' Slewfoot ain't scared of you neither, son. You might even look like an easy meal to him. It's only an old bear that would come around here, or maybe he's ailing. The last thing you want to do is corner a bear like that."

His warning delivered, McGlothlin gave Deke a nod, climbed into the rattletrap truck, and drove away.

THE NEXT DAY, sure enough, Deke had seen the tracks out behind the barn. Ol' Slewfoot had come sniffing around. He'd certainly been expecting it, thanks to the warning from their neighbor. It would have

been a whole lot better for them if the bear had just kept on his way.
Maybe he had figured the Cole farm would be easy pickings.

Deke crouched down and placed his hand inside the track left by
the damaged paw. He was surprised to see that the track swallowed up
his hand. He stood up and tried his foot next, but the bear's track was
still larger. Nearby, he spotted a drop or two of blood. Wounded, all
right. A big, wounded bear wasn't good news.

After McGlothlin's warning, he had started carrying the old Iver
Johnson double-barreled twelve gauge around the farm with him.
Both barrels were loaded with buckshot. He looked down again at
the massive size of the tracks left by the bear's paw. Two barrels.
Two shots. If it came down to it, would that be enough? A couple of
shotgun shells suddenly seemed like a puny thing compared to a
bear.

He looked over his shoulder, feeling a ripple along his spine, but
there was nothing to see but the empty fields crisscrossed by a few
leaning fences. The dark line of woods began beyond the fields and
sloped up toward the mountains. Maybe the bear had run off into
those hills, but Deke didn't think so. Ol' Slewfoot would be hungry,
and possibly mad with pain if he was wounded. Deke had an uneasy
feeling, like maybe the bear was watching him right now from those
trees, making up his mind to stay or retreat into the hills.

That night when the dogs started barking, he knew that he'd
gotten his answer. A frightened squeal cut through the sound of the
commotion outside.

"He's after the pig!" Sadie said, wide eyed and angry. They both
knew that the pig was their only hope of getting through the winter.
Most families raised one up through the summer, feeding it scraps and
slop, fattening it up.

Deke reached for the shotgun in the corner. "I'm going out there."

"Not alone, you're not!" Sadie took the rifle down from where it
hung above the fireplace.

He didn't bother to argue. It wouldn't have done any good where
Sadie was concerned. His sister was stubborn as a mule.

She was also a good shot—maybe even better than her brother.
The Coles owned a shotgun and a hunting rifle. What they didn't own

was a lot of shells for either gun. Those cost money that they didn't have. Each shot would need to count.

Still sitting at the table, Ma looked as though her thoughts were a million miles away. The presence of the bear on the farm didn't seem to concern her. Since Pa had died, she had turned inward, growing quieter and somehow more childlike each day. The normal thing would have been to tell her children not to go out into the dark that was filled with the awful squeals of the pig and the excited yelping of the dogs.

Mutely, she watched her son and daughter standing by the door, guns in their hands, gathering their courage before going into the night to confront the bear. Nobody would have blamed them if they stayed in the house. In fact, you might say that was the smart thing to do under the circumstances. But avoiding danger wasn't the Cole way.

Sadie followed Deke out the door.

Their two dogs were raising a ruckus down by the barn, and they ran in that direction.

They heard what sounded like boards being ripped aside, then more squeals from their pig, so high pitched that it hurt their ears. Had the bear already gotten to him?

Shouting to scare off the bear, Deke ran around the barn, shotgun at the ready. In the moonlight, he could see the hole in the back of the barn where the boards had been torn loose. The pig had gone quiet. That didn't make any sense. With a sinking heart, Deke realized that the bear must have already made off with the pig. He realized that he could now hear the dogs barking off in the field.

"We're too late!" Sadie cried out, her voice taut with anger. "He already took the pig!"

"Maybe we can get it back."

"What are you talking about, Deke?"

"Come on," he said.

He led the way toward the sound of the barking dogs. They weren't letting the bear get away scot-free. Maybe, just maybe, they could get the pig back and salvage something from it. There was an outraged growl that must be from the bear. One of the dogs yelped—it sounded like their old hound, Boomer—then went quiet.

"Oh no," Sadie said.

Deke ran faster, his feet light and sure-footed across the dark field. The night pressed in around them, and his eyes strained to see anything in the moonlight. Vaguely, he was aware of Sadie calling to him to come back, but he kept running.

Finally, he saw the bear, a heaving black lump even blacker than the darkness around it. Without thinking, his pumping legs carried him closer, and a savage sound came from his throat, a keening wail that was a mix of fear and outrage. Some would have called it a rebel yell.

Closer now, he could see the bear in the moonlight, the black lump coalescing into a creature that looked impossibly big. Its paws straddled the freshly killed pig. His outraged yell had gotten the bear's attention. When the bear turned its grizzled muzzle toward Deke, he could see that it was wet and dripping with gore from the pig. The sight was made even more horrible because the bear's face was scarred and hairless on one side, presumably burned, like some unearthly creature.

Deke raised the shotgun, but his heart hammered from all the running, and his arms wouldn't hold the twelve gauge steady. *Two shots,* he reminded himself. *That's all you get.*

Behind him, a gunshot split the night, taking him by surprise. Sadie had fired into the air, once, twice, hoping to scare off the bear. Their other dog, Banger, was still snarling at Ol' Slewfoot and darting in to nip at him, but the bear paid him no more attention than he would give a mosquito. Another shadow lay in the frosty grass nearby, and Deke realized it was old Boomer's lifeless form.

The bear held its ground and roared. He rose up on his hind legs. A full-grown black bear could stand over six feet high, and this one weighed at least four hundred pounds, looking nearly as broad as he was tall. He would have dwarfed a full-grown man, and Deke was just a boy.

"He killed Boomer!" Sadie cried. Anger seemed to get the best of her. She came up even with Deke and fired again, aiming right at the bear this time. The bear roared. He dropped to all fours, and for a moment it looked as if Sadie had gotten him.

"That was my last bullet. Shoot him, Deke. Shoot him!"

Deke raised the shotgun, looking for a good shot. If Sadie had hit the bear, it had only made him even more mad with pain. He rolled his massive head, roaring again.

And then Ol' Slewfoot charged.

Right at Sadie.

A bear, even an old one, can move with lightning speed. All four hundred pounds of the bear exploded into motion, a furious mountain of pain, matted fur, yellow teeth, and claws like reaping hooks.

They couldn't have outrun the bear even if they'd tried. Sadie seemed to brace herself, watching the bear come like she was daring it. She held the empty rifle like a club, standing her ground. The bear was headed right for her.

"Deke, shoot him!"

Deke stepped in front of his sister. He put the bead of the shotgun on the bear and fired.

Then the bear was upon him. It was like being hit by a hay bale fired from a cannon. He slammed to the ground, all the breath going out of him. He felt the bear's claws raking him, tearing away his coat and shirt. There wasn't any pain at first, even when he felt a claw snag a rib and snap it as easily as Deke might have broken a stick of kindling for the woodstove.

Through it all, he didn't let go of the shotgun. One part of him registered that the bear was ripping him to pieces, while another part of him ignored that and focused on the shotgun. It was his only hope. The twelve gauge was all that mattered. He still had one finger through the trigger guard. One live shell in the chamber. If he could just get the muzzle turned into the bear, he would pull that trigger.

Sadie hadn't run off. She was beating the bear with the rifle, shouting at him to let her brother go. Deke could hear her over the roaring that filled his ears.

The dog hadn't given up, either, but was still biting at the bear, coming at him whenever the bear's snapping jaws turned away.

Deke heard someone shrieking in pain and realized that he was the one doing the screaming.

Maybe Sadie and the dog kept the bear from immediately ripping him to shreds. He tried hard to maneuver the shotgun, but the weight of the bear's body kept him pinned to the ground.

Then he smelled the bear's hot breath, right in his face. It was like some awful dog's breath, hot and fetid, stinking of rotting meat. That was when the bear's jaws closed around his head.

He felt teeth grating across his skull, sliding over the bone, looking for a grip. The bear was going to pop his head open like a walnut. The paws shifted to hold him down while the bear's jaws slid around to get a better hold, peeling his flesh away from the bone in the process. The sound of Deke's own screaming intensified.

By turning its attention to his head, the bear had moved enough to give Deke some wiggle room. His side felt like it was on fire, as if the bear's claws had been hot coals. Deke started to fade, but the bear shook his head for him, clearing it. Not yet. He tugged the muzzle of the shotgun up another inch and pressed the trigger. He heard the gun go off, but the blast was muffled by the mountain of bear crushing him to the ground.

At first, nothing happened. The bear kept working at his skull like a dog with a bone. Sadie kept hitting the bear, clubbing it in the head with the rifle butt. Then the bear's jaws moved more slowly, like it was bored with him, or getting tired, and finally stopped.

Grunting with the effort, Sadie pulled him out from under the bear.

She was sobbing. "Oh, Deke, oh, Deke."

"I'm all right," he said, then slipped into a welcome blackness.

* * *

THERE WAS nothing for Sadie and his ma to do but sew him up and pray. Truth be told, the lion's share of both tasks fell to Sadie. The country doctor came by and shook his head. The closest thing to a real hospital that could do surgery on Deke, maybe patch him back together, was more than fifty miles away. Old Man McGlothlin offered to take him in his truck, but they all knew the boy would never survive the ride. Nature would just have to take its course.

"I done warned him about that bear," the farmer said.

Shaking his head, he went off to butcher what was left of the pig, skin the bear, and dig young Deacon's grave.

For the next week, then two, Deke lingered. His life flickered and threatened to go out like a candle in a drafty room. He took his time dying. Autumn leaves filled the hole where he was meant to be buried. Without anyone knowing, Sadie cut off one of the bear's claws and saved it as a talisman.

Instead of dying, Deke got stronger. The candle flame burned stronger. He came from hardy mountain stock, after all, and the young were resilient. Still, it was two months before he could get out of bed. He moved slowly, painfully, but the bones and muscles were knitting back together.

As for the scars, there was nothing much that anyone could do about that. Sadie and Ma rubbed bear grease on the angry red furrows to help them heal. The scars on his body were hidden easily by his shirt. New hair grew on his scalp. When he turned his face slightly away, he looked like the same old Deke. But on his left side, his face and ear remained badly mangled, a reminder of the bear.

Deke would live, but there was a price to pay. As if the physical injuries hadn't been enough, all these years later, he still had nightmares about that bear. It was as if in taking the bear's life, Ol' Slewfoot had passed on its own scars and pain to Deke, like a dying curse. In the same way, the bear must have passed on some of its power and wild spirit.

On the ship, Deke tossed and turned in the narrow bunk, trying to get comfortable. After a while, he stopped fighting it, grabbed a blanket, and curled up in a corner of the deck. The breeze on deck helped to clear the fog of bad memories from his head. He was sure some squid would come along and roust him out, but until then, he let the night air wash over him as he finally slept.

CHAPTER TWELVE

Leyte, Philippines

THE REST of the voyage to the shores of Leyte was mostly filled by days of boredom, mixed with a few moments of terror whenever there was a scare about a Jap plane or sub. Sure, these squids slept in a bunk and ate three squares a day, but it was hard to forget that at any moment they could end up feeding the sharks if the Japs got lucky with a torpedo.

Finally, the monotony broke when Lieutenant Steele gathered them together on deck.

"Here we are, boys," Steele announced. He pointed toward the west. All that they could see was more endless ocean. "Leyte is just over there."

"What, is it invisible?" Philly wondered. "I don't see a thing."

Steele shook his head, then assured them that while land was nowhere in sight, Leyte was just over the horizon. The horizon was currently being churned by large waves that caused the deck to roll—a feeling that Deke was never going to get used to, no matter how much time he spent at sea. He definitely had granite running through his veins, not salt water.

They were launching in less-than-ideal conditions, but their timetable didn't give them the luxury of waiting for calmer seas. Night was falling, and the men were not pleased that they would be landing in the dark, but that was their best hope of making it to shore undetected.

"We can't go in any closer," Steele explained. "That big gun that we're trying to knock out would send this destroyer straight to the bottom. The captain tells me that the ship may already be in range, but that the Japs may not want to reveal more than they have to at this point. In any case, he doesn't want to make it any easier for the Japs to sink him than he has to."

"If he knows where the Japs are, why the hell doesn't he drop some shells on their heads? That's what I'd like to know. This floating tin can has plenty of firepower."

"In case you haven't figured it out yet, we're trying to get ashore without letting the whole Japanese army know about it. Opening fire on them right now wouldn't be very smart, now would it? We don't want to ring the doorbell."

Instead of the destroyer itself, a smaller launch was taking them in to shore. The craft was piloted by a single sailor. To Deke's surprise, he recognized the gruff petty officer that he had seen on deck. The man had the air of an old salt about him and hadn't been overly friendly toward the ship's "passengers," but he had volunteered to pilot the launch. "I figured that I'd take you in myself," he said. "That way, you'll have a chance of making it to shore."

Skilled though the petty officer might be, the smaller boat still bucked and bobbed in the swell. He did manage to keep the launch tight against the sides of the much larger destroyer as the men of Patrol Easy climbed down the ladder and dropped the last few feet into the boat.

Deke was the third man over the side, following Lieutenant Steele and Philly. He concentrated on handholds and footholds as he made his way down the ladder. It wasn't at all like climbing the ladder to fix the barn roof, but just two ropes with wooden slats in between. At first glance, descending the ladder looked like an easy enough task, and maybe it was for a man unencumbered by equipment. At five foot ten with a lean build, Deke wasn't a big man, but he was solid as a locust fence post. That was a good thing, because he soon found his body being pounded against the steel sides of the ship.

The pack on his back created an awkward weight trying to pull him off the ladder. It didn't help that the motion of the ship caused the ladder to sway like a pendulum. One moment he was swinging into space, and the next he was slamming back against the side of the ship. It seemed to Deke that the hardest part of the whole damn mission might be getting off this ship in one piece.

His foot slipped off and he frantically sought for a new foothold, his heart hammering. If he slipped, Deke knew that he would plunge right into the ocean. The weight of his gear would take him straight down to the bottom. Some of the sailors had rather gleefully informed him that the ocean here was more than a mile deep—a fact that he didn't need to know.

If he could have picked the last place on earth that he wanted to be right now, his current situation would have been near the top of that list. Deke wasn't afraid of much, but he hated anything to do with the ocean. Give him dry land any day.

As if the ladder wasn't bad enough, the final challenge was to drop the last few feet into the launch itself. For whatever reason, the ladder stopped short of the water. Couldn't those navy bastards have added a few rungs?

Deke glanced below him. The sea made the small launch bob wildly.

"That last step is a doozy," warned Philly, who had come down the ladder just ahead of him. "Wait for it . . . hold on . . . now!"

Deke let go and tumbled into the launch, landing in a heap. It wasn't pretty, but at least he hadn't gotten wet. Nothing seemed to be broken.

Aboard the launch, they had no choice but to squat shoulder to shoulder on the small deck.

"I've seen bathtubs that are bigger than this boat," Deke muttered.

"Good. You didn't want us to be a bigger target for the Japs, did you?"

If Deke had a tough time of it due to his pack, he realized that he had little reason to complain when he saw Rodeo climbing down with the added weight of the radio that would be their lifeline to the fleet once they were ashore. Even so, the radio would be at the outer limits of its range. Their best hope would be to broadcast from higher elevations.

That was, if Rodeo even made it off the ship in one piece. As the destroyer fell into the trough of a wave, the ladder swung wildly, far over their heads. As the ship righted itself, Rodeo slammed hard against the steel sides. They heard him curse mightily before continuing down the ladder.

Yoshio followed. He was by far the smallest and lightest of them all, and he climbed down nimbly.

Next, the satchel charges that they would use to blow up the Japanese installation were lowered down. They all held their breath when the charges bounced hard against the side of the ship.

"Easy!" Lieutenant Steele shouted.

They all breathed again once the explosives were safely stowed aboard the launch.

The marines climbed down last. Bat was surprisingly agile for a big, gangly guy. When the ladder swung him far out to sea, he whooped with delight, like he was on a ride at the county fair. Ball was just the opposite, seeming to be pure deadweight on the ladder. He dropped the last few feet and landed in a heap that made even Deke's arrival in the launch look graceful.

"That's everybody," Steele said.

The petty officer nodded curtly. He had been doing his best to keep the launch pinned against the side of the massive ship so that the soldiers could drop into the boat without getting the launch crushed in the process. He reversed the motor and backed away from the destroyer. He swung the bow around, checked his compass, and then headed due west toward where the land was supposed to be.

For now, there was only open water in sight—or as far as they could see on the starlit sea, at least. Deke gazed back almost regretfully toward the ship. From a distance, the roll of the ship in the big Pacific waves wasn't even noticeable. USS *Ingersoll* looked like a small steel island.

Nonetheless, Deke was glad to get off the destroyer and to be heading for land, but at the moment they seemed to be on a very small boat on a very big ocean. Deke appreciated the fact that the salty old pilot seemed completely at ease as he worked the wheel, trying to dodge the biggest of the waves.

If the men had pictured racing toward shore under the cover of night, they were sadly mistaken. The launch made steady progress, but the petty officer was trying to avoid going so fast that he would cause a wake. Even the wake from a small boat, luminous on the dark surface of the sea, was enough to alert the watchful Japanese of their presence.

Given the heavy seas and the distance involved, any number of things could go wrong, but the occupants of the cramped launch had no choice but to say their prayers and hope for the best. The few words of conversation they attempted felt hollow, swept away by the wind into the vastness of the dark ocean around them.

"Here we come," Philly said. "I hope the Japanese are ready for us."

"Don't you mean that you're hoping that they're *not* ready?" Deke asked.

"What I mean is that I hope their bunker is done so we can blow it up good and proper."

"So you're hoping the Japs have done a good job building that bunker?"

"What am I, a politician? Don't go putting words in my mouth."

They fell quiet after that, the only sound coming from the motor and the bow of the launch cutting through the water. The plan was to get Patrol Easy to shore under cover of darkness. Once the men were ashore, the boat would be making its way back to the *Ingersoll*. The boat would return for them in daylight, though, at noon on the second day, giving them roughly thirty-six hours to get the job done. If they needed more time, or an earlier extraction, they could contact the ship using the radio they were bringing along.

However, their time frame was limited. Not only that, but how long could they possibly hope to dodge the Japanese, who would surely be looking for them? If they didn't succeed, the big guns would still be there to greet the troops who came ashore a few days hence.

"I see it!" Yoshio said excitedly, pointing west.

"You must be eating your carrots," Philly replied. "I don't see a damn thing."

Deke squinted. Yoshio was right; there was a darker smudge on the horizon that could only be land. As the launch closed the gap, details began to emerge. A white line of surf seemed to glow in the distance. Above, a dark promontory loomed. This must be what had been dubbed Hill 522, on account of it being exactly that many feet high. This was where the Japanese ship-killer battery was supposed to be hidden.

The pilot began to cut back on the throttle as they came closer to land. With any luck, the breeze would carry the sound of the motor back out to sea before the Japs could figure out what was going on. If they were met at the shoreline by a Japanese patrol or if, God forbid, that big gun opened fire, the mission would be over before it even started.

"I can't take you all the way in," the pilot said. "The coral would tear the bottom right out of this boat. But I'll get you in as close as possible."

Lieutenant Steele nodded. "Do what you can."

Close to shore, the pilot cut the motor to a whisper, then shut it off completely, relying on the momentum of the boat to glide them over the water. Deke looked down and saw coral glowing up at him through the water, no more than a few feet below the surface. The coral appeared to have some sort of natural phosphorescence. It might have been beautiful, if he hadn't been aware that the tropical coral was sharp enough to shred the hull and cut any bare feet or hands that came in contact with it.

Soon they could hear waves crashing ahead, where the coral created shallows that the boat couldn't cross. The foaming white line of surf was visible in the night. Just beyond the edge of the reef lay a wide beach that was their ultimate destination.

"That's as close as I can get," said the pilot, who still guided the drifting launch toward the shallows where the waves churned. His hands were poised over the controls, ready to nudge the motor back into life if he needed to.

"All right, boys, this is where we get off," the lieutenant said. "For God's sake, try not to drown on the way in."

As it turned out, the lieutenant had not issued an idle warning. From the launch, the water hadn't seemed all that deep, and the waves hadn't looked all that big. However, once they were in the water, it was a different story. They splashed into the sea, their boots on the coral shelf. The tricky part was getting through the surf line where the waves were breaking.

Deke barely heard the pilot's gruff voice say as if to himself, "Godspeed." Then the motor kicked into life, the bow turned toward the sea, and the launch glided smoothly away into deeper water, leaving them behind in the churning surf.

It was now up to each man whether he lived or drowned. Seafoam and salt water filled Deke's nostrils and throat so that he gasped for air. In the darkness, it was hard to tell where the sky ended and the sea started, adding to his difficulties. He struggled to keep his boots under him as the current surged against his legs and waist. He held his rifle over his head, trying to keep it dry. Before leaving the ship, he had wrapped the entire rifle and scope in plastic, but he still didn't want to take a chance of getting it wet, considering that they might find themselves in a fight as soon as they set foot on shore.

He stepped in a hole in the coral shelf and felt water surge to his armpits. Despite the tropical climate, the dark water felt cold. It would be a hell of a thing, he thought, to come across the whole damn ocean and drown within sight of shore.

He fought the urge to call out for help—which wouldn't be coming, anyhow. The men around him were also doing their darnedest not to drown in the surf.

To make matters worse, Deke thought about how their silhouettes must have shown plainly against the backdrop of sky. It wasn't an ideal situation. The sooner that they got to shore, the better.

He took another step, holding his breath, half expecting to sink in over his head, but, gratefully, he stepped out of the hole.

"Watch your step," Deke whispered to Rodeo, who was right behind him.

Like Deke with his rifle, Rodeo was struggling to keep the radio out of the water. The precious radio was their only communications link. It, too, had been wrapped tightly in plastic. But the radio was a lot heavier than a rifle, not to mention ungainly, and Rodeo was a couple of inches shorter than Deke. When he stepped into the hole, it reached to his chin. Then a wave came in and Rodeo disappeared underwater. He still held the radio out of the water, but the weight of it was keeping him bogged down in the watery hole.

No one could blame him for what happened next. It was simple human nature. Rodeo's survival instincts kicked in. He let go of the radio and struggled back up to the surface.

Realizing what he had done, Rodeo dove under and tried to retrieve the radio, which had sunk like a stone. Deke saw that he wasn't coming back up. He cursed, waded back, and held his rifle out of the surf with his left hand while he groped in the water with his right. He grabbed hold of the back of Rodeo's collar and dragged him to the surface.

They struggled across what remained of the coral reef and reached the shallow water of the beach, then made it to the sand, where they both collapsed, panting.

Steele came over, limping from where he had banged his knee on the coral. "What the hell happened?"

Rodeo still held on to the radio. He was muttering, "Please, please, please." He tore off the plastic covering. Water ran out. Though intact, the radio was as dead as a drowned baby.

"I'm sorry, Honcho," Rodeo sputtered. "I don't even know what the hell happened."

"No use crying over spilled milk," Steele said. "Let's just get the hell off this beach before somebody spots us and we have even bigger problems than a dead radio."

If they had been vulnerable in the surf, then it went without saying that their dark silhouettes made even more obvious targets against the sand. If any Jap sentries spotted them, they'd be done for. Considering the intelligence reports that there were thousands of enemy troops stationed within a stone's throw of the beach, to say that they were vastly outnumbered was an understatement.

Steele ran for the tree line, leading the men off the beach. He kept his shotgun ready—he hadn't bothered to wrap it up in plastic. A twelve gauge could take a lot of abuse and still fire, even after being dunked in the ocean. Deke didn't stop to unwrap the plastic from his sniper rifle but held the rifle in one hand and drew a pistol with the other.

Looking down, he could see the tracks that they were all leaving in the sand. It couldn't be helped. If they were lucky, maybe the tide would come in and wash away the tracks. If not, some Jap patrol would find them in the morning.

Deke also took a quick glance upward, at the hill that rose high above the beach. Not a light showed up there. In the night, the hill was nothing more than a hulking darkness, as sinister as a natural feature of the landscape could be. Deke was reminded of mountains back home that were supposedly haunted—old wives' tales to laugh about in the daylight and think twice about at night. This was their ultimate destination. Somewhere up there, the Japanese battery was hidden. The hill was located about a mile inland, so they sure as hell had a long way to go to get there.

For the first time, it began to dawn on Deke that maybe—just maybe—they had been given an impossible task.

But there was no time to dwell on that now. Deke put his head down and ran, which wasn't easy in the deep sand. The lieutenant had managed to outpace them all. You had to hand it to Steele. Once again, he showed that he was in good shape, considering that he was the oldest one here. He was also a natural athlete. He'd gone easy on the cigarettes and scotch so that they didn't affect his wind. He trotted across the sand on his long legs, forcing the rest of them to keep up.

Deke half expected to see the night light up with tracer fire, but so far all was quiet. Steele dashed into the cover offered by the trees, and the rest of the men followed.

Having reached cover, they fell to their knees, panting from the sheer effort of wading to shore and crossing that beach. In the backs of their minds, they were grateful for the shakedown hike that had been an effort to keep them in shape.

Safely hidden in the trees, they took stock. All of them had made it to shore, although Rodeo was still coughing up salt water after his attempt to rescue the radio. Yoshio had a deep gash on his leg from the coral. The two marines had managed to keep their explosives dry, which was good news.

"You should have let me carry that radio," Bat said to Rodeo. "I wouldn't have dropped the damn thing in the water."

"Go to hell."

"Yeah? I've got news for you. We were supposed to use that radio to call for a ride when we're done with shoving these explosives up the ass of these Japanese."

Steele had heard enough. "All right, can it. This isn't the time for a blame game. Radio or not, there's going to be a boat waiting for us in a day and a half. We just need to get the job done by then."

But Bat wasn't ready to let it go. Like everyone else, he knew that plans change. "Without the radio, what are we gonna do, sir? Shout at them?"

"I said that's enough. And if you call me *sir* again, the only place those explosives are going is up *your* ass. You might as well put a target on my back for every Jap sniper to see when you call me that. Call me Honcho like everybody else."

"Whatever you say, Honcho."

"That's more like it." The lieutenant turned to Rodeo. "Any chance that thing might work once it dries out?"

Rodeo shook his head. "The salt water will have wrecked the electronics, Honcho."

"All right. No sense lugging deadweight around or leaving that radio where the Japs might find it. Better bury it, then."

Rodeo used his entrenching tool to quickly dig a hole in the sand. The metal blade struck a rock, and the grating noise seemed loud as a gunshot.

They all held their breath until the night insects resumed their song. Thankfully, there didn't seem to be any Japanese ears in the vicinity.

"Jeez, why don't you just send the Japs a telegram that we're here?" Philly said.

"Sorry," Rodeo replied, pulling sand over the dead radio.

"Now what, Honcho?"

"We were sent here to blow up those guns, so that's just what we're going to do." He stood up and started through the jungle in the direction of the hill. "Let's get to it."

CHAPTER THIRTEEN

NOT LONG AFTER FIRST LIGHT, Ikeda was leading a reconnaissance patrol on the beach. He found that it kept him and the men sharp, giving them a little exercise away from the hill. He got tired of all the fresh dirt and concrete. The greenery of the forest or the sandy beach was a welcome change of scenery.

In fact, so much attention had been focused on the hill and its defense that it was almost possible to forget that there was far more to the island.

Ikeda breathed in the fresh salt air, enjoying the feel of the sea breeze on his face. What man did not feel energized by the start of a new day? The sun was rising, a big red ball of fire coming out of the Pacific, but the heat of the day was not yet present. There was nothing so glorious as a Pacific sunrise. Later on, they would swelter in that heat, but for now, the rising sun was a thing of beauty, a reminder of Japan itself.

They walked on, some of the men talking quietly in hushed tones. Ikeda permitted it—on the beach, out in the open, there was not much worry about giving away their position, was there? The Filipino guerrillas were not much threat to an armed patrol. As for the Americans, all reports indicated that they must still be many thousands of miles away.

Up ahead, though, something didn't look right in the sand. The smooth surface of the beach had been disturbed. Moving closer, he could see that several sets of footsteps led from the water, across the beach, and disappeared into the fringe of forest beyond the sand.

"Sir?"

"I see it," Ikeda said.

Instantly, he was on alert, the sniper rifle gripped tightly in his hands. The men sensed that something wasn't right and looked around them, but what was there to see but more beach, surf, and sand? Whoever had made those tracks was long gone, the tide having erased many of the tracks.

Ikeda bent closer to examine the marks. He was puzzled as to why the tracks only led away from the sea, as if whoever had left them had materialized out of the water. Also, most of the tracks showed footsteps that were fairly large, sunk deep into the sand. These marks had been left by big men—bigger than the average Japanese soldier or Filipino laborer, at least.

Slowly, a realization began to sink in for Ikeda. The morning calm that he had been experiencing had vanished. If these were not Japanese tracks, or Filipino tracks, then that left one possibility.

Enemy soldiers had landed on this beach and made their way into the jungle at the base of the hill.

This was the only explanation that Ikeda could think of for the tracks on the beach, which clearly showed an organized team had landed here. There had been warnings of commando raids. At long last, those warnings appeared to have come true.

Reluctantly, he dismissed the idea of following the tracks. He would have liked nothing better than to hunt down the invaders and put his rifle to use. However, it was possible that the men who had left these tracks had a head start of several hours. Instead, the reason these men were here seemed far more important. Had the raiders come to attack the hilltop battery?

"We must get back to the hill immediately," Ikeda said, preparing to set off at a trot back the way that they had come. It would be the fastest way to sound a warning, even if it meant letting the raiders get away—for now. "We must warn the others. There is no time to lose."

* * *

IT HAD TAKEN the men of Patrol Easy most of the night to make their way to the base of the hill. The forest between the beach and the hill had not been very dense, much of it having been cleared by the Japanese, in part for defense of the island, but also for the raw materials needed to construct the defenses on the hill. In fact, they would have felt more confident if the forest had offered more cover. They proceeded cautiously, but by some miracle they did not encounter a single enemy soldier.

"I don't get it," Philly wondered aloud. "Where are all the Japs?"

"It's spooky," Deke whispered, looking in every direction, rifle at the ready. "I hope we ain't walkin' into a trap."

"They're not expecting us yet," Honcho said. "When the fleet gets here, they'll see it. They'll have plenty of time to slither into whatever hidey-holes they have prepared for their snipers and machine guns before our boys come ashore. Until then, I suppose they're all still up on this hill, working to dig themselves in even deeper."

"You think we can reach those guns?"

"One way or another, we're gonna have to."

Lieutenant Steele was correct that most of the Japanese seemed to be working on the hill. They could see work parties busy digging or hauling buckets or rocks and dirt. It was a little surprising that not a single piece of heavy machinery was visible. Japanese soldiers were not the only laborers. A large number of civilian Filipino men appeared to have been pressed into service, ranging in age from boys to gray-haired older men.

It was a miserable existence. They appeared to be constantly abused by the Japanese, punched, kicked, and beaten with sticks whenever they stumbled or moved too slowly to satisfy the cruel Japanese overseers. It was clear that the Filipinos amounted to little more than slave labor.

All that work had produced results. To Deke's eye, the entire hillside appeared to be a network of trenches, bunkers, and pillboxes. It had all been accomplished with a backbreaking amount of effort, using basic tools.

"It's like these guys are straight out of the Stone Age," Philly said.

"Lucky for us," Deke replied. "Imagine what they could have done with a few bulldozers."

They could see what must be their destination near the top of the hill. The dark maw of a large bunker was visible. Whatever guns were inside would have a commanding view of the approach to the beach and could rain destruction down on any fleet that approached.

"That's got to be the big guns we're after," Philly said, voicing what everyone was already thinking.

"No doubt about it," Steele agreed.

"How the hell do we get up there?"

Steele grinned. "We walk on in, bold as brass, that's how. Luckily, nobody seems to be expecting us."

Deke could see that the lieutenant was on to something. They could have planned the attack for days and never have had such an opportunity as the one that now presented itself. The attack was bold and spontaneous. It remained to be seen if they could pull it off, but they had total surprise on their side.

While there were plenty of Japanese soldiers in sight, very few of them were armed. These were work details, with the men carrying shovels rather than rifles. Many had their shirts off, no helmets on, or were wearing only the traditional loincloth that the Japanese called a *fundoshi*. It was the only clothing needed in the tropical heat, but it was basically the same as working in your underwear. *Talk about being caught with your pants down,* Deke thought.

He could also see that the Japanese troops looked thin, dirty, and exhausted. There were a lot of them, but they were definitely not in top condition.

Hidden in a trench at the bottom of the hill, Lieutenant Steele used a finger to map out their route, drawing in the dirt.

"See how these trenches zigzag up the hill?" Honcho asked. "We can follow them right to the top."

"That's crazy," Philly said.

"Sometimes crazy is what works. We'll be done and out of here before the Japs know what hit them. That said, I don't want any shooting."

"Honcho, in case you haven't noticed, those are Japs!"

"Japs who don't even know we're here, so don't go shooting anyone and telling them otherwise. Got it?"

"You're the boss."

"I'll lead. Bat and Ball, you're next. Have those charges ready. Rodeo, Yoshio, Alphabet, you cover them when they go to toss those satchels into the bunker. Deke, you watch our tail."

It was a simple plan, and sometimes simple plans worked best— even when they were fraught with danger.

They started up the hill, Steele leading the way. By keeping to the network of trenches, and staying crouched low, they managed not to attract any attention to themselves.

In fact, most of the Japanese soldiers were so intent on their work that they didn't pay any attention to the soldiers moving through the trenches. Maybe they were too exhausted to notice or maybe even to care. Besides, most of the rank-and-file Japanese soldiers had learned a long time ago that it wasn't smart to pay too much attention—it was best to keep their heads down and do what they were told.

The exception was a soldier who spotted the movement through the trench and the uniforms that looked out of place. He stared at Deke bringing up the rear, and his eyes went wide in disbelief. Deke brought his rifle up, ready to pop him, but he remembered Honcho's warning not to spoil the surprise by firing any shots. Besides, the poor bastard wasn't armed with anything but a shovel.

Instead, Deke put a finger to his lips in the universal gesture to keep quiet. The soldier seemed to realize that if he shouted an alarm, Deke would shoot him. It was all the warning that he needed. He just stared quietly as Deke disappeared around a switchback in the trench.

They climbed higher. It took just a few minutes to approach the top. Below, the beach and the blue water of the gulf stretched out before them. Deke had sharp eyes, but he didn't see any sign of the destroyer that had brought them to the Japanese doorstep. If the USS *Ingersoll* was still out there, it must be over the horizon.

With a sinking feeling, Deke realized that all it would take was to position a few machine guns up here, along with some artillery, and that beach would be very hard to take. Not impossible—after all, US forces had already taken Guadalcanal and Guam, among other places— but there would be a heavy price to pay. *I reckon that's why we're here.*

At the top of the promontory, they reached the bunker where the big naval guns were hidden. Deke caught up to the others but hung behind a few feet, watching their back trail. At any moment, the soldier he'd seen earlier might change his mind and sound the alarm. He didn't even want to think about fighting his way back down the hill.

He pushed that thought from his mind and studied the bunker instead. The sight of the massive guns was enough to give anyone pause. He could just see the barrels in the gloom inside the bunker. Three guns, side by side, each barrel at least thirty feet long. The muzzles looked big enough for a man to put his head into. The barrels were set at a forty-five degree angle, probably to give them the greatest range. It was no different from firing a rifle a long distance—you had to aim high because gravity constantly worked to pull things back to earth. He didn't even want to think about the damage those guns could do if they were aimed at the invasion fleet that would appear soon.

"I don't know," Bat said. He looked at Ball, who shook his head.

They both had the satchel charges ready. The plan had been for them to throw them into the bunker, starting with Bat, but he was hesitating. "Heavy as those guns are, I'm not sure we've got enough bang here to take them out."

"Maybe you'll get lucky and set off the ammunition," the lieutenant said.

"Maybe. But with batteries like this, I'd say most of the ammunition is stored separately, just to prevent any accidents," Bat said knowingly.

"What are you telling me?"

"That I want to get closer. If I can get one of these charges into the magazine, it will take the top off this hill. Otherwise, I'm not sure how much damage we'll really do."

The lieutenant nodded reluctantly. "All right, get in there and get as close as you can."

"What about the Japs?" Philly asked.

"We've been lucky so far. Let's hope our luck holds."

It was easy to see why Bat was concerned that the demolition charge might not be enough. The guns looked massively heavy. Then again, how close did he really want to be when that charge detonated? Each satchel contained eight half-pound blocks of TNT. That ought to be enough to blow the battery to kingdom come—along with anybody who happened to get too close to the explosion.

With Ball hanging back with his own satchel charge in reserve, Bat crept closer. Each moment that they lingered up here at the bunker, where there were surely alert guards, increased their danger. The element of surprise could be lost at any moment—and then what?

Deke held his breath as Bat moved toward the entrance to the bunker. He could see movement within—perhaps the gun crew putting finishing touches on the defenses or guards on duty.

Almost there.

Bat stood up to his full height, then pulled his arm back so that he could whip the satchel deep into the bunker. It seemed impossible that none of the Japanese had noticed him.

But his luck didn't hold.

A shot rang out.

"I'm hit!" he cried.

He had been in the process of releasing the satchel charge when he'd been shot. The explosives were now in the air, but his pitch had been thrown off when he'd been hit. They watched helplessly as the satchel struck the side of the bunker entrance and bounced off, landing just outside the mouth of the bunker.

When he saw that the throw had gone wrong, Bat started to haul himself out of the trench, favoring his wounded arm. Deke had to hand it to the marine. It looked as if the determined son of a bitch was going to try to throw the charge deeper into the bunker—even if it meant getting himself blown up in the process.

Another shot followed, striking the lip of the trench that Bat was crawling out of. His natural reflex was to duck back down, costing him the few seconds he needed to get to the bunker.

Too late. With a tremendous blast, the satchel charge went off. At least four pounds of TNT sent dirt flying everywhere, raining rocks and debris across the top of the hill. The Japanese sentries in the vicinity of the bunker entrance had been sent to join their ancestors. As the air cleared, it became evident that the explosion hadn't been close enough to the battery to do it any real harm. Deke could see the three massive barrels still pointing toward the sea, ready to pulverize any Allied ships that appeared.

Dazed soldiers began pouring out of the bunker, but an officer emerged, getting them organized. There was no hope now of getting the second satchel charge anywhere near that bunker.

That was when the other marine sprang into action. Ball hurried forward, got an arm around Bat, and dragged him away from the bunker entrance. Bat was covered in dust from the blast, and bloody, but he still seemed to be alive.

Ball didn't even attempt to throw his own satchel charge. More and more Japanese appeared from the swirling dust at the bunker entrance —and they were carrying more than shovels. Their rifles cracked as they opened fire, although it wasn't clear that they knew yet what they were shooting at through the billowing dust and smoke. No matter— the message was clear. It was time to get out of Dodge.

In the midst of the chaos, a single rifle cracked with accurate fire, kicked up dirt near Ball's head as he helped Bat get away from the bunker entrance. Deke realized the shots had come from below them, and he swung his rifle in that direction, searching through the telescopic sight for a target.

The two marines tumbled into a ditch and kept going. They ran stooped over, but the ditch wasn't very deep. Another shot struck near Ball's head, even closer this time. If he hadn't been on the move, he would have been a dead man.

Deke spotted the Japanese sniper. To his surprise, the enemy soldier carried a rifle with a telescope. No wonder the bastard had nailed Bat in the first place. Also, he wasn't alone. He was accompanied by a half dozen men who took their time aiming and firing their rifles with telling effect. A shorter, squat man who stood just behind the sniper, holding binoculars, was clearly his spotter.

One thing was clear—these Japs were trained marksmen. Patrol Easy had been lucky so far, but bullets began to sing past their ears or strike the ground around them.

Deke put his crosshairs on the enemy sniper and was in the process of squeezing the trigger when something exploded nearby with a flash-bang that threw off his aim. His bullet passed close enough to the enemy sniper to give him a close shave, like a pitcher brushing back a batter.

He had certainly gotten the other sniper's attention. For a split second, they regarded each other through their riflescopes. Deke didn't have a live round in the chamber—and lucky for him, he didn't suppose that the Jap did either. Instead, they regarded each other coolly through their telescopic sights. Like Deke, the other sniper was not wearing a helmet but had on the billed cap that noncommissioned officers wore.

It was only a split second, but it was enough to leave an impression of the other sniper burned into his brain.

He worked the bolt, but by then it was too late. The moment had passed. The enemy sniper took cover, and Deke did the same. Given time, they might have hunted each other through the network of trenches, but this wasn't how things were playing out.

Still, Deke wasn't about to give up on fighting the sniper. He was like a dog with a bone. He slid his rifle over the lip of the trench. He was careful to keep his head behind a big rock. The Jap had already proved himself to be a good shot, so Deke wasn't about to give him a target. Silently, he willed the Jap sniper to show himself.

But like Deke, the sniper had found good cover. Unseen, he sent shot after well-placed shot in the direction of the US soldiers. So far, he hadn't hit anyone other than Bat, but the rifle shots weren't making their retreat off the hill any easier.

Deke observed that the report of the lighter-caliber rifle was drowned out by the sound of other gunshots—especially a Nambu machine gun that the Japanese had gotten into action that now churned up the dirt in all directions. In their haste, the machine-gun crew was firing at anything that moved. Hit by a burst, a whole group of civilian laborers were mowed down.

Out of frustration, Deke gave up looking for the sniper and put his crosshairs on the machine-gun crew. A quick shot took out the gunner.

Next, he spotted a Japanese officer who stood atop a pillbox, waving a sword and shouting in an effort to organize the troops.

Deke squeezed the trigger and the officer went down. He worked the bolt, looking for another target.

"Let's get the hell out of here!" Honcho shouted.

Deke wasn't inclined to listen, thinking that he would hold off the enemy while the others got away.

But Honcho was having none of it. He grabbed Deke's shoulder as he went past and pulled Deke after him.

Their spur-of-the-moment attack had failed to destroy the guns, but they had stirred up the hornet's nest. Soldiers ran everywhere in confusion and officers shouted orders. The element of surprise was long gone. It had been a gamble that didn't pay off. Deke didn't even want to think about what that meant. Getting anywhere near the bunker again was going to be damn near impossible.

There was no time to think about that now as they raced back through the trenches, dodging fire as they ran. The civilian laborers scattered. One or two of the Japanese leaped at them, wildly swinging their shovels. One Jap made the mistake of trying to stop Philly, waving his shovel at him, and got a rifle butt in the face for his trouble. Philly jumped over the writhing body and kept going.

Getting down off the hill was much faster than climbing it had been. It wasn't quite fear or panic, but the need for self-preservation had given wings to their feet. They raced back down the way that they had come. Their best hope of survival was to get off the hill as fast as possible, before they could be pinned down.

Deke was the last man off the hill. He and the rest of Patrol Easy fled into the jungle as bullets and bursts of machine-gun fire shredded the lush green leaves of the trees like confetti. From the hill behind them, above the sound of the furious guns, they heard screams of outrage growing closer.

The Japanese were now on the attack, pursuing them like dogs running after rabbits.

Sometimes you didn't have any choice but to be a rabbit.

Deke ran like hell.

CHAPTER FOURTEEN

RUNNING FOR THEIR LIVES, the soldiers of Patrol Easy headed for cover in the forest. To their surprise, the Japanese did not bother to give chase. The angry shouts of pursuit faded, although the occasional rifle still cracked behind them. But the soldiers were out of sight and under cover—the Japanese were shooting at nothing.

Despite the furious cries of outrage over the surprise attack, the Japanese officers had called their men back before they reached the line of vegetation at the bottom of Hill 522. Lucky for them, the Japanese had not bothered to clear out the jungle growth at the base of the hill, although the hillside itself was mostly bare of trees. Deke and the others were more than happy to lose themselves in the lush greenery. They caught their breath and regrouped.

"Why the hell aren't they coming after us?" Philly wanted to know, pausing in his flight just long enough to look back toward the hill.

"They probably don't know if this is a raid or the start of the big attack they've been waiting for," Steele explained. "For all the Japs know, there could be an entire division down here, waiting to hit them where it hurts."

"You mean they're afraid of us?" Philly asked in disbelief. "You could have fooled me."

"I wouldn't go that far. Say what you want about the Japs, but they're not stupid. Maybe they thought this was a feint to draw them off the hill. The last thing they want to do is leave that hill unprotected."

"Thank God for that!"

"Don't count your blessings yet, Philly. There's still an awful lot of Japs and just a few of us. Let's just be grateful that they aren't coming after us."

Nobody could argue with that. As he loped along at the back of the group, Deke kept looking behind him, expecting at any moment to see a horde of angry enemy soldiers emerge from the wall of vegetation, no matter what Honcho said.

But Honcho seemed to have called it right as usual, and no one came after them. The Japanese had grown cautious. The hill quickly disappeared behind a screen of trees and brush. They could have been utterly alone if they hadn't known about the thousands of Japanese, just out of sight. The jungle growth was both a blessing and a curse. On the one hand, it hid them well. On the other hand, an entire enemy reconnaissance patrol might be lurking behind the next shrub.

Right now, they had more immediate concerns. First of all, they had a wounded man. Ball was helping Bat along. The tall marine had been wounded in the shoulder by the Japanese sniper. Fortunately, there was nothing wrong with his legs. He was mobile, but he was in plenty of pain.

Once they had gone deep into the brush, Steele called a halt.

"All right, everybody, no sense running scared if nobody's chasing us. Deke, keep an eye out and shoot anything that moves."

"Yep," Deke replied laconically. It went without saying that Deke was already on it, with his rifle pointed in the direction of their back trail.

"How's that shoulder?" the lieutenant asked Bat.

"I guess I'll live."

"Let me take a look." Honcho crouched beside Bat, who was taking a drink from his canteen. He grimaced as Lieutenant Steele poked at the wound. "It looks like the bullet went through and through, as far as I can tell. You're lucky."

"The Japs are gonna have to do better than that to take me out," Bat said. "It's just a scratch."

"A scratch, huh? If you say so. All right, let's patch you up as best as we can for now. Rodeo, have you still got some of that sulfa powder I gave you? I've got to say, I wish Egan was still here. He might not be an actual medic, but he did a good job of patching us up on Guam."

But Egan wasn't there, so they would have to fix Bat up as best as they could. Having a wounded man weighing them down was one of the worst scenarios that they could find themselves in, given their current situation. Considering their mission, it would have been much better for a man to simply be killed outright. However, Bat still seemed mobile enough. He gritted his teeth and didn't say a word as Honcho moved to patch him up. One thing for sure, the marine was a tough son of a bitch. As for Honcho, he had patched up his share of wounds, and his fingers deftly bandaged the arm.

"What's the plan now, Honcho?" Philly wondered. He scowled at Rodeo. "If we still had that radio, I guess we'd be calling for help right about now. There's no way we can get anywhere near those guns now that the Japs know we're here."

Steele glared in Philly's direction. "Look, it doesn't matter. Radio or not, we're not going anywhere until we take out those guns. That was why we were sent here, and that's what we're going to do. In just a few days, there will be thousands of our boys headed for that beach, not to mention who knows how many ships just offshore. Do you want that battery to still be in operation?"

Philly looked away and shook his head. "I guess not."

"I hope to hell not. It would be a slaughter. No, it's our job to take out that battery, no matter what. If there's just one of us left who can still crawl up there and toss a grenade at it, then that's what we have to do. Understood?"

Philly nodded. "Yes, sir."

The others grunted. Nobody liked this situation, but they all knew what they needed to do, one way or another. Those guns had to be destroyed.

"Good," the lieutenant said. "I don't want to hear any more talk of radios or rescue. We can worry about that once we take out that gun."

"You got it, Honcho."

The lieutenant gave orders to keep moving, just to put added distance between themselves and the enemy soldiers on the hill.

* * *

KEEPING his eyes wide open and his finger on the trigger, Deke threaded his way through the forest at the base of the hill, sticking to the thickest vegetation to stay under cover. This was not the heaviest jungle that he had encountered in the Pacific, but there was no doubt that a Japanese patrol might be heading toward them, and they would have no warning before the two groups ran right into each other.

On hyperalert, something caught Deke's ears—or maybe his eyes. He couldn't even identify if it was a flicker in the bush or an unnatural sound that didn't belong, but it was there all the same. A boyhood spent in the mountains had made him keenly attuned to anything out of place in the natural world, much the way that a musician's senses might be jarred by a false note.

He signaled to the others behind him to halt, and then moved forward silently on his own. Was it a Japanese patrol? Surely, the enemy must be combing the forest, looking for them. Deke doubted that he could do much against an enemy force of any size, except hold them off long enough to buy the others time to slip away.

The long green fronds of a small tree hung down in front of him, and he used his rifle barrel to push them aside. It was like pulling back a curtain, revealing a small clearing in the forest.

What Deke saw next was unexpected.

Within the middle of the clearing stood a man in a black robe and a clerical collar. Deke was no expert on religion, but he knew enough to recognize a Catholic priest when he saw one.

Beside him stood two tough-looking Filipinos wearing rope-soled sandals and ragged clothing. They held Japanese rifles that had most likely been liberated from the occupying enemy. Improbably, one of the men wore a bedraggled pinstriped dress shirt with a contrasting collar that made him look like a disgraced banker. When they saw Deke emerging from the forest and realized that he wasn't a Japanese soldier, the two Filipinos lowered their weapons. Slowly, Deke did the same.

The priest put his finger to his lips. Deke nodded. The priest pointed into the wall of vegetation to one side of the clearing.

All at once, Deke heard footsteps and muffled voices moving through the forest. Definitely a Japanese patrol, and there was no doubt as to their purpose. They were hunting the infiltrators. It was hard to say how far away the enemy patrol was—hidden from view, and considering how the vegetation played tricks with how sound traveled, the Japanese might have been fifty feet away, or a quarter of a mile.

All four men held their breath until the sounds of the patrol faded and disappeared. Behind Deke, the rest of Patrol Easy moved up. Soon, they all stood in the clearing, regarding the three men they had discovered in the forest.

The priest spoke first.

"I am Father Francisco," the priest said in gently accented English. "I heard the shooting and knew that it wasn't any of my men. I was wondering what was going on and thought it might be American commandos. We heard rumors that a boat had landed during the night. We were hoping that we might find you before the Japanese did."

"There's just the three of you?" the lieutenant asked.

"There are others nearby," the priest said, then looked around at the soldiers, seeming puzzled. "I am afraid that you are going to need more men than that to fight the Japanese."

"Don't worry about that, Padre," said Honcho, stepping forward to shake the priest's hand. "I'm Lieutenant Steele."

"Father Francisco de los Santos."

"Good to meet you, Padre. Like I said, there's plenty more where we came from. They'll be landing on this island soon enough."

"I am glad to hear it."

"What are you doing out here in the jungle? Last time I saw a priest, he was in a church."

The priest shook his head. "Sadly, the Japanese have little use for priests or churches. Since the occupation, they have arrested most of the priests and even our sisters." The priest shuddered, and it was hard to tell whether it was from anger or sadness. "I have been living out here for the last year, doing what I can to minister to men like these who are fighting against the occupiers. I pray with them, I bandage their wounds, I help them bury their dead."

It was clear that the two Filipinos didn't understand a word of English. The priest turned to them and seemed to offer an explanation in their own language, nodding at the Americans. The two men nodded curtly, watching the GIs and marines with wary eyes. These guerrilla fighters were clearly tough customers. However, their stony faces melted into smiles as the priest apparently went into more detail. Finally, it seemed, help was on the way after their lonely fight against the occupation forces.

"I have told them that you are the first of many more soldiers," Father Francisco said. "Our prayers have been answered. They won't be fighting on their own for much longer."

On closer inspection, it was clear that Father Francisco had been living rough. His cassock was torn in places and roughly sewn back together, but clean enough, considering the circumstances. His collar must have been bright white once, but it was now a grayish brown. He was taller and heavier than the two guerrilla fighters and lighter skinned, hinting at Spanish ancestry. He was overdue for a shave, his chin covered in graying stubble, and the priest's hair reached nearly to his collar. With his unkempt appearance and the tattered clerical robes, he could have passed for a mad holy man in the wilderness.

"With all due respect, Padre, it's going to take more than prayers to defeat the Japanese," Honcho said.

The priest gave a devilish smile that was disconcerting to see on the face of a man of God. Deke decided that this was no milksop preacher, but more of a fire-and-brimstone sort. Then again, he had explained that he was a Jesuit, and they hadn't been known for backing down from any challenge. Deke took an instant liking to him.

"I am not a soldier," Father Francisco said. "I carry no weapons but my faith. I cannot harm another human being. That would be wrong, of course. But I do not think God will mind if I help men like these do what I cannot do myself. They will see to the bullets. I will see to their souls."

"Seems like a good arrangement," Honcho agreed. "Can't argue with that."

"As I said before, we heard the shooting," the priest said. "What happened?"

"That was us. I suppose the Japanese are looking for us."

"They tend to be noisy when they are on patrol, thank God," the priest said. "That's the second patrol we've heard today. You've certainly stirred them up."

"Unfortunately, we're going to have to stir them up some more," Honcho said. "You see, there's a gun battery at the top of the hill, and we're here to take it out."

The priest nodded. "The Father, Son, and Holy Spirit."

"The what?"

"Sorry, I am afraid that's just a poor attempt at humor on my part. That is the nickname that I've given those three guns. We know all about them."

"Our code name for those guns is Cerberus."

Father Francisco nodded. "Of course. The three-headed monster that guards the entrance to Hades."

"I wouldn't have thought that a Catholic priest would be versed in mythology."

"And I would not have thought that I would be living in the jungle, having been ejected from my church by the Japanese. These are strange times."

"Good point," Honcho agreed.

"How do you propose to 'take it out,' as you say?"

"I don't think we have much choice but to attack right up the middle. That's our plan for now. With any luck, we'll get close enough, especially if we can surprise them again."

Father Francisco scratched his chin, seeming to think that over. "I am sorry, but that is not a very good plan."

"Is that right?" The lieutenant scratched his own chin, thinking it over. "Have you got a better plan, Padre?"

The priest smiled devilishly again. His brown eyes sparkled. There was definitely some Spanish conquistador in him somewhere. "You want to reach the top of the hill? As a matter of fact, I do have a better plan for doing just that. But first, I suggest that we leave this area. The Japanese are very methodical in their patrols. I believe they search using a grid pattern. They missed us last time, but they won't miss us again. We need to move to a more secure area to wait for dark, and then to spend the night."

"Where would we go?"

"Leave that to me," the priest said. He nodded at the Filipino guerrilla on his left flank—the one wearing the pinstriped shirt—and the man immediately turned and led the way into the jungle.

At a signal from Honcho, Deke was the first to follow him. Immediately, Deke was impressed by the Filipino's woodcraft. He slipped through the jungle with barely a sound or without any hesitation, apparently sure of exactly where he was going, although there wasn't any trail to speak of. Once or twice, the man looked back as if to see if Deke was following him. He grunted with satisfaction, apparently pleased at Deke's own ability to move silently through the greenery, then pressed on deeper into the tangle of vegetation. The rest of Patrol Easy, along with the priest and the other Filipino guerrilla, followed in their wake.

CHAPTER FIFTEEN

THERE DIDN'T SEEM to be any reason not to trust the priest or the Filipinos. They were the furthest thing possible from Japanese agents. Not only that, but the Americans desperately needed friends at the moment, considering that the enemy was combing the forest for them. Given their situation, the soldiers of Patrol Easy didn't have much choice but to put their faith in this mad priest and his Filipino henchmen.

Anyhow, if these Filipinos had wanted to turn them over to the Japanese, all they would have needed to do was to shout as the Japanese patrol passed earlier.

Finally, they reached wherever it was that they were going. Deke could see that they had skirted the base and come around to the back side of the hill, managing to avoid the enemy patrols in the process.

The Filipino brought them into another clearing that was surrounded on all sides by dense jungle. Deke realized that the clearing was a kind of camp, with hammocks hung between trees at the edge of the clearing and even a chair set up. A high, rough-hewn bench stood to one side, with a crucifix hanging from the tree trunk behind it.

And not just any tree trunk. The trunk was several feet across at the base, with the tree itself rising above the neighboring forest canopy—although many of its branches appeared conspicuously gray and withered. With the ancient, dying tree as a backdrop, the priest had built a makeshift altar in front of it.

Deke had to admit that he was impressed by the faith of these people. The Japanese occupiers had denied them use of their church, but they could not keep them from practicing their religion. Deke's family never had been much on churchgoing, but that didn't mean his mother hadn't read aloud from the Bible on occasion or that they hadn't given thanks during meals.

He didn't really know what religion he was. He supposed you might call it Pentecostal, in that mountain people were always seeking manifestations of the Holy Spirit in the world around them—everyday miracles.

The bottom line was that Deke was as God-fearing as the next soldier. After all, you couldn't be a soldier without some form of faith, not when you were hunkered down in a foxhole with bullets flying all around.

"We will be relatively safe here for the time being," the priest said. Again, he spoke to the Filipinos in their own language, and the men slipped away into the surrounding jungle, perhaps to keep an eye out for any Japanese.

"We're not here to hide out," Honcho said. "We need to take out those guns, and the clock is ticking. If Cerberus is still in place when the invasion fleet arrives, it's going to be a goddamn massacre. Sorry, Padre. I meant no offense."

"None taken," the priest said. "It is God you should worry about offending, my friend."

"If you say so. Considering the things I've seen the last few months, I have to wonder if there even is a God."

The priest nodded. "I am sure you have your doubts, my son, and maybe not without good reason. But let us set aside the mystery of God for the time being, and consider how to defeat the Japanese."

"Sounds like a good plan," Honcho agreed.

The priest continued, "I have not been out here in the forest all this time for nothing. This whole time, I have watched the Japanese turn this hill into a fortress."

"That's for damn sure. Oh, sorry again, Padre. For darn sure."

Father Francisco shrugged, as if mild profanity was the least of his concerns. "It is indeed a formidable fortress. But you see, the Japanese are expecting an attack from the beaches. Their defenses are facing that direction. Toward the sea."

"Agreed. That's the direction we hit them from this morning. I've got to say, the only reason we got on that hill was that they weren't expecting us. It will be a different story when we try again, but we don't have much choice."

The priest nodded. "The Japanese are expecting a frontal assault. As you said, they will be ready for an attack, whether it is your small patrol or a regiment. But where do you think the Japanese bring in supplies for the men on the hill or communicate with their other forces in the area? For that, there is a trail up the north slope of the hillside."

This time, it was Lieutenant Steele who offered a predatory smile. "Go on. I'm listening."

It was true that the hill made an outstanding natural fortress. On two sides, it was bordered by the Bangon River, which created a moat of sorts, almost like the moats surrounding ancient castles. The steep hillside sloping down toward what would surely be the beach landing area was indeed well defended, bristling with pillboxes, trenches, and machine-gun nests.

But as Father Francisco explained it, the Japanese had created a supply route—actually a series of trails and trenches—right up the northern face of the hillside to bring in ammunition and reinforcements. It would be the last direction that they expected an attack to come from.

"It is what you would call a back door," the priest said with a grin.

"Then I supposed I'm what you might call a backdoor man," Honcho said, grinning back. "Please tell me everything you know, Padre."

* * *

THE PLAN that evolved was simple enough—and downright devious. They had the priest to thank for the devious parts. It was kind of impressive for a man of God. In fact, come to think of it, maybe they should have been a little worried about his soul.

There in the clearing, the lieutenant explained the plan. "We'll rest here tonight. If the priest is right, the Japs will be looking for us toward the front of the hill, maybe expecting us to make a run for the beach."

"They will not be expecting you on their back porch," the priest said.

Out of the group, only Philly did not seem entirely convinced. He shared his doubts with Deke. "If you ask me, it sounds like we're putting our lives in the hands of this priest," he muttered. "Hell, we don't know anything about him. Can we even trust him?"

As it turned out, Father Francisco had overheard Philly. "I understand your concerns, my son. However, you are not putting your lives in my hands," the priest said.

"Coulda fooled me."

The priest smiled, not unkindly. He seemed to appreciate their doubts. "No, my son, you are putting your lives in God's hands."

"I'm not sure that makes me feel any better."

"Pipe down, Philly," Deke said. To him, the priest appeared trustworthy enough. Besides, they didn't seem to have many options. "Have you got any better ideas? I don't know about you, but I'd rather not make a run straight up that hill. Like Honcho said, the Japs will be expecting us next time."

"I guess you're right," Philly grumbled, not sounding entirely convinced.

If the others had doubts, they kept them to themselves—as Deke had pointed out, they didn't have much choice. They were on a Japanese-occupied island, being hunted, their radio was gone, and they had no hope of rescue if they missed their window of opportunity. The priest and his knowledge of the local geography seemed to be their best chance.

Lieutenant Steele gathered them around and reviewed even more details of the plan. Once again, he had put his head together with the priest. The result was that the priest had produced several piles of Japanese uniforms—torn, dirty, and sometimes bloodstained, but recognizable as Japanese. There were even a few Japanese helmets. Nobody came right out and explained it, but Deke suspected that the uniforms had come off Japanese troops who had run afoul of the guerrillas.

"What's all this for?" Philly wondered.

"I'll get to that Japanese gear in a minute," Honcho said. "This is going to be a three-pronged attack. With any luck, we'll be able to use this back door that Father Francisco gave us to get close enough to those guns for Bat and Ball to destroy them."

Using a stick, Honcho sketched out a rough map in the dirt of the clearing.

"Father Francisco and the Filipinos will lead us up the hill using the supply path that's the back door. There will likely be some sentries, so we'll have to do what we can to take them out before they can sound the alarm. Our job will be to get Bat and Ball as close as we can to that battery. Bat, how's that shoulder? Can you make it?"

"Can a camel cross the desert? You're talking to a marine here, sir. I'll get up that hill no matter what."

"All right. I know you will. But those are all the explosives we have, so don't foul it up by getting shot again. That's an order."

"Yes, sir." The two marines exchanged a look. Bat seemed to hesitate, but then added, "Ball and I have been talking. The thing is, we're a little worried that the satchel charge won't be enough. You saw the size of those guns, sir. We may need to ram something right down the barrels to blow them up. Either that or we need to set off the magazine and blow that entire hilltop."

"I don't disagree. The question is, Can you get that close?"

"We can sure as hell try. The problem is that the Japs will be expecting us."

Honcho nodded. "Maybe not. That's what these Jap uniforms are for. That's where Yoshio comes in."

"Me?" Yoshio sounded surprised.

"What you're going to do is take a handful of the good priest's Filipinos and come right up the hill, shouting that the Americans are after you. In other words, your job is to create confusion and raise havoc. Get as close as possible. The last thing that the Japanese will expect is that one of the Americans is shouting at them in Japanese. Meanwhile, that will give Bat and Ball a chance to make another run at the bunker."

"*Hai*," Yoshio replied in Japanese, sounding more than a little convincing.

"You'll be wearing those Japanese helmets and uniforms that Father Francisco was good enough to provide us with—with any luck, they'll hold their fire until it's too late. You and the Filipinos will start shooting, and all their attention will be on you. In other words, you are going to be sort of a walking, talking Trojan horse."

Yoshio just nodded. It went without saying that he had been given the most dangerous prong of the attack to carry out. If the Japanese on Hill 522 became at all suspicious of Yoshio and the disguised guerrillas, they wouldn't last more than a few seconds once those Nambu machine guns opened fire.

Finally, Lieutenant Steele turned to Deke. "Yoshio isn't the only one who is going to create havoc. We'll need you and your rifle on that hill, picking off any officers you see. They're easy to spot. They're the ones waving swords around." Honcho shook his head. "*Swords*. Would you ever imagine such a thing? These Japs are a piece of work, all right."

If the swords were a badge of office, even the lieutenant would have to admit that they were also a powerful psychological weapon. A soldier expected to be shot at. But being sliced to bits by a sword was something else altogether.

It was common for snipers to work in pairs, with one man serving as a spotter and also watching the sniper's back while he stayed on the riflescope. Honcho added that he could spare Philly to accompany Deke.

"Hold on, sir. Just to be clear, you're saying that just me, Deke, and Yoshio are going to attack that hill?" Philly wondered.

Deke had been wondering the same thing, but he put too much faith in Lieutenant Steele to say it out loud.

"You'll also have the guerrillas," Honcho reminded him. "If this is going to work, we need every man we can spare on that back trail. Remember that what we really have to do is get those guns destroyed. You're just the sideshow, Philly."

The shadows of the day had been growing longer. Between the two of them, Honcho and the priest agreed that it would be best not to attempt their plan at night when they would have to stumble along the unfamiliar trails, but to wait for first light. That would mean spending the night hidden from Japanese view.

Given that a few enemy planes flew low over the forest, staying hidden seemed challenging, but the priest and Filipinos did not seem concerned by the presence of the aircraft.

"We'll make camp here," Steele said. "It's as good a place as any. The jungle offers us enough cover that the Japs can't see us, even from the air—or so says the padre."

With their orders received, the men prepared to sleep in the clearing as best as they could. It might not have been the most comfortable spot, but it helped that they were all exhausted.

As for whether or not any of them would be alive by this time tomorrow night, that was anybody's guess.

CHAPTER SIXTEEN

HAVING MADE their rough camp for the night, they soon learned that they were not alone. Along with the Filipino guerrillas, a handful of women emerged from the forest, appearing silently out of the shadows. They carried jugs of water and baskets of food, which they quickly distributed to the guerrilla soldiers.

The soldiers spanned many ages, but most were young men. After all, such a rugged existence, not to mention following the steep jungle trails, was a young man's game.

Deke didn't know the language, but it was clear to him that many of the women seemed to know these rough soldiers. There was a tenderness between them, smiles and looks of concern over fresh wounds. Surely these women must be the mothers, wives, and sisters of the Filipino soldiers.

The priest moved among the men and women. He had a rough-but-gentle manner that made him a natural leader. He laughed with some and bowed his head in prayer with others. He seemed to know just what each person needed to tap their inner strength. After a few minutes, the women made their goodbyes and slipped back into the tropical forest. Apparently it was too dangerous for them to stay.

Eventually, Father Francisco came around to the soldiers of Patrol Easy, who had claimed a corner of the clearing as their own.

"I've got to warn you that we're a difficult flock, Padre," Lieutenant Steele said.

"Yeah, we're sure as hell not a flock of sheep," Philly said.

Deke noted that the priest did not seem daunted in any way as he approached.

"Here, let me take a look at that shoulder," the priest said. "It looks as if it has bled through the bandage."

"It's just a scratch," Bat said gruffly. Far be it from a marine to complain about being shot—never mind the fact that his shoulder was now covered in a bloody bandage. Honcho had done the best that he could earlier. However, it was just a field dressing. Bat's shoulder would need more medical attention soon.

"Then you will not mind if I take a look," the priest persisted. "I have had quite a lot of practice attending to wounds, unfortunately."

Bat shrugged, which turned out to be a mistake, because the motion caused him to wince.

Deftly, the priest pulled back the bandages to inspect the wound. "Through and through, praise God. You are fortunate, my son. Another inch lower, or to the left, and you would be speaking with Saint Peter right now rather than a lowly priest."

Deke also couldn't help but wonder about the caliber of the Japanese sniper rifle. There was no doubt that the Japanese snipers were deadly enough. However, if he'd been firing a heavier round, the outcome for Bat might have been very different.

Father Francisco inspected the wound and changed the bandage expertly, doing so with practiced hands that barely caused Bat to grimace. "There, you will heal now. Just do not get shot again."

"Easier said than done, Padre," Bat said. "You know all about that hill we've got to go up in the morning to take out that battery. Easier said than done."

"Do not worry, my son. I will be there with you—and so will God."

Nearby, Ball snorted. "Padre, I know this guy pretty well. If that bullet had hit a little harder, I can guarantee that he'd be roasting like a marshmallow over a campfire right now. Down in that other place, you know."

Father Francisco shook his head. "Do not be so sure. What you might think of as 'sin' would probably not get Saint Peter to so much as raise his eyebrows these days. Did you drink too much or enjoy the company of women? Play cards? These are merely the foibles of young men. I am sure that God did not intend for us to live as saints all the time. No, my son. Men are fools and will always do weak, foolish things. Usually, these are sins against ourselves. God can forgive us those sins. This is why there is confession and purgatory." The priest shook his head. "Other sins cannot be forgiven so easily. I am talking about cruelty. I have seen terrible things these last two years during the Japanese occupation. Innocent men shot for no reason. Women raped. Churches destroyed. Our sisters in faith terrorized. Things so terrible that I have been caused to question my faith at times."

Deke was sure that the priest could have found an easier refuge than the jungle, hiding out with these guerrilla fighters, but he had some inkling as to the path the priest had chosen. "Has being out here in the jungle, helping these Filipino guerrillas, helped you keep your faith?" Deke asked.

"Indeed, it has, my young friend." The priest studied the raking scars on Deke's face. "Did you get those in the war?"

"No."

When Deke didn't elaborate, the priest didn't press him for an answer. Instead, he nodded in the lieutenant's direction. "I also noticed that your lieutenant has one eye. How unusual. Under the rules of your army, he could go home, could he not?"

"I reckon he wants to stay and fight."

"Good," the priest said. "He seems to see more than some men who have two good eyes."

If the priest had chosen to do so, he could have gone into far more detail about the atrocities carried out by the Japanese against the church—indeed, against the entire civilian population. After all, the story of the Catholic church in the Philippines was a long and thorny one. Jesuit priests had arrived with the Spanish in the early fifteen hundreds, and the first mass had been celebrated on Leyte. The

Filipinos had quickly embraced their new religion. The church had brought education with it, and Western ideals, even if they were sometimes imperfect.

But the church had not been without enemies. Pirates raided the coastal towns and villages established by the Spanish, killing the priests and enslaving the Christian converts. Spanish forces had finally put an end to the pirates.

The church had taken another blow centuries later when United States forces had won the Spanish-American War. The Philippines became a US possession, and all Spanish citizens had been required to leave—including the priests who had been educated in Spain and were thus considered to harbor a colonial mindset and foreign loyalties. In their place, a new generation of priests ran the churches and tended to the flock. These priests had been born in the Philippines and were thus closer to the people.

Father Francisco was part of this new generation that had grown and flourished during the decades of American administration. Of course, the US promoted freedom of religion as well as a healthy separation of church and state.

Then came the arrival of the Japanese in 1941. Since then, the church had suffered greatly at the cruel hands of the Japanese, who targeted any organization that they thought might undermine their authority.

Bat nodded as he inspected the neatly wrapped bandage, and the priest moved off to talk with some of the Filipinos. "It's all well and good to have a priest and God on your side, but what I'd really like tomorrow morning is a company of marines to go up that hill with us," he said.

"This is all we've got," Ball pointed out.

"Then I guess it's gonna have to do."

* * *

THE SOLDIERS HAD SPREAD out in the space between the low-growing molave trees. In reality, there wasn't much of a camp to make. They had been traveling as light as they could. Aside from weapons and explosives and ammunition, they didn't even have a blanket between them, but it didn't matter.

This was the tropics—the temperature never fell below seventy-five degrees, even at night. They settled for tugging their jackets more tightly around themselves as best as they could and fell asleep almost instantly. They'd been awake for most of the previous night, and so they were exhausted, to say the least.

After the long tropical twilight, night came on, and the soldiers around Deke slept fitfully. There was a lot riding on what would happen in the morning—not only were their own lives at stake, but they couldn't help but think of the hundreds or thousands who might die if they couldn't knock out that battery.

Deke cleaned his rifle using the small bottle of gun oil and patches that he'd brought along for that purpose. It was too dark to really see if he was doing a good job, but it didn't matter. The feel of the metal under his fingertips was reassuring, and he worked the oil into the action until the steel was almost silky to the touch.

He felt a hand squeeze his shoulder. It was the lieutenant, who had taken the first watch.

"Better get some sleep, son," he said. The lieutenant was old enough that Deke almost felt like an actual son at times. Not for the first time, he realized how much he missed his own father. He just hoped that if his pa was looking down on him from somewhere above, that Deke would make him proud. "I know for a fact that you and that rifle won't let us down."

Deke said, "I just want to finish up here."

The lieutenant nodded and moved off.

Deke reassembled the rifle, finally sliding the bolt back into place.

He recalled the Japanese sniper that he'd seen earlier that day. He wasn't afraid of the enemy sniper—not exactly. After all, he had managed to survive the Samurai Sniper that he'd run into on Guam, a marksman who had been every bit his equal. The Samurai Sniper had escaped with the small number of Japanese troops who had managed to flee Guam as the American noose tightened. Deke wasn't in any hurry to meet him again.

If the sniper that he'd crossed paths with today was half as good, reaching those guns at the top of the hill wouldn't be easy. He reassembled the rifle carefully, knowing that tomorrow might put him and the Springfield to the test.

Not for the first time, Deke wondered just what he had gotten himself into. He sure was a long way from the mountains. Back home, the mountains would be well into fall, with crisp mornings, cool nights where the stars shone clear over the peaks, maybe a fox barking in the distance, and the leaves turning orange and red so that it almost looked as if the hills were on fire.

The warm, humid jungle was a long way from that. The only sounds came from singing insects and the distant drone of an aircraft—most likely a Jap plane on patrol. To be sure, they were deep in enemy territory. At the moment, it seemed almost impossible that they would ever wrest this island—not to mention the entire Philippines—from Japanese control.

Still, Deke couldn't think of a place where he'd rather be—among these good men, helping these people, fighting the Japanese. He sometimes wondered if that meant there was something wrong with him.

The others would do their duty, but for Deke, this was something else altogether. This was what he was meant to do, the same way that a wolf was meant to hunt.

The only other member of Patrol Easy who seemed to feel the same way was Lieutenant Steele. In his own way, the lieutenant seemed just as content as Deke to be here.

Steele was still awake, pulling the wrapper off a chocolate tropical bar and munching it slowly. The look on his face indicated that his thoughts were elsewhere—probably on their next move. He kept his shotgun upright between his knees. Deke also kept awake and stared into the jungle, his ears straining for the slightest sound. But all he could hear were a few birds and the ever-present insects gossiping in the treetops.

Deke closed his eyes and fell asleep almost instantly. It was like when he'd been a boy on the farm and had barely been able to get into bed before falling asleep.

Before he drifted off, Deke took some satisfaction in the fact that they'd been on the run from the Japanese troops most of the day,

hiding out, but in the morning, it would be time to bring the fight back
to the enemy.

* * *

THE SURPRISE ATTACK on their hilltop fortress had put the Japanese
on high alert. No enemy ships had been spotted, and yet a small enemy
force had launched an attack. This brought on a flurry of doubt and
questions that struck at the confidence of the Japanese. Where had
the enemy come from? What was their mission? The appearance of
the enemy soldiers had created uncertainty—and anger.

One of those angry soldiers was Ikeda, who was holding his sniper
rifle with a white-knuckled grip. Truth be told, Ikeda felt thoroughly
red-faced in the wake of the surprise attack. After all, he had seen the
signs that raiders had landed on the beach. If only he had been a little
faster, he might have cut them off or given Noguchi more of a warning
so that they could have been prepared.

In part, he thought that the attack on the hill was his fault. Somehow, it felt as if he had allowed or enabled the attack. Over and over
again, he reviewed his actions, wondering where he had failed.

Ikeda knew that he had held off making any warning shots because
he had hoped to overtake the raiders and didn't want to give himself
away. Some part of him had wanted to play the hero, and he realized
that had been a costly mistake.

Given his personal failures, his only thought now was to go after
the raiders. He had shot at least one of them with his sniper rifle, even
if he evidently hadn't killed the enemy soldier outright, and he would
be more than happy to finish the job.

"Sir, I will organize a squad to pursue the enemy," he said to
Noguchi. He had found the officer outside the bunker to the massive
battery, busy directing new machine-gun emplacements.

Noguchi put his hands on his hips and blew out a big breath of air.
"No," he said.

Ikeda was stunned. "Sir? I do not understand. What if they come
back? We must hunt them down first."

Noguchi appeared surprisingly calm, despite the fact that the enemy soldiers had attacked the hill. The rest of the Japanese soldiers on the hill, men and officers alike, did not look nearly as calm. They ran in all directions, jumping into trenches, having traded their shovels for rifles. The officer watched it all and nodded with satisfaction. Rotund and short, he suddenly resembled a Buddha figure more than ever, a reminder that Noguchi was not a career military man but an engineer who had been pressed into service as an officer.

Ikeda scowled, thinking that a real officer would have ordered him after the raiders. He shifted from foot to foot, unable to contain his energy and his anger.

"The enemy will not return anytime soon. Not today," Noguchi said. "Maybe tonight, under cover of darkness. There were no more than a dozen raiders, if even that many. What can so few hope to accomplish? They will need to rely on stealth—and darkness, if they have any hope of a successful attack on the battery."

"The battery?"

"Of course, Ikeda. Why else would American soldiers be here? There is no doubt that they plan an invasion. They know that they must destroy this battery before their invasion of our little beach. But their hopes are misguided."

"With all respect, sir, let me take a group of men and track them down."

Noguchi clapped a meaty hand on Ikeda's shoulder. While the sniper looked grim and angry, Noguchi had a smile on his face. "I want you here, Ikeda. Why chase the fox when he will come to you? It is likely that these enemy soldiers are highly trained. On this hill, we have every advantage that in the jungle we do not have. Not only that, we all know that there are Filipino guerrillas at work under the direction of that Jesuit priest."

The Japanese knew all about the priest who lived in the forest alongside the Filipino fighters. It was true that the guerrillas had been a constant thorn in their side during the months of work. While the Filipinos stopped short of an all-out attack, they had constantly harassed the Japanese supply lines. The guerrillas knew better than to attack organized troops and patrols. However, soldiers who made the mistake of venturing too far into the undergrowth often did not come back. It had been a great cause of frustration to Ikeda, who found it hard to chase ghosts that simply melted into the jungle and who knew every animal trail and ravine so well.

But he wasn't about to admit as much to this officer.

"I do not fear a few peasants and their filthy monk!" he shouted.

Noguchi raised his eyebrows at the outburst. As casual as Noguchi seemed compared to other officers, considering that he was an engineer and builder first and foremost, even he had his limits to breaches of discipline, and that included questioning orders.

"I appreciate your fighting spirit, Ikeda. Truly I do, and we will put it to use yet. You see, I am not talking about fear, but about strategy."

Ikeda still wasn't sure that he understood. His every instinct was still to go on the hunt. Yet he had no choice but to respond, "Of course, sir."

"Our orders are not to chase raiders but to prepare for the defense of this hill—which is a key to defending this island. It may seem like a distant outpost, an unimportant task, but make no mistake that Leyte is a stepping-stone to our homeland. That is why the Americans want this hill, and this island. You and that rifle of yours will *not* allow the raiders to get this far, will you, Ikeda? Your men will be in position to defend this hill at any cost against another attempt to destroy this bunker and those guns. That is why I want you here, not chasing shadows around the forest."

Chastened, Ikeda's doubts about Noguchi had abated. The officer seemed well aware of the threat but was not allowing himself to make a hotheaded reaction.

Ikeda straightened, coming to attention. *"Hai!"*

"Good. We shall wait for the Americans to return—and when they do, this time we shall be ready." Noguchi nodded at the crew that was busy around the entrance to the bunker, digging frantically. "Besides, if the raiders do make it this far, to the top of the hill, there will be a surprise waiting for them."

CHAPTER SEVENTEEN

DAWN'S gray light filtered ever so slowly down through the jungle canopy. None of the men had expected to sleep well, given their surroundings, but exhaustion was a tremendous soporific. The soldiers of Patrol Easy awoke with new energy, along with apprehension, knowing that the operation to attack the Japanese bunker and destroy the enemy battery was about to begin.

To his surprise, Deke awoke feeling more or less himself. The worst of it was his right hand, which ached from having gripped the rifle all night in his sleep. He shook it out and accepted half a tropical chocolate bar that Philly handed him, saying, "Breakfast."

"Where's my biscuits and white gravy at?" Deke asked.

"Ugh. That sounds like something they'd feed to inmates at the Eastern State Penitentiary. As punishment, you know. I'll never understand you hillbillies."

"No reason to get sore. I'll settle for some grits and scrapple for breakfast."

"Aw, shut up and eat your damn C rations."

Grinning, Deke did just that, washing the chow down with a few swigs of water. It wasn't much of a breakfast, but at least it was something. The warm water tasted strongly of metal from the canteen and halazone tablets. He wouldn't have minded a hot mug of coffee, just to chase the cobwebs out of his brain.

The Filipino guerrillas in the clearing were also having their version of breakfast, something called *bilo bilo*, which were basically rice balls cooked in coconut milk. It looked a whole lot better than what Deke had just eaten.

They had started small fires just for the purpose of making breakfast. The fires were so circumspect that Deke could have held them in one hand—just big enough to heat a small amount of water or coconut milk. Deke found himself impressed. It was just the sort of fire a sly woodsy back home would have built to cook a rabbit but stay hidden from revenuers—or Indians in the olden days.

The guerrillas were skilled in jungle-craft and they knew to use dry, sap-free wood so that their fires scarcely made any smoke that would have given away their position to Japanese patrols—or aircraft. To Deke's surprise, they also brewed coffee, and Deke gratefully accepted a tin cup of java, gulping it down while it was still too hot.

Each Filipino ate a handful of the rice balls between double-checking his equipment. With their short pants, rope-soled sandals, and ragged shirts, they hardly resembled soldiers. Considering that a few women and even a couple of children had joined them for the night, there was a family aspect of the guerrilla unit that was generally lacking in most military camps.

However, there was no mistaking that these were soldiers, all the same. The guerrillas all handled their rifles with easy familiarity, and their weapons gleamed from the care that they'd been given. Several of the Filipinos also wore bare-bladed bolo knives that swung from their belts. The bolo knives with their curved blades were meant to hack their way through the underbrush. If it came down to it, those would be savage weapons in close-quarters fighting.

The Japs might have their swords, but Deke shuddered at the thought of facing a swinging bolo. Some of the Filipinos also carried a short, wickedly curved knife known as a kris. Nope, definitely not the sort of knife he would want to go up against. With their captured Japanese rifles, bolo knives, and kris blades, these Filipino guerrillas were armed to the teeth.

It was no wonder that the Japanese had gained true control of only the more urban areas. In the more remote provinces, the Japanese remained under constant threat of attack—and often retaliated or took out their frustrations on the helpless civilian population in the towns and small villages.

Deke looked around, noting that the only one who hadn't seemed to sleep was Lieutenant Steele. The ring of cigarette butts surrounding the spot where he'd spent the night on a tree stump indicated that he'd been awake most of the night, keeping watch, and probably planning out in minute detail exactly what had to happen in the morning. It was just what good officers did. Deke shook his head, filled with new admiration for the lieutenant. Didn't the man ever sleep?

The other man who hadn't seemed to sleep was the priest. He'd already been up and moving before anyone else. He seemed to have many small tasks to do while the Filipinos slept. Eventually, one of the older Filipinos—the one wearing the pinstriped shirt, who seemed to have a leadership position in the guerrilla band—went around waking the others by nudging them with his sandaled foot. The priest found time to visit with each small group of guerrillas around the cooking fires. He prayed with some quietly, or simply gave their shoulders a quick squeeze of encouragement.

Breakfast eaten, they were soon up and on their feet, but they weren't quite ready to set out yet. Apparently, the individual prayers were not enough, because the guerrillas gathered around to pray as a group.

The lieutenant shifted the shotgun to his shoulder and watched impatiently as the Filipinos bent their heads. Quietly, Father Francisco spoke a prayer. Deke wasn't really the praying type, but he noticed that the marines, along with Rodeo, Alphabet, and Yoshio, all bowed their heads. The priest added a few words in English for the benefit of the Americans, praying for a successful mission and their safe return.

When he had finished, the priest nodded at the lieutenant.

"All right, let's move out, Padre," Steele said. "Keep it quiet. There's no telling if the Japs have any sentries, but I'm willing to bet that they do. Deke, I want you up front."

The Filipino guerrilla who had been wearing the tattered pinstripe shirt yesterday led the way, which made sense considering that he knew the territory, while Deke was just behind him. He didn't know the guerrilla's name, but in his mind Deke had nicknamed him "Pinstripe." This morning he had put on a Japanese fatigue jacket over the shirt, but the contrasting collar was still visible. The rest of Patrol Easy followed Pinstripe and Deke, with the guerrillas and Father Francisco next. Thanks to the soft forest floor underfoot, they managed to make very little noise.

Pinstripe picked his way quietly through the thick underbrush, and they soon reached the "back door" trail that would take them up the hill. This was the trail used to bring supplies up the far side of the hill —the opposite of the beach side, where the Japanese expected an attack.

Deke hoped that they didn't encounter any supply trains coming up the hill that morning—it was the last thing they would need. So much of the plan depended on surprise, and a single rifle shot or warning shout would upset all their plans.

In the gloom, Deke saw the Filipino ahead of him halt and go into a crouch. He did the same, wondering what the guerrilla soldier had seen. Considering that it was still nearly dark, the man must have had eyes like a panther.

That was when Deke spotted the sentry, keeping watch over the trail. He stood near a post that had a covered box on it, and Deke realized that this was probably a telephone with a line directly to Jap headquarters. Maybe this was a back door, but the Japanese hadn't left it completely unprotected. Once again, it was a good reminder that the Japanese should never be underestimated. *I wonder what other surprises they've got for us.*

Pinstripe raised his rifle as if he was about to shoot the Jap sentry, but Deke moved forward and touched the man on the shoulder. Now that he had the guerrilla's attention, Deke shook his head at him. *No.* The last thing that they needed was a rifle shot that would alert every Jap on the hill that something was happening. Their plan of attack would have gone out the window before it had barely begun.

Shooting him wasn't an option, but the sentry had to be eliminated if the rest of the patrol was to get past him.

He could have waited for Lieutenant Steele to catch up, so that Deke could ask him what to do, but the more time that elapsed, the greater the odds that the sentry might hear something. If he picked up that phone and warned the rest of the Japanese, the gig was up.

Deke made a decision, even if he didn't like it. He handed his rifle to the Filipino and whispered, "Hold this." Even though the guerrilla couldn't understand the words, good ol' Pinstripe seemed to get the meaning. He gave Deke a quick nod.

Deke drew his knife. The blade of the drop-point bowie knife made for him by Hollis Bailey at his mountain forge was razor sharp. The Filipino raised his eyebrows in admiration. Sure, the guerrillas had some wicked blades, but there was no doubt that a bowie knife meant business. Silently, Deke crept forward, the knife held in one hand.

He could see the Japanese sentry in the predawn gloom, the man's lighter-colored uniform showing against the darkness of the surrounding vegetation. The Jap's rifle was slung over one shoulder, and the man did not appear particularly alert. There was a kind of padded covering on his helmet that must have been intended as some sort of camouflage.

So far the sentry hadn't spotted him, but for how long would his luck hold out? Deke didn't like the idea of what was coming next, but he had to do it—and fast.

Deke gripped the knife tightly, his hand sweaty on the antler grip. On the farm and in the fields, he had helped butcher pigs and put wounded deer out of their misery. He was no stranger to ending life. But this was different.

Sure, they had gone over this kind of thing in training—how to kill a man with a knife—but to actually do it was something else altogether. He had killed the enemy before, but always with his rifle. The exception had been the Japanese soldier that he had stabbed with a bayonet on Guam. Then again, that soldier had just shot Ben, his friend from training. His reaction had been one of rage, not cold-blooded murder.

This was just another soldier, doing his duty. Maybe this wasn't necessary. Maybe they could try to slip past the man—or overpower him and tie him up.

But deep down, Deke knew there was no hope of that. One shout from the sentry, one gunshot, and their whole plan of attack would be in the wind.

He would have liked to work his way behind the sentry. After all, Deke could move as quietly as a fox when he wanted to. Even quieter —back home, he had been known to sneak up on a fox or two while hunting. But he also didn't want to push his luck. He really didn't have time to circle around the sentry, so he would have to come at him head-on. It was risky, to say the least. Anything could go wrong.

Deke crouched in the brush at the edge of the trail, no more than ten feet away. He was directly in front of the sentry. The trail opened up in front of him, and there was no more cover between him and the sentry.

Now or never.

Deke jumped up and covered the distance to the sentry in two quick bounds, holding the knife high.

The Jap went wide eyed at the soldier who had materialized out of the jungle. In a panic, he groped at the rifle strap over his shoulder. The Jap opened his mouth to shout something.

Deke never gave him the chance. He jammed his left hand over the sentry's mouth. He felt the man's hot breath and the words trying to form—or perhaps not words at all, but only a scream. He shoved the Jap right up against the sentry's call box. He pressed harder against the soldier's mouth to keep the man silent. Above Deke's hand, he got a glimpse of the soldier's eyes, wide with terror. With his right hand, he stabbed the point of the bowie knife into the base of the sentry's throat.

For a split second, the blade seemed to get hung up on something, maybe the collar of the sentry's uniform, or maybe the cartilage of the other man's larynx, but then the point slid home.

It was like plunging a knife into a raw roast. There was even the same sound of the blade going deep into wet meat. Deke twisted the knife free and rammed it home again, wrenching it back and forth viciously as he did so. In training, the instructors always acted like death was instantaneous for the enemy, that they went quietly to sleep, but that wasn't the case here. The sentry thrashed and strained, but

Deke pinned him in place against the telephone post, keeping his hand pressed tight to seal in the man's screams.

Finally, Deke started to feel the deadweight of the sentry sliding down the post. He pulled out the knife and let the body slump to the ground. The dying Jap made an awful croaking sound, like a bullfrog when you cut off its legs for the frying pan. The sentry's eyes stayed open, even after his hands no longer clawed at his ruined throat. Deke gave the body a push so that the dying Jap fell clear of the phone box.

Under normal circumstances, Deke knew that he would have been horrified by what he had just done, but he didn't allow himself any time to process those thoughts. Some part of him realized that he'd been as savage to the Jap as that bear had been to him all those years ago. But what choice did he have? If they didn't keep moving, he and the rest of the raiders were going to end up as dead as that sentry.

Quickly, he wiped the knife blade on the sentry's uniform and returned to the Filipino guide, who was staring at him—and no wonder, because Deke's face and shirt were now streaked with the enemy soldier's blood. Pinstripe shifted away, putting some distance between them. Deke had taken it for granted that the guerrillas did this sort of killing on a daily basis, but maybe not.

He took his rifle back and whispered, "What are you lookin' at? Get going." He gave the man an angry shove in the direction that would take them up the hill. "Go!"

Soon the rest of the patrol came rushing up the supply path. No one gave the dead sentry a second glance, aside from Father Francisco, who briefly knelt beside the body and made the sign of the cross before moving on.

"You mean that Japs have souls? Coulda fooled me," Philly said. "Jesus, did you just kill that Jap?"

"I reckon I did."

"No wonder you're covered in blood. Looks like you just about sawed his head off."

"Go to hell, Philly."

Deke picked up his rifle and resumed his place at the head of the column. They didn't encounter any more sentries, which was just fine with Deke. He was in no hurry for a repeat performance of what he had been forced to do with his knife to keep the patrol from being discovered. Lucky for them, the Japanese didn't seem to be expecting any trouble from this direction.

Once they were halfway up the hill, Honcho called a halt.

"This is where we split up," he said. "Yoshio, you go with the Filipinos to create that diversion. Make some noise, son. You know the old saying—you've got to break a few eggs to make an omelet. Deke, you and Philly see if you can pin those Japs down once Yoshio hits them. Remember, take out any officers that you can see. The rest of us are going to ram a big fat bomb down the Japs' throats—or die trying, anyhow."

"You got it, Honcho."

The lieutenant hesitated. He seemed to understand that this might be the last time that he would see any of them alive. "I wish I didn't have to ask you to do any of this, fellas, I really do, but we've got no choice. We've got to get this done if the landing is going to succeed. Otherwise, if those big guns are still in place, thousands more of our boys could die."

Nobody said anything, but the soldiers nodded grimly as Lieutenant Steele met their gaze. They knew the stakes. They knew what they were being asked to do.

"All right," Steele said after a moment. "If any of us make it out, the rendezvous is that clearing where we spent the night. Father Francisco will look after you until the cavalry arrives on that beach."

Orders given, they moved out into the brightening day, wondering if it would be their last day on earth. Here in the Pacific War, that was starting to be a familiar feeling.

CHAPTER EIGHTEEN

DEKE AND PHILLY struck out on their own, leaving the trail to bushwhack their way across the face of the hill. They could see blue sky above the treetops, but down among the palm fronds the morning remained dark and shadowy, which worked in their favor. The surrounding vegetation was lush, green, and silent, absorbing the sound of them passing through.

Deke put his head down and ran hard up the path, not worrying about stealth at this point. He doubted that there would be enemy troops on this part of the hill. Besides, the earlier that they hit the Japs on the slope, the better.

Lean and hard from years of working on the farm, not to mention boot camp and hard living in the Pacific, Deke maintained a pace that forced Philly and the others to struggle to keep up. Despite the shady surroundings, they were all soon sweating mightily in the tropical heat and humidity.

"You must be in a hurry to get shot," Philly grumbled.

"Sooner we get there, the better our chances," Deke replied, and lengthened his stride so that Philly had to struggle even harder to keep up.

Yoshio and the guerrillas accompanied them for part of the way. It was more than a little disconcerting to see Yoshio decked out like a Japanese soldier, right down to the familiar fatigue cap that Jap officers favored. It was nice to see that Yoshio had promoted himself to officer status, Deke thought. Then again, having Yoshio look the part of an officer was part of the subterfuge.

The Filipino guerrillas also wore bits and pieces of Japanese uniforms. They sure as hell wouldn't pass a parade inspection, but from a distance, it ought to be enough to fool the Japs—at least for a few crucial minutes.

Philly had also taken notice and said, "Yoshio sure looks like a Nip."

"Yeah, but at least he's our Nip."

There remained a language barrier between the Americans and the Filipinos, but Father Francisco had given the guerrillas their instructions that morning. They seemed to understand the mission well enough.

Deke was reassured by the presence of his old pal, Pinstripe. Unlike Philly, the wiry Filipino had no trouble keeping up with Deke, although, after the incident with the Jap sentry, Pinstripe remained wary of him. He kept his fellow guerrillas moving along in Deke's wake.

Pinstripe also seemed to know a few words of English. When they came to a thick wall of vegetation that blocked their progress, Deke was suddenly aware of a whirring sound and the flash of a blade past his ear. He flinched, taken by surprise by the sight of Pinstripe hacking through the underbrush with his bolo knife, which had a blade at least a foot and a half in length. The other guerrillas followed suit.

"*Andale*," Pinstripe said, wielding the bolo until a kind of doorway opened in the undergrowth, revealing an animal path ahead. "Hurry."

Deke didn't need to be told twice, but surged ahead. They were still far enough down the slope that there were trees and jungle scrub to give them cover. The tall palm shrubs reached above their heads, keeping them obscured from any curious eyes above. They moved steadily uphill, rushing to get into position before the second half of the team began their attack on the bunker high above.

"Are we going in the right direction?" Philly asked, gasping for breath.

"Gonna find out."

Soon, it was time for Yoshio and the band of Filipinos to go their own way. They were going to strike out directly across the face of the hill, while Deke and Philly moved still higher.

"Good luck, Yoshio," Deke said. "I'll see you at the rendezvous."

"Kōun o," Yoshio replied, then trotted away with the guerrillas who were going to impersonate Japanese troops. Pinstripe brought up the rear, watching for any stray Japanese who might give them away.

"I wish people would talk English around here. What do you think Yoshio just said?" Philly asked.

"I'm pretty sure it was Japanese for, 'Stop asking so many damn questions.' You're making everybody nervous."

"Yeah, yeah."

They reached the front part of the steep hillside that had been transformed into the Japanese defenses. Most of the trees and vegetation had been cleared, leaving the hillside open. Of course, the ground was veined with trenches and pockmarked with pillboxes and firing pits. Some were clearly marked by the baskets of earth and even concrete that had been used to fortify them, while others were cleverly hidden.

Deke hoped that he never had to attack and capture this hill—it would be a nightmare. What they planned on doing was going to be hard enough. To take this hill would require boots on the ground because bombing alone from ships or from the air would never be enough to completely wipe out these defenses.

He looked toward the summit. The top of Hill 522 was basically divided into two ridges that branched out from the main spine of the hill to create a kind of Y shape, one branch of the Y being slightly higher than the other. Near the peak of the topmost branch of the Y, Deke could see the cave-like entrance of the bunker that protected the powerful Japanese battery. From up there, the Japanese gunners would have a commanding view of the approaches from the sea and beach. With any luck, the rest of Patrol Easy would be hitting that bunker soon.

Deke would leave them to it. His plan was to climb to the lower branch of the Y that formed the summit. Up there, he would make himself at home in one of the Japanese rifle pits. He and his Springfield would give the Japs plenty to think about.

But first, they had to get there, which was easier said than done. Having entered the cleared portion of the hill, they had lost their cover and now had to rely on the series of Japanese trenches to traverse the face of the slope. The trenches would have been fine if it hadn't been for all the damn Japanese.

Sprinting up a trench, they went around a switchback and came face-to-face with a soldier holding a shovel. Apparently, the Japanese still weren't finished with their fortification efforts.

The Jap shouted something that sounded like, "Hey!"

Deke was so startled that he froze. Lucky for him, the Jap did too. They stood for a split second, staring at each other.

Deke didn't want to fire a shot or risk damaging the rifle and its delicate telescopic sight by swatting the soldier with it. Still shaken by the incident this morning, he was reluctant to use his knife again.

The Jap started to open his mouth and might have shouted more to sound the alarm, if Philly hadn't surged past Deke and hit the soldier in the forehead with the butt of his rifle. *Whunk*. The Jap went down instantly and didn't move.

"Thanks," Deke muttered.

"Aren't you glad you brought me along? That probably messed up my rifle, though. I hope it can still shoot straight."

"Is he dead?"

"If he isn't, then he's going to have one hell of a headache when he wakes up. Either way, who the hell cares? Let's keep moving."

They kept going, this time with Philly in the lead. He kept his rifle ready, butt first; however, they didn't encounter any other enemy troops. Apparently it was still too early for the work crews to be out in full force.

After another minute of hard climbing, they reached the secondary ridge, from which they could look down and see the rest of the hill sweeping away. Slightly above them was the topmost ridge with the brooding presence of the bunker. All in all, Deke had a good view in all directions.

That was when Deke spotted what he was looking for. It was a Japanese version of a foxhole, encircled by roughly woven baskets filled with soil and partially covered with a tarp that must have been intended to hide the hole from above. He slid into the hole, with Philly right behind him. The hole smelled of dirt, of course, but something else—dirty canvas on account of the tarp, and urine, like maybe some Jap had taken a leak in the hole.

Never mind that. This was prime real estate, a good shooting spot, even if it smelled bad. He was sure the location was exactly why the Japanese had put a sniper nest here. This morning, he would be using it against them.

"This is where I set up shop," Deke said. He pointed to a similar foxhole nearby, close enough that the two men could communicate easily. "You take that one. If the Japs drop a mortar on my head, no sense in both of us gettin' killed. If they get me, you keep shooting. Remember, every Jap we kill is one less to shoot at Yoshio or the rest of our boys up on that hill."

"I'll be damned. It's gonna be like a shooting gallery!" Philly exclaimed. There was no doubt this was a good position, offering a clear field of fire down the slope, which was why the defenders had put a foxhole here in the first place.

"It will be a turkey shoot, all right, at least until they figure out we're here." In the back of Deke's mind, it nagged at him that anyone shooting down at them from the ridge with the bunker would have a distinct advantage. He hoped to hell that the Jap sniper that he'd run into yesterday didn't figure that out, or it was going to be a pretty lousy morning dodging bullets.

Besides that, the Japs had all sorts of nasty surprises up their sleeve, from their grenades that looked like cans of beans, to so-called knee mortars for close combat, to the Nambu machine guns that could plow up a field quicker than Farmer Brown's prize mule.

"Listen up, your job is to watch my back. Shoot any of those Nip bastards who come sneaking around up here."

"You got it."

They'd been hurrying all morning, but now was the time to take it slow. In his deliberate way, Deke got organized. Haste makes waste, Pa used to say. He took off the small haversack that he had carried up the hill on his back and set it on the edge of the hole, then laid his rifle across it to make a passable benchrest for his rifle. He scooped dirt over the haversack and the rifle barrel where it protruded from the hole to help disguise them. He kept the muzzle clear, of course.

It helped that he had already wrapped strips of dirty fabric across the rifle and the telescopic sight itself to break up the outline of the weapon. He worried about the glint of glass from the telescopic sight, but that couldn't be helped. If the Japs figured out where he was hunkered down, they would be sure to rain hellfire upon his head—and on Philly's head as well.

He backed himself deeper into the hole, then pulled the tarp across. Once he started shooting, enemy eyes would be hard-pressed to spot him unless they did happen to pick up on that reflection off his riflescope. He reached for his canteen and took a long drink of water, which might be his last for a while.

In stark contrast to the jungle growth, the hill spread out below him was barren of any vegetation, a vast network of trenches, pillboxes, and dugouts. The scene before him looked like one of those pictures of the trenches in an old photograph from World War I, but all built on a slope. Jap soldiers moved about, carrying shovels or bossing around the crews of Filipino workers, oblivious to the US sniper who had them in his sights.

Then he settled himself behind the rifle, butt pressed into the cup of his shoulder, cheek to stock, eye to the scope, finger on the trigger. He breathed in, breathed out.

It nagged at him that if some Jap sneaked up behind him, he'd be a goner. He'd have to trust that Philly was watching his back. Now he'd just have to wait for the show to begin, and that depended on Yoshio and his band of Filipino guerrillas.

Right on cue, he heard shouting down the slope. Through the scope, he saw a small group of what appeared to be Japanese soldiers running up the hillside. The man in front was waving his arms and hollering something in Japanese. Deke couldn't understand the words, but they sounded urgent.

He grinned, realizing that this was Yoshio and his band of guerrillas in disguise. Yoshio was doing a damn fine job of sounding like a Jap officer. From a distance, Yoshio and the guerrillas looked convincingly like enemy soldiers.

The Japs seemed to think so too. Heads popped up from hidey-holes around the slope, sentries that Deke hadn't seen before. Good thing he and Philly had taken the back door onto the hill, or they wouldn't have gotten far before stumbling right into a nest of Japs.

An officer stood up from a trench, hand on the hilt of a sword, and shouted something at Yoshio, who shouted back and pointed down the hill.

Yoshio's ruse was very convincing in that the last thing this seemed like was an attack. It looked for all the world like Yoshio and his men were fleeing from American soldiers who must be on their heels, still hidden in the greenery below. All eyes were now looking down the hill, away from the summit where, Deke hoped, Lieutenant Steele and the rest of the gang were trying to blow up the bunker.

But the ruse couldn't last forever. Yoshio spoke the language, but he and his group of Filipino guerrillas were only passable as Japanese soldiers from a distance. Their uniforms were piecemeal, and Deke could even see the collar of Pinstripe's shirt sticking out from the Japanese tunic. Up close, he felt sure that the officers could tell the difference between a Jap and a Filipino.

Already, two or three officers were moving to intercept Yoshio—probably trying to determine what the hell was going on.

Maybe they were wondering if the Americans had landed. That seemed unlikely, considering that the sea was visible from these heights, and Leyte Gulf remained blue and empty of ships.

Deke tracked the lead officer in his scope, finger on the trigger. Not yet.

He could hear Philly muttering from his own foxhole, as if urging Deke to shoot. "Come on, come on."

Deke ignored him. Soon enough, there was going to be all kinds of shooting.

Below, the officer had reached Yoshio and stood a few feet away, shouting at him in Japanese. Realization seemed to dawn on the Japanese officer. He stopped shouting. He stared at Yoshio, momentarily speechless, then reached for the pistol on his belt.

Deke squeezed the trigger and shot the officer in the back, leaving a coin-size wound visible through the scope. The officer crumpled as if somebody had cut his puppet strings.

Deke squeezed off another shot, managing to take out a soldier who had been standing at the officer's elbow.

That was when all hell broke loose on Hill 522.

That morning, the Filipinos had been given orders to pick targets as they came up the hill. Now they opened fire. A guerrilla who had been passing a machine-gun nest quickly shot all three soldiers before they knew what was happening. He and another guerrilla slid into the hole, swung the Nambu machine gun around, and opened up on the Japanese. The satisfying rhythm of the machine gun firing at enemy soldiers soon filled the air.

Elsewhere, a guerrilla had gotten hold of a grenade. He tossed it into a trench, taking out the Japanese squad waiting there. The work crews of Filipino men ran for cover.

Yoshio was shooting in all directions like a wild man, but he was too exposed, making himself a target for every Jap on that hill.

"Get down, you dang fool," Deke muttered. He fired at a soldier who was charging in Yoshio's direction with a fixed bayonet, dropping him.

But Deke's mission wasn't to protect Yoshio. He tore his eyes away from his squad mate and scanned the slope for Japanese officers. Truth be told, they were the brains of the operation. The Japanese didn't trust their enlisted men to think for themselves and relied on officers far more than did the Americans.

If you wanted to create chaos, you had to shoot the officers.

Deke took his time picking out his targets, swinging the crosshairs through and past any enlisted men.

His sights settled on an officer waving a sword, and Deke shot him through the chest.

Looking around for another target, he spotted an officer trying to organize a charge to sweep the guerrillas off the hillside.

Deke dropped him.

From above, he had a clear view of the hillside below and its defenses. Some of the machine gunners were dug too far into the hill for him to get a good shot at them. One by one, their nests came into play as they figured out what was happening on the hill. The Japanese had set up fields of fire to cover the open ground, and he saw two guerrillas mowed down in a single burst of machine-gun fire.

He spotted a stab of flame coming from a dugout hiding one of the deadly Nambu guns and fired at the flashes. It took three shots before the machine gun fell silent.

He fired again and again.

He was in the process of reloading when the first bullet plucked at the tarp. He heard the round ricochet and go winging off into the distance with an unpleasant metallic whine that made his spine tighten.

"Philly!" he shouted. There was no point in being quiet anymore, not with all the shooting going on.

He heard Philly shout back, "Hey, Deke, somebody is shooting at you."

"You don't say. Where's it coming from?"

"To hell if I know."

"See if you can find out."

Another bullet whistled in, apparently not aimed at Deke's hidey-hole this time, but at Philly. "Dammit!"

"Keep your head down."

A Jap sniper had found them.

CHAPTER NINETEEN

DEKE HAD HOPED for more time to pick off targets without attracting attention. But he'd been overdue for someone to notice him, considering the number of shots that he had taken from the same location.

The truth was that Deke was still relatively inexperienced at sniper warfare, but one basic rule had come through loud and clear, which was that a sniper had to keep moving if he wanted to stay alive. Either that, or he had to be extremely well hidden—invisible was best. It was a rule that the Japanese snipers who tied themselves into trees tended to ignore, which was why they didn't last long. They did their fair share of damage nonetheless.

Deke had violated that rule this morning, and somebody had noticed him, all right. That somebody had to be another sniper. He figured it took one to know one.

Deke was still busy picking off targets below, but somewhere in the back of his mind, he had time to hope that it wasn't the same Jap sniper that he'd run into yesterday.

On the hillside below, the attack was faltering. Several of the Filipinos were down. Deke reckoned that the dead guerrillas would be the lucky ones. If the Japanese captured any of the Filipino guerrillas, wounded or not, he didn't like their chances. The Japanese wouldn't like having been duped, and they might consider any captured Filipinos to be spies, considering that they had been dressed as Japanese soldiers. The punishment for spies was swift and merciless.

For the Filipino soldiers, the stakes were high. This was one of those situations where if it came down to being captured or killed, then they were truly better off dead than alive.

What about Yoshio? Deke spotted him working his way back down the hill. Given the odds arrayed against him as more and more Japanese poured into the fight, overwhelming the small guerrilla force, Yoshio was doing the sensible thing and retreating—but it looked like he might be too late.

He could see Japanese soldiers moving to work their way in behind Yoshio, trying to cut him off before he reached cover. The worst part was that the Japs weren't shooting at Yoshio—they seemed intent on taking him alive.

Deke was having none of that. He had to at least give Yoshio a fighting chance of reaching the trees, where he could lose himself in the jungle cover. Deke shot one of the soldiers, and the rest scattered for cover. He fired again to make them keep their heads down. Yoshio saw his opening and ran for the trees.

But Deke's interference had come at a price, revealing his position and helping the Japanese sniper zero in on him. Another bullet struck the tarp, punching a fresh hole in the canvas that let in more daylight. With a sinking feeling, he realized that the enemy sniper was probably above him, a position that was allowing the Jap to shoot down at the tarp. Just what he had been afraid of. Whoever was up there knew his business. Sure, Deke had found a good vantage point, but the Jap sniper had done him one better and found an even higher position.

Maybe the tarp gave Deke some concealment, but it sure as hell wasn't bulletproof. The Jap sniper might not be able to see him, not exactly, and the tarp might end up with more holes in it than a screen door, but it was only a matter of time before he made a lucky shot.

"Philly, where is that guy?"

"I'm looking!"

Another bullet perforated the tarp. And another. His hiding place had definitely been detected, and the tarp now had several holes that

Deke could look up and see daylight through. He was just starting to debate taking his chances and making a run for it when Philly called out, "I see him!"

"Where's he at?"

"On the peak above us. My ten o'clock."

Deke might never have known where the Jap was hiding if it hadn't been for Philly, which spoke to the value of working with a spotter. With the binoculars, Philly had been able to detect some sign of the enemy sniper. Philly might be a loudmouth and a pain in Deke's back-side at times, but silently he praised the fact that he had the best spotter in the Pacific working with him.

It was time to get a move on. He'd had enough of that Jap sniper. Deke slipped his rifle under the tarp and worked his way around to the other side, being careful to keep low so that he didn't brush the canvas with his head and give away his position. Once he was on the other side of the foxhole, he eased the muzzle out from under the canvas.

From here, he had a much better view up the slope, although he could still see a slice of the hill below, which was now swarming with the enemy. Philly was in a foxhole just off to Deke's left, and figuring about where Philly's ten o'clock was located, he began to survey the hillside above through his riflescope.

"How far up?" Deke asked.

"About a hundred feet down from the bunker, to the left a little. There's kind of a darker spot in the dirt—might be a dugout."

Another bullet crashed in, making another singsong whine as it ricocheted away. That was the thing about the Jap bullets—they tended to bounce off things because they were lighter, hitting more like a varmint round than a .30-06 bullet. Would you rather get shot with a varmint rifle or a deer rifle? It was a moot point, because in the hands of an experienced marksman, either one would kill you all the same.

At the sharp crack of the Japanese rifle, Deke had been able to focus on what appeared to be a rifle pit, in just the right spot. He'd bet a jug of moonshine that was where the Jap was hiding. Philly had called it. He had done his job as a spotter and found the target, more or less.

Now it was Deke's turn to do his job as a sniper and take out that target.

Easier said than done, considering that all he really had to shoot at was a patch of dirt. There wasn't any real target, just some promising real estate. If he missed by an inch, he'd miss by a mile.

With a sinking feeling, he wondered if it was the same sniper that he had tangled with during yesterday's ill-fated attack on the hillside. He got his answer when he saw a familiar figure break from the dugout, run about ten feet, and dive into the nearest trench.

Taken by surprise, Deke wasn't able to get a shot at him. There was something familiar about the enemy soldier. Deke realized it was the same heavyset, squat figure that he had seen accompanying the sniper yesterday. The man must be the spotter, doing for the Jap the same thing Philly was doing for Deke. These Jap snipers had their act together.

The question was, Where was the Jap spotter going? There were several possibilities—none of them good. Maybe the Jap sniper was low on ammo and the spotter was running to find more. Or maybe the spotter was going to relay Deke's position to Japs equipped with those wicked knee mortars. They'd zero in on the foxholes occupied by Deke and Philly in no time.

Wouldn't be good, Deke thought.

He had to take out that Jap, and soon, before somebody called in the cavalry.

Also, he hadn't lost sight of the fact that there were a lot more Japanese soldiers on this hillside than there were Americans. As a matter of fact, he and Philly were the *only* American soldiers on this hillside. If they became surrounded, he sure didn't want to become a prisoner of the Japanese.

Deke pressed his eye closer to the end of the telescopic sight, practically screwing it into his eye socket. He had a good idea of where the sniper was hiding, but he needed something more—a hint of motion, or a muzzle flash—to pinpoint his location. Once Deke could see a target, there was pretty much nothing he couldn't hit.

But he had to see it.

"Hey, Philly," he called. His view of Philly's foxhole was blocked by the tarp. "You ain't dead yet, are you?"

"Not yet."

"Good. We need to get out of this pickle barrel. I want you to try something."

"I'm all ears."

"Put your helmet on the end of your rifle and stick it out of your foxhole. Let's see if he takes the bait."

Next door, Deke heard muttered curses, followed by metallic scraping noises. "All right. Here goes."

Deke waited behind the rifle, eye pressed to the scope, carefully studying the spot where he suspected that the enemy sniper was hidden. All he needed was a hint of a muzzle flash, a puff of smoke, the glint of sunlight off a telescopic sight. Then he'd know where to put his bullet.

He could hear another scrape of metal on metal nearby as Philly raised up his helmet. Deke tensed, ready to take the shot.

Nothing happened.

"He's not buying it," Philly called out.

"Keep trying. Maybe he'll get annoyed enough to shoot."

After another minute, Philly announced that he was done with the ploy. "My arms are getting tired. Now what?"

"Now we wait."

"I hate to tell you this, but we don't have a lot of time. I vote for getting out of here."

"The second either one of us shows ourselves, we're dead men. That sniper has got the drop on us."

"Then you'd better work some hillbilly magic with that rifle of yours—and fast. We're not going to be alone up here for long."

Deke was nothing but patient, but he had to admit that Philly was right. They didn't have a lot of time. The Jap sniper's spotter had likely gone to relay the fact that there were two American soldiers hiding out on this ridge. It was only a matter of time before the Japanese attacked in force.

He stared at the spot where he thought that the sniper was hidden, but nothing presented itself as a target.

Down the slope behind him, Deke heard angry shouting. Was it the Japs coming after them? He took his eye off the scope long enough to look down the slice of slope that he could still see.

A terrible spectacle was taking place there. It appeared that the Japanese forces had captured four of the Filipino guerrillas. Fortunately, Deke didn't see Yoshio, who must have gotten away.

The Filipino guerrillas had been forced to kneel in the dirt. With a sense of dread, Deke realized that one of the men was Pinstripe. Somehow he had survived the raid only to be captured by the Japanese. He had still been wearing the Japanese uniform tunic, but a soldier ripped it off him, none too gently, revealing the Filipino's trademark pinstripe shirt with its contrasting collar. The other guerrillas were also stripped of their Japanese uniforms. It was as if the Japanese did not want their precious uniforms sullied by the guerrillas.

The Japanese had a reputation for being cruel to prisoners, and with a sinking feeling, Deke realized that he now had a front-row seat to see just how those prisoners were treated.

Next, an officer appeared. Ominously, he carried a drawn sword. He approached the prisoners and stopped behind the first man, looming over him. The officer set his feet, got a good grip on the samurai sword with both hands, and raised the gleaming blade over his head.

A soldier stepped forward and forced the kneeling man to tilt his chin down to better expose his neck. The captured man knew what was coming and had little choice but to cooperate. As the soldier moved away, the blade slashed down. Deke watched in horror as the Filipino's head separated from his body and rolled in the dirt.

The officer moved behind the next man, careful to avoid the dark pool of blood spreading across the dirt.

Ever so slightly, Deke started to shift his rifle around. He settled the crosshairs on the Japanese officer as the Jap raised his sword once again.

"Don't even think about it," Philly whispered.

"You saw what he just did. I can't let those bastards get away with that."

"Right now, that Jap sniper is the only one who seems to know where we are. He hasn't been able to get word to anyone else yet. If

you shoot Errol Flynn down there, the rest of the Japs will know we're
here."

"Dammit, Philly—"

"See all those guns down there pointed at the Filipinos? It's not like
they're going to stand up and walk away if you shoot that guy with the
sword."

Deke kept his sights on the officer. Deep down, he knew Philly was
right.

But still.

He held his fire.

The sword swung down, decapitating another man.

Then the officer got to Pinstripe. The sword rose.

Philly uttered one last warning, "Deke, don't you do it."

Ignoring Philly, he put the crosshairs on the Japanese officer—and
held steady. He couldn't miss.

But Deke took his finger off the trigger, hating himself for doing it.
In the end, he supposed that he didn't really owe Pinstripe anything.
Besides, they still had the mission to complete. But he hated to see a
brave man slaughtered like a hog or a steer.

The sword swept down. Pinstripe's body joined the others, spilling
their life's blood into the soil that they had fought for against the
Japanese. The Filipinos had been incredibly brave and determined.

Gritting his teeth, Deke put his rifle sights back on the spot where
they thought the Jap sniper was hidden. There was still no sign of him,
however. They seemed to have each other pinned down. Just how long
could they keep this up?

Deke heard another shout from the hillside below.

Now what?

He took his eye off the scope long enough to see that the Japanese
spotter had reached the group of soldiers who had overseen the execu-
tions. The man was pointing up the slope toward the spot where Deke
and Philly lay hidden.

"Uh-oh," Philly said. "Looks like we're about to have company."

"I'll keep an eye out for that sniper. See if you can hold off the rest
of them."

Philly opened fire, causing more angry shouts from the hillside below. Instantly, bullets began to churn the dirt around them as the soldiers figured out where they were hidden. Their foxholes sheltered them from most of the fusillade, but now they were seriously pinned down. They were stuck between a rock and a hard place, between the troops coming at them from below and the sniper perched above them. So far the sniper still hadn't shown himself, although Deke still kept his attention focused on the scope while Philly fired downhill at the Japanese.

Come on, come on.

He could hear the firing and the shouts of the enemy drawing closer from below. From the constant crack of Philly's rifle, it was clear that he was trying to hold them off, but there were just too many enemy troops coming at them.

Deke reached down and touched the pistol in his belt. If it came down to it, he'd save the last bullet for himself rather than be taken alive. He had already seen how the Japanese treated their prisoners. *I'll be damned if some Jap is gonna cut my head off.*

He forced himself to focus on the limited field of view through his telescope that had reduced his world to a narrow circle of red-tinged dirt and shadows that might have been the hiding spot for the Japanese sniper.

Finally, there it was. Just the hint of a muzzle flash.

Over in his foxhole, Philly yelped in pain.

Deke fired at where he'd seen the muzzle flash.

He ran the bolt, fired again. Impossible to tell if he'd hit anything. But the Jap sniper had fallen silent for now.

The fact that they weren't being shot at had emboldened the other Japanese, who now surged up the hill. Ominously, Philly had stopped firing at them.

"Philly, are you all right?" Deke shouted.

"Punched a hole in my helmet, but I'll live. Did you get him?"

"Don't know yet, but here come the rest of the Nips."

It wasn't looking good. If they'd had M1 rifles, rather than the slower-firing bolt-action Springfield rifles, maybe they would've had a chance. Deke touched the handle of the pistol once again, just to reassure himself. If it came down to it, all he needed were a few seconds, and one bullet.

That was when a tremendous explosion ripped across the hilltop beyond them. Deke looked up to see smoke and debris swirling around the entrance to the bunker.

It looked as if the rest of the team had gotten to those guns, after all.

The blast took the Japanese by surprise, prompting a momentary lull in the firing.

It was now or never.

Deke jumped out of the foxhole. Nearby, Philly had the same idea and came scrambling out of his own foxhole.

"They did it," Philly said in amazement.

But Deke didn't want to stand around and discuss it. "Run!"

They both headed back down the ridge, running full tilt for the trees, expecting at any moment to catch a bullet in the back.

CHAPTER TWENTY

GIVEN AN OPPORTUNITY TO RETREAT, Deke and Philly ran like hell for the rendezvous point. The first leg meant getting off Hill 522 in one piece. Lucky for them, it was all downhill, first along the spine of the Y at the top of Hill 522, and then down the slope of the hill itself.

Not far behind them, they could hear shouts and small arms fire.

"Here they come!" Philly warned.

"Don't look back. Just run."

The blast from the bunker had startled the Japanese troops, but not for long. Murderous cries and gunshots followed them as they ran, with bullets clipping the air around them. They jumped into a trench for cover, ran down its length, and jumped back out, that much closer to the relative safety of the forest's edge.

From their vantage point on the hill, they could easily spot the massive, dying tree that served as a landmark for the clearing in the forest where they had spent the night. That was where they were headed. The massive Philippine rosewood—known locally as a toog tree—towered above the rest of the jungle canopy. Scarred from lightning strikes, the gray, grizzled trunk stood out against the green forest surrounding it like a lighthouse on the shore. The old tree drew them now like a beacon.

Deke made the mistake of ignoring his own advice and looking back at the Japanese pursuing them. He could see several soldiers not more than a couple hundred feet away, led by an officer waving a pistol in one hand and a sword in the other. There seemed to be no shortage of fanatical officers.

Beyond a doubt, he knew now what those Japs did with their swords. He could almost feel his neck itching. He shouldn't have looked back.

They entered the cover of the forest and raced pell-mell through the trees, dodging the trunks like downhill skiers, propelled by fear and gravity. Bullets still followed them, but the shots went high, punching holes in the fronds of the big palm leaves overhead and raining green confetti on their heads.

Before entering the forest, Deke had gotten a glimpse of the landmark rosewood tree and held its position in his mind. He didn't like their chances if they missed the rendezvous point. The jungle stretched beyond, so in its own way, it was a bit like trying to reach an island in the vastness of the Pacific.

He felt relieved that the sounds of the Japanese had faded somewhat. It was no wonder—he and Philly were running like madmen. At any moment, he was sure that one of them was going to fall and break his fool neck. But Deke sure as hell didn't slow down.

Back when he'd been a boy on the farm, play and games had been rare. His ma and pa had seen play as a waste of time and energy. Why run around when you could haul water to the stock and split firewood? Still, that hadn't stopped him and Sadie from playing fox and hound on occasion. It was a simple game in which he or his sister got a head start through the woods, while the other one gave chase. Sadie could track him as well as any boy—or grown man, for that matter. It wasn't just about who could run the fastest and catch the other one, because they constantly came up with ways to give the other one the slip by disguising their tracks or leaving a false trail. She could also run like the wind, and there had been times when Deke was hard-pressed to catch her. That game always had been thrilling, but it was nothing compared to the game taking place now.

The sight and sound of all those Japs had given wings to Philly's feet, Deke decided. For all his smoking, and despite his shorter legs, Philly managed to pull ahead—and sure enough, that city boy started to run in the wrong direction.

"This way!" Deke shouted, when Philly got off course at a ravine.

"You sure?" Philly didn't look convinced. Wild eyed, he was about to run off in the wrong direction.

"Sure I'm sure." Deke still had the picture of that big tree held in his head.

"All right, I'll trust your redneck instincts out here in the boonies. But if you ever need to find a trolley station, let me know."

After a few minutes of hard running, they burst into the clearing. The big tree stood just a few feet away. Deke hoped that they had somehow lost the Japanese.

But maybe he was wrong about that. No sooner had they quit running and stood bent over in the clearing, hands on knees, gasping for breath, than they heard someone crashing through the forest, coming right at them. Both men swung their rifles in that direction.

To their relief, it was Yoshio who came bursting from the jungle undergrowth.

"I'll be damned, but you're a sight for sore eyes," Deke said.

"You're lucky I didn't plug you," said Philly, finally lowering his rifle. "I thought you might be a Jap coming after us."

Yoshio looked around. "Where are the others? Where's Honcho?"

Deke shook his head. "No sign of 'em yet."

"Do you think they made it?"

"Let's give them some time. They were farther away than we were."

"None of my Filipinos made it," Yoshio said in disbelief. "Some were captured. They cut off their heads!"

"Yeah, we saw what happened to them." Deke shook his head in disgust. "Damn Japs!"

From the forest, they heard the sounds of more men crashing through the trees, headed in their direction.

All three men swung their weapons toward the sounds, not sure if they were about to see friendly faces—or Japanese soldiers.

* * *

IT HADN'T BEEN easy taking out the gun battery. In fact, it had been a near thing. Just as Lieutenant Steele and the others had feared, the Japanese had been expecting them and were well prepared. A couple of machine guns had been set up to cover the approach to the cave that had been carved into the hillside, inside of which was the three-gun battery waiting to blast anything that moved out of Leyte Gulf—or out of the air, for that matter. In addition to the machine guns, there were at least two dozen soldiers spread out in rifle pits as well.

While those were ordinary riflemen, they couldn't have known that one of the Jap's best snipers, Sergeant Akio Ikeda, was positioned here as well, with his rifle covering the slope leading up to the cave mouth. Ikeda and his spotter were well hidden in a rifle pit, out of sight. Some of the men scattered throughout the trenches were his sniper trainees.

Something else that the Japanese probably hadn't intended for them to see were the land mines directly in front of the bunker. If any attackers made it that far, the mines created one final line of defense. The Japanese probably thought that those mines would be a big surprise for any raiders. And they would have been, if Bat's practiced eyes hadn't picked out the tiny flags the Japanese had left to mark the mines for their own troops.

"You've got to hand it to the Japs. They thought of *almost* everything," Lieutenant Steele said, looking over the defenses as he crouched in a nearby trench with the rest of Patrol Easy, the priest, and a handful of Filipino guerrillas. Most of the Filipinos had gone with Yoshio to join the diversion attack. "Then again, they didn't think of *absolutely* everything."

Father Francisco smiled. "The back door."

"Exactly. You might say our prayers are answered, Padre."

The very fact that they had reached this point undetected spoke to the reality that the Japanese were expecting any assault on the bunker to come front and center, up the hillside itself. It was just the direction that their attack yesterday had taken. What the enemy wasn't expecting was an incursion from one side of the bunker—slightly behind it, in fact, where the supply trail emptied out near the summit of the hill. They definitely had Father Francisco to thank for letting them know about that route.

If the Japanese did have any worries about the supply trail, they probably figured that their sentries had it covered. The only problem was that Deke had taken out the sentry at the bottom of the hill, and a similar fate had befallen another sentry at the hands of one of the Filipino guerrillas.

Even so, it wouldn't have taken much for the defenders to shift their machine guns and their rifles to meet an attack from another direction.

That was where the diversion led by Yoshio had come in. Deke and Philly would also play a role, with Deke picking off as many Japs as he could and sowing confusion. One thing for sure, Honcho had been glad that he wouldn't be the one in Deacon Cole's rifle sights. That farm boy could shoot.

"Sit tight, everybody," Honcho whispered. "Let's wait for the show to begin down there."

"What if it doesn't work?" Bat asked. The marine looked pale—it was clear that his wounded shoulder had been causing him some pain.

"It will work, all right," Honcho said confidently. He added more quietly, "Because it has to."

Any plan was bound to fall apart, but if and when it did, you had to improvise. Lieutenant Steele wasn't entirely sure what their plan B would end up being if it came to that, so he hoped to hell that the diversion involving Yoshio and the Filipino guerrillas, and Deke and Philly, was going to work.

When he heard the shooting begin on the slope below, he felt an enormous sense of relief. It also meant that it was time for him and his team to hold up their end of the bargain.

"All right, boys," he said. "It's showtime. Bat, Ball, you two get that satchel charge into the bunker."

"I dunno, Honcho. It's maybe gonna take more than that to knock out those guns."

"Then get in there and figure it out," he said impatiently. "You two are the demolition experts. The rest of us will cover you."

"Aye, aye, Cap'n."

Ball was carrying the satchel charge, but Bat held up several grenades that he had strung together. They dangled from his big hands like bunches of steel fruit.

"What's that?"

"That's me figuring it out."

Lieutenant Steele waved a hand, and the patrol moved forward. The bunker entrance loomed ahead. Closer, closer. He could see Japanese troops scurrying around inside. What they were up to was anybody's guess.

Approaching one of the Nambu nests, he leveled his twelve gauge. Incredibly, they were only a few yards away. The Japs were so focused on the sounds of combat from down the slope that none of them paid any attention to the crouching forms running at them from the rear.

Honcho pulled the trigger of the shotgun. *Boom!*

Quickly, Rodeo, Alphabet, and the handful of Filipinos spread out and opened fire. There were not enough of them to overwhelm the bunker defenses, but all they needed was a little time.

"Go! Go!" Honcho shouted at Bat and Ball.

The two marines went running straight up the middle, headed for the bunker entrance. It was like they were running a football play, heading for the end zone. The image was helped by the sight of Ball running with the satchel charge tucked under one arm like a football.

Yesterday, the sniper had winged Bat just as he'd been about to throw the satchel, messing up his toss. The charge had bounced off the mouth of the cave. They didn't plan on making the same mistake today.

Somehow, the men had managed to dodge the mines. Bat held back and crouched to one side of the cave entrance while Ball dashed inside, surprising the hell out of the Japanese troops within. He hurled the satchel deep into the bunker, then turned on a dime and raced back out, throwing himself to one side of the bunker entrance as he did so.

Steele could see the shock wave like a clear bubble pushing out of the bunker's mouth. Even so, he wasn't prepared for the deafening blast. Dirt and grit scoured his face. As if through a dusty curtain, he could hear muffled screaming from the poor Jap bastards who had been caught inside the bunker when the satchel charge went off.

The marines had done good, he thought. But apparently, they were not finished. Bat and Ball went running back into the swirling dirt and dust inside the bunker, rather than away from it.

What the hell? Then Steele thought about those bunches of grenades that Bat had carried, and he had an inkling of what the two planned to do. They were going to spike the guns, just in case the satchel charge hadn't been enough.

It was likely that neither man had planned on making it back out, but Steele would be damned if he was going to leave them behind. He pumped the shotgun and fired at the nearest Jap who dared to stick his head up after the blast.

Boom!

Around him, the others kept up a withering fire when they should have been beating it out of there toward the rendezvous point. He glanced at the cave entrance but didn't see anything but more smoke. What the hell was taking Bat and Ball so long?

He fired again and again. *Boom! Boom!*

Then the shotgun shucked out the last empty shell.

Before Steele had a chance to reload, Bat and Ball came barreling out of the bunker. The sounds of the explosions that chased them out were anticlimactic, sounding more like a firecracker going off inside a pipe compared to the massive blast earlier. But judging by the grins on the marines' faces, it had been enough.

"Go!" Steele shouted. "Everybody go!"

They beat a hasty retreat back around the bunker to the supply trail. A couple of the Filipino guerrillas had been killed, but otherwise everyone was none the worse for wear. It was time to head for the rendezvous and maybe, just maybe, there would be a boat waiting for them back down at the beach.

* * *

TWENTY MINUTES LATER, Deke lowered his rifle when he saw that it was Lieutenant Steele who had burst out of the forest and into the clearing. Upon spotting friendly faces, Steele lowered his shotgun.

"I never thought I'd say it, but you guys are a sight for sore eyes. Or sore eye, in my case."

"We were afraid you might be Japs," Philly said.

"I have a feeling they aren't far behind."

More men entered the clearing. First came Rodeo and Alphabet, followed by a handful of Filipinos, and finally Father Francisco.

The priest's gaze swept over the American soldiers, then around the clearing, searching for the men who weren't there. "What happened to the local men?" he asked.

The lieutenant's questioning gaze fell upon Deke, Philly, and Yoshio, who shook their heads in the negative.

"I'm sorry, Padre. It looks like your men didn't make it."

"None of them?"

Deke felt for the priest, who suddenly looked forlorn, standing there in his tattered cassock, in the middle of a jungle clearing, in the shadow of the dying rosewood tree. In places they could still see charred patches where those dead men had built their cooking fires that morning, some of them with wives or children they would never be returning to.

He spoke up. "They didn't die for nothing, though. They bought us the time we needed to take out those guns. They were the real heroes today."

He wasn't going to add that some of them had died from having their heads cut off by the Japanese. The priest didn't necessarily need to know that part—not at the moment, anyhow.

The priest nodded, then made the sign of the cross.

They had no time to mourn the dead, however. Not if the living hoped to stay that way.

"All right, let's get the hell out of here," Honcho said. "We gave the Japs a real gut punch this morning, but they aren't going to stay down for long. You know the Japs. They keep coming no matter what."

There were a few items in the clearing that the priest wanted to retrieve, considering that he likely wouldn't be able to return once the Japanese started beating the bushes for the raiders. While he did that, Philly turned to Bat and Ball. "Did you really blow up those guns? I was starting to wonder if it was even possible."

"We sure as hell did," Bat said, looking pleased with himself. "Ball here shoved that satchel charge right down the Japs' throat."

"It went boom, all right," Ball added. "I think we ended up exploding some of their munitions. But we were worried that the guns would come through all that, you know?"

"So we climbed up there and shoved a handful of grenades down the barrels for good measure. I've always wanted to try that to see what happened. Anyhow, it worked. It was like a firecracker going down your gullet."

"It seemed to do the trick," Ball agreed. "It was like a Boy Scout tied a knot inside those barrels."

"It was a hell of a thing," Steele said, clearly pleased. "Those guns shouldn't be a problem anymore."

Deke was glad that the Jap sniper must have been too intent on his duel with Deke to pay the raiders any attention. In that regard, the diversion had certainly worked.

"What next?" he asked.

"Let's get down to that beach and see if we can hitch a ride off this island."

"What if we can't, Honcho?" Philly wondered aloud. "Maybe those navy boys forgot all about us. You really think they'll go out of their way to help us dogfaces?"

Lieutenant Steele didn't answer. He didn't have to. They all knew the answer to that one. They were the only US troops on an island absolutely crawling with the enemy. An invasion might be coming soon, but it would be too late for them if they didn't escape.

"That's what I was afraid of," Philly said.

The priest and the remaining Filipinos were not going with them. They retrieved packs and supplies that had been hidden beyond the perimeter of the clearing for just such a contingency as having to move deeper into the forest, out of reach of the Japanese patrols who would be bent on revenge. The plan never had been to evacuate the local guerrillas. The navy boat—if it came for them at all—was going to be a small vessel. Anyhow, Father Francisco and the Filipino guerrillas had been doing just fine against the Japanese before the arrival of the Americans, and they planned to do more of the same.

"Go with God," the priest said, shouldering one of the packs. "Perhaps we will meet again, God willing."

"Good luck to you, Padre," the lieutenant said.

The priest led his small party away, and in a moment they were swallowed up by the green wall of vegetation as if they had never been there in the first place.

"I'm gonna miss those guys," Philly said.

"Follow me," Deke said, and led the patrol into the underbrush on the opposite side of the clearing from the direction that the priest and the Filipinos had taken. They were heading west, toward the beach. Honcho brought up the rear. There was no time to waste if they were going to make that rendezvous.

CHAPTER TWENTY-ONE

FROM BEHIND THEM, they heard the horns and bugles that the Japs sometimes blew in battle. The Japs didn't seem to care about being quiet. In fact, it was as if they wanted to let their quarry know that they were being hunted.

The bleating noises made Deke's skin crawl, and he moved even faster through the brush, leading the others toward the sea. If the Japs wanted to make him feel like a hunted rabbit, they were successful. He reached a tangle of vines that had woven themselves into an impenetrable net, blocking the direction that he wanted to go in. He was bushwhacking rather than following any kind of trail—not that there were any trails to follow. The tangle spread in both directions, and he didn't want to take the time to go around it. Each moment that passed, those bleating horns seemed to grow closer.

Sweat ran down from under the brim of his jungle hat and stung his eyes. The still air seemed to wrap around him like a suffocating gauze. He took a moment to catch his breath. He swiped at his face with the back of his hand and thought about what to do next.

He shouldered his rifle and drew his bowie knife. The blade wasn't as long as that of the bolo knives favored by the Filipino guerrillas, but it was hefty enough, and razor sharp.

With a grunt, he swung at the vines in front of his face. The blade cut through most of the way before it lost momentum and got hung up in the thickest of the vines, as big around as his forearm. Deke pulled back his arm and slashed again at the green notch that his knife had made. He swung again and the vine parted. Stroke by stroke, he began hacking a path directly through the net of vines.

"Need some help?" Yoshio asked. One of the Filipinos had given Yoshio a bolo knife, and he stood shoulder to shoulder with Deke, attacking the vines blocking their path.

As if the vines weren't bad enough, there were all sorts of spider-webs here, along with massive spiders that barely troubled themselves to get out of the way. What did these things catch in their webs, he wondered, birds? Snakes and spiders didn't much bother Deke, but these critters were so big that they were hard to ignore. Then again, if the Japs caught up to them, spiders would be the least of their worries. Still, having the sticky webs cling to his face and hands gave him the creepy crawlies.

Once they had an opening big enough to force his body into, he squeezed through the wall of vines and reached relatively open forest on the other side. Yoshio followed right behind him.

"Keep moving," he said to the others. "Ain't nothin' to it from here."

It turned out that Deke had spoken too soon. He took a few more steps through the jungle and started to put his foot down in the patch of greenery ahead, but something didn't feel right. He stopped in mid stride and put out an arm to stop Yoshio, who had come up beside him, ready to surge past Deke.

"What is it?" Yoshio asked, bringing his rifle up.

"It's not Japs," Deke said, nodding at the forest ahead, where the branches opened up, revealing open air. "But don't take another step. It's a long way down."

It became clear that they were standing at the edge of a ravine that plunged down twenty or thirty feet—it was hard to tell exactly because of the dense vegetation at the bottom. Thick vines snaked down from the trees overhead into the shadows below.

A quick investigation showed that the ravine was maybe twelve feet across, fracturing the hill for as far as they could see in both directions, like the crooked smile of a jack-o'-lantern. They just didn't have time to go around it, which meant that they had to get *across*.

Deke wondered if they could jump the ravine. Maybe he could jump it with a running start, if it had been possible to get up enough speed through all the vegetation, and if he wasn't weighed down by soggy combat boots and gear. It was as if the hill itself was playing a final trick on them, keeping the other side of the ravine just out of reach, making sure that they wouldn't leave.

Behind them, the sound of the Japanese bugles became louder and more insistent. The rest of Patrol Easy found itself staring at the ravine, wondering what to do.

"Now what?" Philly asked.

"We have to get across that ravine, that's what," Honcho said.

"I can jump it," Yoshio said.

"No, you can't," said Honcho, who had apparently done his own mental calculations. "It's too wide. You'll end up stuck in the bottom with a broken leg, or worse."

Deke had come too far to give up now. There was only one thing to do, foolhardy as it seemed.

"Aw, to hell with it," he said.

He shouldered his rifle again and took out his bowie knife, then used it to cut through one of the vines hanging within reach. With the bottom end cut loose from the ravine, the vine could now swing freely. He gave it a good tug—it seemed sturdy.

"It'll be just like when me and Sadie used to swing out over the creek at our old swimmin' hole," he said, as much to convince himself as anyone.

"You're not going to—"

Deke grabbed the vine with his wiry arms and pushed off from the edge of the ravine. He felt the burn of friction as his hands slipped a little, and he held on tighter, hugging the vine with his knees to give him momentum. He told himself not to look down, but he did it anyway, glimpsing a blur of rotting tree trunks and moss-covered rocks far below. Then the far side of the ravine was beneath his feet and he dropped down. He barely cleared the gap and would have fallen in if he hadn't caught himself on the vine, holding on to it for dear life.

"You crazy redneck," Philly shouted. Once he saw that Deke had made it, he added, "Hey, swing that vine back over here!"

Lieutenant Steele still seemed to be considering whether or not this was a good idea, but by then Deke had sent the vine back, and Philly was swinging across the ravine.

But he didn't have enough momentum. Or maybe he just hadn't had much occasion to swing on vines back in the city. The arc of his swing ended before he could get his feet on solid ground, and he started to swing back over the void below.

"Oh crap!" he cried.

Seeing that Philly was in trouble, Ball shouted to the men still on the edge of the ravine, "Grab my belt!"

Bat immediately figured out what Ball was up to. The tall marine got one hand on the back of his buddy's belt just before Ball leaned out and gave Philly a powerful shove that sent him flying back in the other direction.

Philly yelped. On the far side, Deke grabbed him by the shirtfront and pulled him the rest of the way until Philly got his boots under him.

Both men stood for a moment, hearts pounding, panting from the effort. But this was no time to rest.

"Hurry it up!" Honcho shouted. "These Japs are getting so close that I can smell what they had for breakfast."

Indeed, they could hear excited shouts mixed in now with the horns. The vine went back across six more times until all the soldiers had crossed the ravine. It had to be some kind of record for the most swings on a jungle vine—it would have put Tarzan to shame. Ball insisted on being the last one across, and he finally came swinging at them with all the momentum of a wrecking ball before he crashed into the brush on what was now their side of the ravine.

They were not a moment too soon. Amid the forest vegetation on the other side, they detected movement. At first, it seemed as if their eyes might be playing tricks on them. Then dozens of Japanese soldiers slowly materialized, spread out in a wide line. Several of the Japanese had twigs or leaves stuck into their helmets, helping them blend into the vegetation. Most of the Japs had bayonets on the ends of their rifles, poking at the shrubs and clumps of brush. They still hadn't spotted the Americans on the other side of the ravine.

It was time to slip away, but not quite yet.

"Let's give them something to think about," Honcho said.

He raised his shotgun and fired, peppering the Japs with buckshot. The other raiders opened fire. Deke picked out a man who had reached the edge of the ravine and was in the process of raising his rifle to return fire. Deke's bullet caught him in the belly, and the man lost his balance and fell into the ravine, his scream cut short when he crashed into the rocks and fallen logs at the bottom.

The Japanese were not surprised for long, however. They began to return fire, their bullets chewing up the greenery. The two groups were almost within spitting distance. More and more Japanese emerged from the forest and congregated at the edge of the ravine, quickly outnumbering the raiders.

"Go!" Honcho shouted, and they kept going down the hill. Ahead of them, the trees were already starting to clear, and glimpses of blue water became visible in the distance.

Philly whooped. "That ravine will slow down those Japs. I'd sure like to see them cross that thing. Knowing the Japs, they'll probably stop and build a bridge."

"I wonder why they don't all just swing across like we did?"

"Maybe they've never seen a Tarzan movie in Japan."

"Don't matter," Deke said, leading the patrol a couple of steps ahead of Philly. He had his rifle held in his hands again, eyes roving in all directions on the landscape ahead. "They don't have to cross the ravine."

"Sure they do! They'll never catch us."

"Philly, if you were a Jap, where do you think we'd be headed?"

"To the beach." Then Philly got it. "Uh-oh."

"Deke is right," said Honcho. "They know where we're going, so there might be a welcome party for us down there. Everybody stay alert."

Behind them, the ravine must have thwarted the Japanese pursuers, at least for now. The Nips had even given up on blowing their annoying horns while they worked out a way around the ravine.

They reached the beach, but what they saw in the ocean nearby prompted them to remain in the cover provided by the forest's edge. To their astonishment, they saw that it was some kind of Japanese naval vessel, slowly cruising past the beach area. Even without the scope, Deke could see the meatball flag flying from the pagoda mast. He put the rifle to his shoulder so he could get a better view through the scope. The ship was close enough that he could see the Jap sailors on it. Sailors stood at the rail, scanning the beach and surrounding waters. He figured it must be some sort of Jap battleship. The ship certainly bristled with guns.

"Don't tell me you're going to try and sink that ship with your rifle?" Philly said nervously. "Their guns are a whole lot bigger than ours."

"I reckon it might be worth a try," Deke remarked. "If I pick off a couple of those Japs on deck, they'll never know what hit 'em."

"Hold your fire," said Honcho, who was glassing the ship through binoculars. "Philly is right, for once. I guess the Jap navy isn't done yet."

As the ship sailed out of sight, the raiders emerged onto the sand and discovered that, so far, they had the beach to themselves. There wasn't a Jap around, but for how long?

Honcho looked at his wristwatch. Almost high noon. They were right on schedule for the pickup, but there was no rescue boat in sight, and no sound of any approaching motor. With the Jap navy on patrol, who could blame them?

With a sinking feeling, the men realized that the lack of any rescue boat meant that the navy boys had either forgotten them or had decided that they weren't worth the risk. These were still Japanese waters, after all, as evidenced by the enemy ship they had just seen. Getting even a small US Navy vessel to the beach—and back to the ship—wasn't going to be a pleasure cruise. Another possibility was that things had gotten too hot for the ship that must be waiting just over the horizon. The Jap navy was still out there, along with all their snooper planes and Betty bombers, which were hell on navy ships. The nervous skipper might have withdrawn to a safer distance.

"Rodeo, do you still have that flare gun?"

"Sure do, Honcho."

"Then go ahead and fire a flare, just to remind those navy boys that we're here."

Philly spoke up. "Sir, you do know that once we fire that flare, we're going to let every Jap in the vicinity know that we're here too?"

"Geez, Philly. Since when do you get paid to think? I wouldn't worry too much about alerting the Japs, because I'm sure they'll figure out where we are soon enough," the lieutenant said. "Besides, I don't know about you, but I'd sure as hell like to get off this beach. The sooner, the better. Does anyone else have any bright ideas on how to do that?"

When no one else spoke up, Lieutenant Steele nodded at Rodeo. "Fire the flare, son."

Rodeo stepped a few feet away, raised the flare gun, and fired it into the tropical sky. The flare ignited and arced down toward the sea, burning brightly until it disappeared far from land.

"If those navy squids didn't see that, they must be blind," Philly muttered. "I know that the Japs sure as hell didn't miss it."

"I'd tell you to smoke 'em if you've got 'em," Honcho said. "But that would be a really bad idea right now."

All that they could do was settle down and wait. There wasn't a bit of cover, aside from a few scattered chunks of tropical driftwood. Deke didn't like being so exposed, not one bit. They were putting an awful lot of faith in the hope that the navy had not forgotten them.

He took up a prone position, his boots practically in the surf, literally at the edge of the island, his elbows propped in the sand. From there he could see the entire sweep of beach in both directions.

He didn't have to wait long for the enemy to show up. To Deke's surprise, they materialized from the edge of the jungle growth where it met the beach. This must be the same Japanese who had pursued them off the hill until they had been thwarted by the ravine. Deke was curious as to how the Japs had finally gotten around the ravine, but he doubted that he'd be able to ask them that anytime soon.

The others were so busy intently watching the ocean for any sign of the navy boat that they didn't even see the Japanese appear.

"We've got company," Deke said.

There were no more than thirty Japanese, but they far outnumbered the men of Patrol Easy, who were exposed on the beach. Deke was reminded of that day on Guam when they had decided to go swimming and they had been caught out in the open by Japanese snipers. Once again, they had nowhere to go.

Deke decided to make the first move. He spotted an officer, who wore a field cap instead of the helmets worn by the enlisted men. He hoped that it was the same Jap officer who had cut off the Filipinos' heads. Nothing would have given him more pleasure, he thought, as he lined up the crosshairs on the officer and squeezed the trigger.

The man crumpled.

He ran the bolt and picked out another target.

Deke had picked off the officer, but the Jap soldiers didn't need any commands to know what to do next. They began firing at the Americans, but they did not advance toward them across the beach. *Why should they,* Deke thought, *when they could just take their time and pick off our guys out here in the open?*

Bullets whined overhead, snapping through the humid air.

"Everybody down!" Honcho shouted, and the others threw themselves flat onto the sand, joining Deke.

Deke noticed that one of the Japanese hadn't retreated into the relative cover of the jungle fringe. He also hadn't thrown himself flat but stood in plain sight, as if taunting the Americans, or perhaps showing his disdain for them. He was just far enough away that he made a difficult target.

But he wasn't so far away that Deke couldn't study him through the scope, picking out a few details. He realized that the soldier also had a scoped rifle. He wasn't wearing a helmet, but he wasn't an officer either. He wore the Japanese field cap that was emblazoned with a star, with cloth hanging from the back of the hat to shelter the neck from the sun. The cap was practical for use in the tropics and uniquely oriental in appearance. Deke thought the Jap looked awfully familiar.

With a jolt, Deke realized that this must be the same Japanese sniper he had tangled with back on the hill. He was definitely a cocky son of a bitch, reminding him in some ways of the Samurai Sniper that Deke had run into on Guam. Two different snipers, but cut from the same cloth. What was with these Japs? He wondered if they all thought of themselves as ancient samurai warriors for the Emperor.

But the days of spears and swords were long over, he thought, lining up the rifle for a shot at the man.

As he did so, a bullet passed within inches of his head, reminding Deke that the Jap was also a good shot. He willed his prone body to sink deeper into the sand, the mad hornet whine of the small-caliber bullet sending shivers down to his toes. He couldn't tell for certain at this distance, but he was pretty sure that the Jap sniper had been looking right at him when he'd fired, delivering a taunt along with the bullet.

Have it your way, Deke thought.

Letting out a breath, he put the crosshairs on the Jap's chest, held a little high. It was kind of a long poke. Nothing fancy at this distance, he told himself. If he hit the Jap anywhere in the chest, a rifle round traveling at more than two thousand feet per second would take care of business.

There was always wind at the beach, but it was coming in off the sea, getting behind his shot, which suited Deke just fine. The good side of his face was pressed against the stock, making the angry scars more visible. His gray eyes were hard as mountain granite as he fixed them on the target through the scope.

His finger started to take up tension on the trigger. Through the scope, he'd have sworn that the Jap sniper was aiming right back at *him*. It was anybody's guess whose bullet was going to leave the muzzle first.

"Hey, here comes a boat!" Philly shouted. "It's got to be one of our guys. I guess those squids didn't forget us, after all."

A volley of whoops and cheers rose from the throats of the men on the beach. Distracted, Deke eased up on the trigger.

They had heard the roaring motor before they saw it, but sure enough, a small craft came racing in from just beyond the surf line. It looked as if he'd been waiting far enough out that the gray hull blended in with the surrounding Pacific, maybe even just over the nautical horizon visible from the beach. No matter, the boat was here now, piloted by a lone man.

The extraction time had been chosen in part because it would be high tide, enabling the boat to come in much closer than it had when dropping them off a day and a half ago. Had it really been just thirty-six hours? Deke thought that it felt like a century.

He turned his full attention back to the Jap, but the enemy sniper's attention seemed to have shifted. He was no longer aiming at Deke but had shifted his rifle to point in another direction.

At the boat.

The Jap wasn't aiming at Deke anymore because he was going to shoot the helmsman in the rescue boat. With their escape route cut off, the Japs could then take their time picking off the raiders—or capturing them and cutting off their heads.

Deke wasn't the only one who had noticed that the sniper planned to target the rescue boat. Nearby, Lieutenant Steele was watching the Japanese through a pair of binoculars.

"Deke—"

"I see him."

Deke knew that he had to shoot this son of a bitch—and fast. Quickly, he realigned the rifle—

His attention was interrupted by a sound that drowned out the pop of the enemy rifles. It was louder than the boat motor, growing in intensity to a screech, then building to a terrible sky-splitting roar, like a whole freight train was rumbling through the sky.

"Everybody down!" Honcho shouted.

The Jap sniper forgotten for the moment, Deke buried his face in the sand as a volley of five-inch shells arrived. The shells plowed into the forest where it grew close to the beach. Entire trees shattered and cracked, scattering splinters in all directions. Great gouts of dirt and rock erupted like volcanoes.

Somebody on that navy ship was looking out for them. Still, they had been taking a huge chance that the team had managed to knock out the deadly battery on Hill 522. That was faith for you, all right. If the shoreline was within range of the *Ingersoll*, it also meant that the *Ingersoll* was within range of any shore batteries.

Deke had thought that he was a good shot, but he had to give those navy gunners credit. Talk about a long poke. The ship was nowhere in sight. It was all the more impressive, considering that they couldn't even *see* the target. Then again, all they had to do was get their shells close. The several pounds of high explosives in each shell did the rest.

An instant later, another volley roared in, striking a little farther inland. Again, the destruction looked spectacular, a bit of Armageddon visited upon the forest.

It was hard to say if the Japanese troops had been killed or not, but when Deke raised his head again, they were nowhere in sight. Bits of shattered trees and even boulders littered the sand near where the Japanese had been, with a blackened shell crater smoking nearby.

As for the Japanese sniper, it looked as if Deke wasn't going to get his chance to see who the better shot was, after all. The sniper was gone, either blasted into oblivion or hiding within the jungle perimeter.

"Let's go!"

The men didn't need to be told twice. The boat had come in as close to shore as it could, but the men still had to splash their way toward the boat. The water was deep enough that it made climbing aboard difficult. The helmsman couldn't help much because he was occupied trying to keep the boat from capsizing in the six-foot waves cresting as they rolled toward the beach. Luckily, the Japanese ship that they had seen earlier had not reappeared or opened fire on the US ship over the horizon. Perhaps it suited the Japanese to stay out of sight for now.

Yoshio managed to wriggle up the side, then helped the others aboard, one by one.

To their surprise, at the helm was the same sailor who had brought them in.

"Boy, are we glad to see you," Philly announced.

"You dogfaces will do anything for a boat ride, won't you?" said the tough old salt, a grin creasing his leathery face. "Maybe you want to take a little shoreline cruise and see the sights?"

"Aw, wouldn't you know it that we forgot our picnic basket," Philly said.

"All right, all right," Honcho said. "You guys are cracking us up. Just get us the hell out of here."

The helmsman obliged by swinging the wheel around and ramming the throttle forward, leaving a foaming wake behind as they raced toward the navy vessel waiting over the horizon.

CHAPTER TWENTY-TWO

A FEW DAYS LATER, Deke was in another cramped bunk, feeling the ship roll beneath him and trying to ignore that familiar queasy feeling in his belly.

"I've got to say that I'm almost wishing I was back on Leyte, scrambling through the jungle," he said. The words came out closer to sounding like a groan than he would have liked. "Anything has got to be better than being stuck on this damn ship."

"You can keep your jungle," said Philly, jammed into another bunk nearby, intent on reading a magazine. "Snakes, spiders, bugs, Japs—and sleeping in a hole in a ground if you're lucky. No sirree, baby. Give me a bunk and three squares any day of the week."

It was a familiar debate. More than one soldier had asked himself why he hadn't had the good sense to join the navy instead. Then again, they had seen firsthand how terrifying it could be on a ship when the Japs came calling. Deke thought of his cousin Jasper, killed at Pearl Harbor. More and more, it was hard not to come across someone who hadn't lost a relative or a buddy in the war, either in the Pacific or in Europe, or even in the cold waters of the North Atlantic.

Deke groaned again. Yoshio was in another bunk, ignoring them both as he turned the pages of a Western novel. Deke doubted that there had been many Japanese gunslingers in the Old West, but the snipers whom he'd run into on Guam and Leyte would have been good candidates. They'd have given any of Zane Grey's heroes a run for their money.

Rodeo and Alphabet were sleeping in their bunks. Bat and Ball weren't there, having been sent back to the marines where they belonged. Rumor had it that they were heading for some island called Iwo Jima.

Stuck without much to do, the men were entertaining themselves as best as they could. Yoshio had his book, and Philly had gotten into a card game or two—somehow, he had managed not to lose his shirt.

Deke had spent some time writing a rare letter to Sadie, off in Washington, DC. He owed her a letter, considering that he'd gotten a note from her when he was still on Guam. That letter had been full of details about city life and police work. To Deke's surprise, he could read between the lines that his sister didn't miss home or their life on the farm the same way that he did. In fact, she seemed to have embraced city life and her new career.

But that was Sadie for you. Like a cat, she always landed on her feet. He had enjoyed visiting her before shipping out, back when the unit was training on the Chesapeake Bay. They'd had a good time, and Deke had enjoyed meeting some of the girls she knew. Sadie must have warned them about his scars, because they hadn't asked questions and hadn't stared. But it didn't change the fact that he was damaged goods compared to all the other soldier boys they had to choose from in the big city.

As for Washington itself, Deke had been impressed by the stately white buildings, places that he'd only heard about, such as the White House, the United States Capitol, and even the Washington Monument. It felt strange, in a way, to see them in person, but also reassuring. These buildings represented the institutions and the ideals that they were all fighting for. Deke respected that and hadn't lost sight of why they were all here, which was easy enough to do.

Dear Sadie,

We have had a hard time here in the Pacific, but we are getting through it all right. There are a lot of good men in my unit and we have a real good officer.

I would follow him anywhere. He reminds me of Pa in some ways. The Japs are a tough nut to crack and many are good shots, but not as good as you. I feel sorry for any man who thinks he can shoot better than you. How are things going for you in Washington? I hope they are giving you more to do than write parking tickets.

Right now we are getting plenty of chow, but I do miss a good breakfast like we used to have on the farm sometimes. That's all for now, I reckon.

Your brother,

Deacon

It was a short letter, but he supposed that something was better than nothing. Besides, once land came into view, it was hard to say when he would ever have a chance to write again. There was a lot more that he couldn't put in the letter, of course. The censors would have struck out any details anyhow.

Deke realized that the last few days had been a confusing whirlwind. After their rescue from the beach on Leyte, their time aboard the destroyer turned out to be relatively short. The *Ingersoll* had backtracked until it came to the invasion fleet making its way across the Pacific.

After a few days, they found themselves transferred to USS *Elmore*. They had been a novelty aboard the destroyer, but *Ingersoll* had returned to its regular duties of escorting aircraft carriers through waters still infested by the enemy, whether on the water, beneath the waves, or in the air.

Elmore was an attack transport, loaded with men ready to launch the invasion of Leyte. The ship itself wouldn't take them to shore. When the time came, they would descend rope netting to Higgins boats waiting to take them to shore, where the Japanese would be waiting.

Deke tried not to think too much about that.

Despite their efforts during the raid, they received no special treatment compared to the rest of the troops aboard. Philly had done some crowing about how they deserved a medal for what they had done, but that was wishful thinking. The way Deke saw it, many others had done plenty more.

Like the other troops, they were more or less confined to their cramped quarters, with the exception being a few hours on deck each day for exercise and fresh air. There were organized calisthenics and weapons inspections just to keep the men on their toes.

The sailors had a ship to run so were busy going about their duties. Hordes of soldiers on deck just got in their way, which was why the troops were kept under wraps for the most part. Also, the army officers didn't want their boys to get the mistaken idea that they were on a pleasure cruise. Lieutenant Steele had disappeared into his officer's quarters, and they had not seen much of him since coming aboard.

"I'm not going to babysit you," he had announced. "Get some sleep, eat all you can, and stay the hell out of trouble. I'll see you when we get back to Leyte."

Leyte. It was a place he'd never heard of until a few weeks ago, and now he was never going to forget it.

Deke had said that he would gladly have traded his seasick state for another stint in the jungle, and it looked as though he was going to get his wish. Leyte was hardly in their rearview mirror. Instead, it was their destination once again, this time with several thousand other troops. It was a good thing those guns had been knocked out.

Almost every man on the ship had seen action in some way, and nobody was looking forward to more of it. Not that they had any choice. As usual, the GIs had been told as little as possible, which meant that the rumor mill was going full tilt.

"I hear we're going to some place called Leyte," one of the soldiers on deck had said to Deke and Philly, like he was letting them in on a big secret.

"Leyte, huh?" Philly turned to the soldier and said, "Take my word for it, buddy, when I say that we don't recommend it."

"What would you know about it?" the soldier asked, but at a look from Deke, he suddenly remembered that he needed to be someplace else.

"There you go again, scaring the neighbors," Philly said.

"All I did was look at him."

"Exactly."

One good thing about being on the transport was that they recognized several people they *did* want to talk to. One of those was Egan.

He had been left behind on Guam because his main skill had been as a war dog handler—not a scout or sniper. At the time, he hadn't even had a dog.

But that was then and this was now. They had reunited earlier with Egan, right after coming aboard.

What they hadn't seen before was his new dog. He was now walking a large, blondish dog on deck. It was hard to say what the dog's lineage was, but there was definitely some German shepherd in there. One of the dog's ears sagged, like maybe he'd already seen some action.

There were a handful of similar war dogs that would be going ashore to sniff out hidden Japs and protect against enemy incursions at night. The dogs were being kept in shape, like the men themselves, with as much exercise and training as the cramped quarters aboard ship allowed. There was one strip of sod that had been laid out on deck for the dogs, the only bit of greenery on the ship. That grass had a distinct purpose.

"Believe me, you don't want to go walking on that grass," Philly said.

"No worries about that."

Egan approached, leading the dog. Philly whistled. "Where'd you get the pony?"

"This is Thor," Egan said, grinning. It had taken him a long time to smile again after Whoa Nelly had been killed in the fighting on Guam. "Best damn dog in the Pacific."

Thor growled when Philly tried to pet him.

"I wouldn't do that if I were you," Egan said, keeping a firm grip on Thor's leash. Philly didn't need to be told twice but had taken a couple of steps back. "These guys aren't trained to be lapdogs, you know."

Deke always did have a soft spot for dogs, having grown up around them, and the big German shepherd mix didn't scare him any. He knelt and scratched the dog's ears.

Thor responded by wagging his tail.

"I'll be damned," Egan said. "He likes you."

"You're all right, ain't you, boy?" Deke said quietly. "Those Japs are going to take one look at you, and they're gonna run the other way."

He gave Thor a final rub and straightened up. As useful as it was to have the dogs guarding them, he felt that it wasn't right to bring a dog into combat. Too many of the dogs had died on Guam when the Japs began to target them out of fear and hatred.

"I've got to say, Deke, that you're about the last person I would have taken for an animal lover," Egan said.

"Sure, I like dogs. It's mainly people I don't like." When Deke saw the expression on his buddies' faces, he added, "Present company excepted."

Philly snorted. "After the war, I'll bet you're gonna go live in a shack in the woods somewhere."

"No," he said. "I'm going to get my family's farm back from the son-of-a-bitch banker who stole it from us, that's what."

"You want that farm back so you can bale hay and milk cows all day? It sounds like maybe he did you a favor," Philly said.

Deke just shook his head. "City folk wouldn't understand."

"I guess not. Listen, I heard Ernie Pyle is somewhere on this ship. I'd like to talk to him and get my name in the newspaper."

"If you want to make a fool out of yourself, then go right ahead," Deke said, but he was grinning. "Go on, then."

Deke watched him go off in search of the famed newspaper reporter. Alone at the ship's rail, he looked across the sparkling sea. He stared at the horizon, a trick he had learned to help with the seasickness. Their ship was just one of many, a convoy heading to kick the Japs out of the Philippines, although the Japs didn't have plans to go anywhere.

I reckon we'll see how that turns out, Deke thought.

* * *

IKEDA STOOD NEAR MAJOR NOGUCHI, both men looking out to sea. He lifted his hand to his eyes to shield them from the glare off the water. A few Japanese vessels were visible near the shore, on patrol. They had been on high alert since the raid a few days ago. Overhead, planes patrolled the skies. There seemed to be constant dogfights between the Japanese planes and the American fighter pilots. Still, some of the enemy planes broke through and managed to bomb or strafe the Japanese defenses.

It was for naught—Major Noguchi had engineered the defenses so well that even the most well-placed bomb or rocket scarcely had any impact on what he had built here.

The deep-blue surface of Leyte Gulf remained empty of enemy ships, but not for much longer. The growing number of planes was a sign that the Americans were coming, and when they arrived, the Japanese would be ready.

"Perhaps we cannot win," Major Noguchi had admitted in a moment of candor. However, he did not appear gloomy or defeated as he said it. Noguchi was simply being pragmatic, as usual. He was a builder, after all, not a warrior. The major had a bandage on his head where a chunk of stone had struck him when the American raiders exploded the bunker. Absently, he touched the bandage. "Rest assured, we shall make them pay dearly."

"And we shall die gloriously," Ikeda added.

The major sighed. "Yes, I suppose that is a possibility."

Neither man had spoken directly of the raid, which they found personally embarrassing. Despite their best efforts, the raiders had managed to destroy the gun battery on Guinhangdan Hill.

However, the shoreline was far from undefended. Even in the days since the raid, more rifle pits and hidden machine-gun nests had been added near the beach. The hill itself was close to an impregnable fortress. The raiders had taken them by surprise, but there would not be much of an element of surprise once American forces stormed the beach.

Although the battery of massive guns had been destroyed, Major Noguchi had lost no time in bringing in more artillery to occupy the same bunker. To be sure, the replacements were smaller, but they would still rain destruction down on the beach and assault craft. It was just the big ships that would now be out of reach.

The rest of the hill remained honeycombed with trenches, tunnels, and firing pits. Again, this was the result of many months of effort.

Ikeda's own team of *sogekihei* marksmen was ready to occupy these fortifications, both here on the hill and closer to the beach. He had worked tirelessly to train these men well, even if one of his best men had been shot and killed at the ravine where they had almost cornered the enemy raiders. The poor man had been hit in the belly and plunged over the side.

Perhaps Major Noguchi was correct and they could not hope to stop the steel wave as it broke upon their shore, but they could make the invaders pay dearly all the same. If they did not stop the Americans here, then they would be that much closer to Japan.

The Japanese high command was well aware of what was at stake. A constant stream of ships had been arriving to bring reinforcements to the Philippines. While the Japanese did seem to have men and ammunition in relative abundance, what they lacked was a supply of food and other basic needs, such as medical supplies, for these men. The Americans had wrought such havoc on their shipping that the supply ships had simply not been able to get through. There was only so much that the Japanese commanders could do to feed an army off the land itself. Many of the Japanese troops who had helped to build the defenses on this hill still looked weak and underfed.

As for the Filipinos themselves, it had become clear that several of those who attacked the hill had been guerrilla soldiers. The few who had been captured had been dealt with severely enough.

Also, there had been reprisals in the nearby village of Palo, which was likely home to many family members of these guerrillas. Ikeda himself had led a search of the village, resulting in gathering several more workers for the crews on the hill and the beach defenses. Those Filipinos who had resisted had not survived—Ikeda had seen to that.

Although he went about his duties enthusiastically, the marksman realized that his role was a small one. Ikeda knew that he probably could not even begin to grasp the sheer scale of the military strategy involved. But he could fight. His own battle would simply be reduced to what he could see in his rifle sights.

He hoped that he might get the chance to again confront the American sniper he had run into. The man was clever and a good shot.

Were American snipers as good as Ikeda himself? Ikeda smiled. That remained to be seen, but he knew that he and his men would soon be put to the test.

NOTE TO READERS

After Guam was secure in the late summer of 1944—except for a few Japanese holdouts who persisted for many years after the war—the United States set its sights on regaining the Philippines. The Japanese had captured the islands from the US right after Pearl Harbor. General Douglas MacArthur had every intention of taking them back—which is where Patrol Easy enters the picture in *Rising Sniper*.

To be honest, the story was inspired more than a bit by a childhood spent watching old WWII movies like *The Guns of Navarone*. But mostly this story was loosely based on the advance raids that Army Rangers made on small islands in Leyte Gulf, in order to secure the approaches to the beaches for the Leyte invasion. From those actual events, a plot was born around Hill 522, a Japanese stronghold on Leyte. The hill really had been turned into a fortress, although the battery that Patrol Easy intends to take out is the stuff of fiction.

That's a good thing in this case, considering that the fight for Leyte would turn out to be difficult and costly enough. The guns in the story were based on those manufactured for the infamous Japanese battleship *Yamato*. As it turned out, even those massive guns couldn't protect the *Yamato*, which was sunk by US forces.

Once again, some of the language and attitudes expressed by the characters are typical of men confronting a deadly enemy in the Pacific theater of 1944 but that we don't find acceptable today. It's also worth noting that while Ernie Pyle, Douglas MacArthur, and Tom O'Connell (my great-uncle) were real people, they are used fictitiously here.

The next book will pick up the story in the waning months of 1944 as the actual battle for the Philippines begins and General MacArthur prepares to wade ashore.

Deacon Cole and the rest of the gang are sure to lend a hand.

ABOUT THE AUTHOR

David Healey lives in Maryland, where he worked as a journalist for more than twenty years. He is a member of International Thriller Writers and a contributing editor to *The Big Thrill* magazine. Join his newsletter list at:

www.davidhealeyauthor.com

or

www.facebook.com/david.healey.books

Made in the USA
Columbia, SC
01 May 2023

16000250R00126